fiction

SO-BEZ-762

FIELDS
OF
FATE

FIELDS OF FATE

A Novel by
Fernando Namora

Translated from the Portuguese
by
Dorothy Ball

CROWN PUBLISHERS, INC., NEW YORK

© 1970 by Crown Publishers, Inc.
First Published in Portuguese as
O TRIGO E O JOIO
Library of Congress Catalog Card Number: 79–101299
Printed in the United States of America
Published simultaneously in Canada by
General Publishing Company Limited
Designed by Iris Kleinman

PART I

PART 1

1

The small town lies along a road that comes down from the eucalyptus trees disturbing the somnolence of the plain, cuts through a junction of roads that carry the call of Spain or of the sea, and then suddenly, in a rush of audacity, climbs up to the plateau to a church that, in days gone by, was the refuge of Moors and abbots, and still stands there, arrogant, challenging the stillness of the plain. Round the church little white houses, with high chimneys boring through their thickest backs, close up in a redoubt that stands firm against the tranquil surge of the wheatland. The women come to their doors, anxious for details of any newcomer, to nose out some firsthand piece of news, or invent it if necessary. The men wear sheepskin smocks, and talk and walk with deliberation, something tragic in their demeanor. The lads run off to the shady spots where acorns drop from the trees by grace of God in the heart of the thickets.

There are taverns along the road, and in them the gentle hum of life sometimes boils up into whirlpools. Numbers of taverns. After the day's work the peasants go and sit in them, near the counter or at the table, leaning their elbows on the marble top. They sit and listen. Talking is weary work. That's why a man who knows the art of throwing off a telling phrase at the right time takes an hour to think it over.

All kinds of people come into the town—stones thrown into a still pool. There are laborers from the north who come looking for work at harvesttime, a shifting but tenacious wave of folk who cross whole provinces on the lookout for someone who will hire their labor. They hurry in and out of shops unobtrusively just to buy bacon and a packet of tobacco, while the resentful eyes of the Alentejanos follow them about. There are

7

herdsmen bringing their flocks and melancholy songs from Baixo Alentejo. There are peddlers and passing visitors. All these people make the taverns lively. They talk, tell tales of high adventure and misfortune. There was pockmarked Crispino, for instance, who had been through the Spanish war, and told the black epic of vandals burning frontier olive groves. There was Galdério, too, a bumptious braggart whose smile easily changed to cold malevolence and who left behind him a wake of legend, astonishing the locals with his tales of the time when he'd done some smuggling in the wolfram line.

I want to tell you about these people. About the town, about hot, primitive Alentejo and the characters in the drama who give it strength or languor, laughter or tragedy. I want to open pages from the past, and trace the story of Loas who could foretell the future; Vieirinha who had sailed the waters of the Amazon, and yet felt queasy if some overhearty companion let his fingers dip into the sauce; Barão who came to a bad end; and Dona Quitéria whose house reeked of mold, prayers, and drops of balsam to ward off influenza. And I want to tell you too about the wheatlands, the fiery sunsets, the herdsmen and farmers, the still trance of the days, the mysterious call of the earth, of solitude, of space.

Let's begin with Barbaças. At first sight you'd take him for a wandering rogue, like that wretched Galdério. Nevertheless, he showed that he could settle down on a patch of ground, out under the parched sky of the heath at that, so long as he had some bread soup, a drink or two of wine, and a scrap of living space, preferably soft, so that he could sit down now and again and not find it too hard for his bottom. A loafer he was, rather than a rogue.

His exact origin was uncertain. His mother had bequeathed to the town sons by various fathers: one with a farmer's blood in his veins; others from casual laborers who came for a season and passed on; from farmhands; and it seems that an itinerant vendor of sardines also played his part in this haphazard procreation. Then, having fulfilled her mission of easing the desire of men inflamed by sun-drenched solitudes, the woman died, leaving her sons to fend each for himself.

8

Latterly, Barbaças and two of his brothers had made their home in an old outhouse belonging to the Misericórdia, but each remained completely independent, relying on his own special gifts to solve the difficult problem of finding a meal each day and a pair of trousers for St. Michael's Day. If one of the lads, with brazen unconcern, sat plucking a stolen fowl at the door, the other two watched the ritual, their mouths watering, but hopeless. They knew very well their brother would leave nothing but a heap of picked bones. Dawdling pleasantly through the days, they were not above earning a copper or two at some farm if the wage were worth the effort; but during the long slack weeks when no work was to be had and day laborers bitterly cursed and complained, for Barbaças and his brothers, with no family to support and no appearances to keep up, idleness was a pleasure and thieving their right.

Barbaças had the advantage over his brothers of enjoying a local reputation. This attracted the generosity of neighbors, a privilege not to be despised when the situation was almost desperate. As a matter of fact, some years earlier the eyes of the whole town had been focused on him. One morning he had woken up with his teeth clenched, unable to speak or eat, the muscles of his jaws as stiff as rods. Loas, who had otherworldly relations, diagnosed an evil spirit. The neighbors said he was moonstruck. At last the doctor, out of curiosity, went to have a look at him where he was lying on his shakedown, rigid and all of a piece, like a corpse awaiting burial. The doctor came out of the hovel with the staggering news: The fellow's got lockjaw!

Lockjaw! The rascal! So crafty he'd even gone and got a rare and horrible illness that would soften the hearts of the comfortably off to the benefit of his own pocket! If he'd been dying all alone, with some commonplace disease, nobody would have thought anything of it. But the rare, the breathtaking word *lockjaw*, sensational whichever way you looked at it, would spread all over the plain like a song—and so the town felt obliged to share in the glory by helping Barbaças either to live or die. And thus it came about that Dona Quitéria went in for dozens of novenas on his behalf, and the Misericórdia—

a charitable institution with a superintendent, treasurers, secretaries, and an annual budget of three hundred milreis—rapidly exhausted its resources on him. Then came the turn of the farmers and well-off to do their bit. Barbaças used up serum and swallowed tonics in the same way that he used to toss off glasses of wine; and on top of it all he took the boluses the healer sent him on the sly; but, to the great satisfaction of the town, he survived. He came back to life to find himself the town hero, with long hair and a mop of beard—and because of this some wag dubbed him Barbaças, or Big Beard. The nickname had its uses. It made people remember the epic event, and Barbaças—rather stunned by the waves of sympathy—was so loaded with eatables before the town got tired of him that he could trade them to other casual laborers. And nobody thought of criticizing him when he lay stretched in the sun on the threshold of his hovel like a full-fed lazy lizard, waiting for the clouds and time to pass slowly overhead. Even some years later, the fish vendor, a pinchpenny if ever there was one, was still leaving a fistful of sardines at Barbaças' door so that his thinness should not be a scandal to strangers.

"You still haven't carried out your promise, Luís," Dona Quitéria would say to him from time to time.

"What promise?" he would answer, on the defensive.

"To our Lady of Fátima, who saved you, you young heathen! You ought to go on foot—it takes two days and three nights—and thank her for her divine favor."

"I don't see any divine favor about going there on foot, lady."

Dona Quitéria crossed herself and cast her eyes up to heaven, from which by rights a dart of flame should come and strike such a blasphemer.

"I'll have to pray for you, sinful as you are!"

"Now then, lady, give me some slices of ham; that's better than prayers. . . ."

But the impudent rascal didn't abuse his position as protégé of the well-to-do. Although by so doing he risked loss of face as a free man, he learned a trade and took up his quarters with a master cobbler. However, he later reasoned logically enough, there was a striking difference between the money the customers paid for half soles and the few coppers his master gave *him* to spend at the café. So he chucked up the job. That is, he decided in favor of returning to the hovel, where a chap could sing or curse the whole day long, call his soul his own, with nobody to make money out of the sweat of his brow, and where there were sometimes pleasant visits from friends bringing perhaps a few perch from the river. When there were neither big fish nor small perch, nor an unwary fowl to catch, when, in short, life began to look sour and sad, then Barbaças would resign himself to the sacrifice and accept some job or other—harvesting, gathering olives, cutting wood—and wade into these tasks with the desperation of someone in a hurry to get back to a quiet life. And with this energy, this free-lance enthusiasm, the scamp earned good money, more than many another skilled in the job, enough for two or three months of dawdling ease.

One day, as was frequently the case, Barbaças was sitting by the roadside where red dust whirled up in stifling puffs when the east wind blew or when flocks passed by. With a delightfully empty mind he sat rubbing his nose, letting the hours slip away. Now, lots of things pass along a road, sometimes a crony who needs some help and is willing to pay for it. And sure enough, about midway through the afternoon, Barbaças caught sight of a blurred group coming slowly along the road, but still too far away to make out who it was. A little later, through the haze of dust stirred up by the travelers, he could just make out a man, a woman, and some way behind them a child. There were some animals, too, a dog and a ram or something of the sort. The ram was tied to the woman's shoulder by a cord, and it was all in a fret because, being tethered, it couldn't butt at the teasing dog. They looked so funny, and fascinated Barbaças so much, that he didn't recognize the leader of the group till they came level with him. It was Loas (he ought to have guessed that sooner) on his way to some task, leading his family, including the bitch and the goat—because the young ram turned

11

out to be a nice white goat with well-filled dugs but horns broken off short in some tussle or other. And the dog was of course the farmer's very lively bitch.

"Hello there, Uncle Loas!"

"Hello, Barbaças!"

That was excuse enough for the leader of the group to rest his bag and implements on the ground. Loas never missed a chance for half an hour's talk, not even when the other party was a poor nobody in the eyes of a man with two acres of land of his own, a machine for drawing water, and the dream of transforming his beloved plot into a nice little property. Lost to the passage of time, he would let his tongue run on (perhaps his way of getting nearer to what he wanted so much), and his family just had to wait for him. Loas had been known to get hold of a person on the road and stand talking endlessly, while his wife sat among the bushes by the roadside, nursing the child overcome with sleep. In fact, you never knew when Loas would decide it was time to end his monologue.

He would begin by thrusting back the hair from his forehead, like someone drawing aside the curtain that divides stage from stalls. Then he would ask some unexpected question. In a world where nothing ever happened and life in flat, open country was uneventful, any man of inquiring mind was either a warlock or a soothsayer. Loas was considered to be both, and as time went on he came to make the most of his reputation.

"What day is it today, Barbaças?" he asked.

"Tuesday."

"What day will it be three years from today?"

"Tuesday, as like as not."

But he was wrong. And Loas smiled because he knew and other men didn't. He didn't need a calendar to tell him about the future. Tides, days of the week, moons, even a century ahead (if he wanted to look so far forward), he knew all about it. He counted up on his gnarled fingers, added something from a table, and there was the answer as quick as from a calculating machine. And even though he may have had man-to-man talks with the devil himself, there was nothing mysterious about these calculations; he had learned about them in books, in old dog-eared almanacs of alchemy and evil eye. This witchcraft lore was useful in that it made old women afraid of him. It came in handy, too, on occasions like the present, when he wanted to inveigle someone into idle conversation.

"Well, you're wrong, Barbaças," Loas went on mildly, "three years from today will be a Thursday, new moon, and, to use your words, as like as not it'll be autumn.... Now, what about it, Barbaças; why not come along to my place?"

"Nothing doing! It's too far!"

Then Loas definitely did set down his bag and sit down as though clearing the way for a long piece of persuasion. Joana, his wife, saw in a twinkling that her husband wouldn't tear himself away till he'd induced Barbaças to go along with them, and in resignation she tied the goat to a big stone and sat down in her turn. Alice the little girl stroked the dog's back and looked round for something nice to pass the time, while the dog skipped about and licked her face and hands. Alice, too, was delighted to be able to sit and play.

"Now, you say it's too far! A young chap like you flinching at a mile or two!"

"It's more than that."

"Bless my soul, a mile and a half at most! You can have supper with us." Here Loas wiped the back of his hand over his mouth, as though after a good meal.

Barbaças, already half persuaded, licked his lips at thought of the food. But he didn't give in without a struggle.

"If you only had a cart and mules like other farmers," he remarked, "I'd be with you like a shot, even if it were leagues and not miles!"

Loas turned pale and brushed the cruel words away with a sweep of his arm. Without knowing it, Barbaças had flicked him on the raw. To put it plainly, you could compare Loas's life to that of a man who carried the burden of a dream of scraping enough together to buy a couple of mules like those he'd had before. It wasn't the mules as such that interested him, but what they represented—earth well stocked, flourishing, and productive; cycles of fertility, and man taking part in the prodigious mystery of renewal.

13

"I'll manage it someday," Loas said in a smothered voice. "You had a fine pair once. . . ."

"Yes, I did."

The reply was curt, quite unlike Loas's usual flow of words. Barbaças, being a rough-and-ready kind of chap, hadn't meant to hurt him by dragging up the past and the plain fact that Loas had once been a proper farmer with hired men, good land, and a pair of mules. And Loas decided that the best thing was to let it pass, put a cheerful face on it, and talk of more agreeable things.

Now, for a pleasant conversation there was no better opening gambit than his famous cure for tuberculosis with mold of rye bread; or the case of his mother-in-law's hip when he'd yanked the bones into place again; or maybe that clash he'd had with the farmer from Ereira. No doubt about it, his cure for tuberculosis had caused a lot of talk. When he'd come away from the doctor who had diagnosed a septic condition, he'd set about rubbing his arms with mold, and when he'd scratched the skin with his nails later they really came away black with microbes—probably dirt, but he swore it was the bacilli of the disease driven out through the pores. People had just had to believe it.

"Now, Barbaças, let's be off, and I'll tell you all about it as we go along."

And without waiting for an answer, he threw the bag over his shoulder; his wife did the same; Alice put her arm around the goat's soft neck, and Barbaças could do no other but follow them. To be polite he held out his hands for the mattock and rake, and Loas grunted his thanks.

Bent under the weight of the bag, Loas's words sounded strained, and the dust made them even gruffer. The air, caught in the hot stagnation of the afternoon, was all adazzle; and when Loas turned his head for his companion to hear better, his words hung still upon the air, as though caught in a spell, and echoed in Barbaças' ears like a recitative aimed solely at hypnotizing him.

Barbaças had heard Loas tell these tales so often that he knew them by heart, but what was the use of interrupting?

14

When the farmer turned on the tap, it was a real flood. And by this time Loas was in a right good humor, and nothing could stop him. He was already looking forward in imagination to the fine afternoon they were going to spend on the holding, opening up soft furrows in the melon beds, watching them grow black when they set the watering machine to work. And good talk into the bargain!

For his part, Barbaças wasn't very keen on this sort of relationship where, under pretense of an outing, a chap was forced to work like a slave, but for once in a way, and just to bring a bit of change into the monotony of life, he could let himself be gulled by Loas's chatter. On the other hand, he could count on getting a good meal at the end of the day—and he was as much in need of that as neighbor Noémia, who never left off telling all and sundry that she was just waiting for the day (still far ahead) when she'd get her first harvesting pay and be able to eat her fill.

And Barbaças hadn't been mistaken. When they came back to the cottage at dusk with sweat making pale streaks on skin ruddy with effort, they had turned the garden over from end to end and weeded the whole wheat patch—but at the finish of all the drudgery, the piece of bacon with bread and olives, and brandy to drink, had been very welcome. Barbaças could claim most of the honor for himself, while Loas, in his passive way, had been content to direct his companion's energy in the proper channels—but Barbaças wasn't the sort to take offense at that. By the end of the meal, such a pleasant torpor came over him that he agreed to spend the night at the holding.

They were both sitting at the cottage door, smoking from Loas's packet of tobacco. The dog, the goat, and the little girl were playing round. The plain in front of them seemed to sweep out more widely in the twilight, and they had the feeling it all belonged to them. The master of the house suddenly exclaimed:

"Now, Barbaças, what I want here is a helper. And a mule, too, to help with the work...."

And there he sat rubbing his chin and nose as though to quicken senses dulled by his jaunt to town. Whenever he had to leave his little plot, on his return he always went and breathed in the odor of plants, animals, straw, renewing himself in the things of the soil.

"A woman?" asked Barbaças in a disinterested voice.

"No, a man, that's what I said. A kind of partner. I've got a woman—my wife. Nobody has any faith in that machine of mine, and I want to show the lot of them that on such a piece of land, with water, even maize is full ripe in August. We could do big things, Barbaças! But that pair of mules—that's the rub."

The youth looked round to make sure the words were meant for him. And the devil, they were! And at that moment, with his stomach full, he felt particularly receptive and in a mood to be impressed by large ambitions. From the warm twilight and still silence of the countryside came a most moving appeal. As though the very bowels of the earth came up at him, came creeping up, hungry to be possessed. The plain had the undulation, the depth and breadth of an ocean. Everything about it was vast and unfathomable, simultaneously offering itself and withdrawing.

This was the spell that had taken hold of Loas long ago. But the flat languorous plain relaxed men's muscles, and Loas, loving the land and desiring to make it fruitful as he would a woman's body, was impotent to translate his desire into action. He would wield the mattock half a dozen times, then stop as if in a trance, expecting the soil to grow fruitful and surge in a tumult of fertility just from that brief stimulus. The physical effort necessary stood between him and the solemn rite of fecundation. He felt a fanatical urge to make his mark on the earth—but a mark of love, not sweat.

Barbaças was far from the complexity of such feelings, but at that moment he felt drawn to this unknown, seductive world. The machine, water, wheat, daily bread assured—a whole epic of achievement. The youth gulped with emotion, and tears almost came into his eyes. He was a loafer, a hanger-on. And Loas's invitation to share his life moved him.

To be sure, the water machine had been the joke of the district from the day when Loas mortgaged his bit of land to a city dealer, to get the money to dig a well and buy a motor to

16

raise water from the bowels of the earth. But Barbaças could now sympathize with the ambitions of the man who had made himself the laughingstock of this stick-in-the-mud place. It was said that Loas had brought a skilled mechanic from the city to set the motor and adjust it to the best effect. He was in such high feather that he'd put the man up at the best inn the town could boast. The mechanic made himself at home, lounging with cigarette dangling from the corner of his mouth, and spitting disdainfully while the landlady served him with good lean pork and glasses of cognac. The locals spotted straight away that only Vieirinha would be able to tackle this smart aleck; and Vieirinha, when he'd been told about it, just sailed in with chest and belly well in front of him and swept Loas off the bench—poor simple Loas who was gazing at the mechanic as though he were some messenger from heaven. But a man who'd traveled the backwoods of Brazil was not to be put out of countenance by some city upstart whose attitude seemed to imply that with a couple of spanners he could change the face of the heath. And Vieirinha lost no time in giving him to understand as much. Maybe these uncouth laborers could talk of nothing but acorns and pigs, and Loas was fit for nothing but chatter about charms and spells, but he, Vieirinha, was ready for any bigmouthed boaster. The fellow wanted to talk about motors? Well, what of it! He himself, with a pair of pincers and some bits of wire, had driven an old Ford from one end of the Amazon to the other. The chap wanted to talk about women and city taverns? Well, he, Vieirinha, could tell a thing or two about that. In South American ports he'd left dozens of brats with his blood in their veins. And every time he spoke he went one better than the mechanic—no doubt about that!

At last the mechanic told Loas that everything was ready for the final test. Interested onlookers saw them set off for the holding, very brash, with a retinue of excited lads after them, as though the fate of the town hung on that machine. But twilight saw them come back, crestfallen and looking as though they'd been in a fight. The blessed thing had led them the devil of a dance, and the town welcomed them with a roar of laughter.

"What was the fight about, Loas?"

"Damn it all, that crank kicks back like the devil!" Loas answered the first man to ask about the bruises on his face, but when he saw they were only making fun of him, he shut his mouth like a trap for the rest of the day. The mechanic slunk away through back alleys, and left by the first train. The big farmers who up to then had looked down their noses at the report that a poor wretch like Loas was going to give them a lesson in farming now perked up and made the most of the fiasco, twitting him mercilessly. Months later they were still quizzing him about it.

"Eh, Loas, I could make a nice garden down at the end of my land, if you'd just fix up a machine for me. . . ."

And Loas laughed. Probably he would have preferred to make a rude gesture. But in his laugh there was amused pity for the obtuseness of these wealthy fellows, rigid in their egotism and routine—and a laugh said more than a coarse oath.

While laying the snare for Barbaças, Loas had been thinking over those past unhappy events. Even now, whenever he opened up a channel and soused it with water from the well, he couldn't help casting a look of mingled resentment and affection at the useless machine now covered with rust. He would console himself with the thought that an Alentejano farmer had one sole destiny to fulfill: wheat, the wheat harvest. Wheat was always with them the year round; from the time of sowing to the time of threshing it filled autumn, winter, spring, and summer, exacting uninterrupted service. But perhaps for that very reason, because eyes had to be unceasingly watchful through long, hazardous gestation, men loved it with the long-suffering, the disquiet, the anxiety that are the lot of all great passions. No sooner do two Alentejanos come together than they look at the sky or the wheat-bearing back of the plain; their silence or their talk is dominated by the thought of the crop. Gadgets and watering and little gardens were only small considerations outside the indolent, infinite, telluric scale of Alentejo. Wheat, that was the only thing.

Now, Loas's wife, Joana, had come to the heathland in a gang of seasonal workers from the north. And till the end of her days never would she forget the damp green north. Perhaps the persistent way she kept raising flowers and close-hearted cabbages round their cottage had helped to fix her husband's wavering purpose, and egged him on to the comic adventure of bartering a wheat crop for a few armfuls of vegetables. But now he had come back with all his heart and soul to the proper epic of the plain. It didn't worry him that the adventure had meant mortgaging his parcel of land—the Alentejano, surrounded by such a wide expanse, doesn't feel bondslave to the two small plots on which he plants his feet. Wheat, yes, wheat was the thing.

Thinking about wheat, he fell to thinking about what he considered the major disaster of his life: the sale of his couple of mules. There was no small farmer who hadn't been obliged to sell his mules. And the cause of it: ruinous years of drought; mildew in spring; resort to mortgage loans in order to buy fertilizers; cutthroat competition from mechanical transport for goods that used to be carted by mules. In former days, a man could use his mules to cart all kinds of goods from one town to another, and earn enough to buy seed and fertilizer, and improve the land with good dressing. With carting as a sideline, he could carry on if the crop failed. The mules helped him to pay the price of his dream. But now railway and trucks cornered all the transport in the district—mules neither carried wealth nor helped to make it. A big farmer with herds, and timber to cut, and a good crop now and again, could more than pay his way, and go on concentrating on wheat. But when a smallholder came to the end of his hard-working life, all he had to leave was an unshakable faith in great days coming for the cornlands.

"Do you know what wheat means?" a farmer asked in a philosophizing mood. "It boils down to this: Joaquim Rovisco's ass died on him one day. And after fifty years of harvesting he hadn't made enough money to buy another donkey to plow his land!"

19

But Loas wouldn't accept defeat. If only he could manage to get a yoke of well-fed mules with nice long tails streaming in the wind!

"Did you say 'partner'?" asked Barbaças. "What would you pay?"

Now, hold on there. Loas had already forgotten what Barbaças was referring to. With his daydreaming he'd left all that far behind. Yes, that was it. A couple of mules, and a man to help him. But a man who could be fobbed off with talk, and his food.

"You're just the man for me, that's sure," answered Loas. "I'll teach you things, Barbaças. I'll teach you to tell fortunes and work spells, and maybe the devil himself will come and show himself to you one day."

"A bottle of wine's worth more than all that put together. The cobbler promised a lot of fine things, too."

"There'd be wine, of course."

"Well, then, speak out plain."

Loas didn't offer anything very concrete, but the partnership had certain points in its favor. To begin with, properly speaking there wouldn't be a boss to make Barbaças get up at cockcrow, and keep him at it on afternoons when the sultry weather was like a sluggish stream seeping dully through the veins; a boss who slept at ease while others had to watch out for his security and prosperity. No, in that respect Loas was a Christian; maybe he liked to talk and philosophize, work one minute and daydream the next—but at least he did give others the right to fold their arms the better to listen to what he had to say.

And so Barbaças stayed at the holding, where many strange things happened to him.

2

Everybody got busy on the holding. Ti Joana slipped about like a frightened shadow near the cottage, absorbed by tasks of her own. She kept apart from the rest of the family as if she didn't want to be noticed or draw attention to what she was doing. Alice led the goat away to clearings in the shrubby heath. She had passionate talks with hens, with the dog, with creeping things. And the master of the house and his partner had done wonderful work—as though the holding had been waiting a long time for such enthusiasm to rouse it from desolation.

At first sight it might seem hard to believe, but the truth was that Loas had no complaint to make about Barbaças as a working partner. Maybe the fellow did prolong his siesta to evenfall, but then a furious energy took possession of him, and in less than no time he'd cut the furrows, sow them, rake them over again before his master had time to voice praise or protest. For a time these fits and starts broke the monotony of confinement in a place where nothing ever happened (except for Loas standing stock-still at times, gazing at the sky and romancing about estates and yokes of mules), but there was no crony for Barbaças to get into mischief with, so it wasn't surprising that he began to feel bored, that his temper got frayed, and very likely he'd soon be wanting to go back to town where something was always happening.

Loas, however, was on his guard. Maybe he was a bit odd, but he was by no means stupid, and Barbaças' sulks hadn't escaped him. He feared these changes of mood for various reasons, and was ready to take all measures to persuade him to stay. He'd shared his food with him, given him ham and plates of bread broth. He'd taught him something he'd

21

never known before: that you can be proud and happy in work that is based on some life ambition. He'd have to harp on these things, or find stronger baits. But was Barbaças ready to feel the call of the earth? Or was he too dense to understand the vastness of the future? How could anyone, however hidebound, resist the appeal of a growing shoot? Old Vieirinha, for instance, was a tippler and a windbag, but he'd come back from wealthy countries on the other side of the world to live in a shack on an arid patch of heath. . . .

So when they were sitting at the cottage door at twilight, looking out over a plain softened by shadows, and the sounds and sap of the land seemed charged with an erotic undertone, ready to fuse up at any moment in the drowsy senses, Loas would lay his broad dark hand on the loafer's knee.

"You see, Barbaças," he would say, "money's just a flash in the pan . . . but we've done great things."

When Loas began talking in metaphors, Barbaças' forehead wrinkled up like the skin of a startled worm, and his eyelids became a curtain of flesh obscuring his eyes and his understanding.

"A flash?"

But Loas had already left that thought behind.

"A man—even nobodies like ourselves—can give big things to the world. The wheat harvest comes from man's hands, doesn't it? We did the reaping and threshing. And we're going to prepare the earth for good sowing. A seed, a grain of corn would be nothing without a man's hands to put life into it. And we've done it all without mules! Bless my soul, Barbaças, give me land rather than money! Land's the thing! Now, am I right or aren't I?"

"Sometimes it's just a damned grind," retorted Barbaças, kicking sullenly at the ground.

"It's true, a man needs help to be able to do really well. When you've got a fine pair of mules in front of you, damn me if your feet don't seem to fly," said Loas, shaking his head wistfully. "But someday we'll manage it. Even a donkey would be better than nothing."

"You're the donkey for talking so much about it!"

It was a waste of time to reason with such a lout, and, discouraged, Loas turned to look at his long strip of land. The long, melancholy landscape was in tune with his mood. Sometimes it looked as though the land were drawing away in disappointment, stretching away toward someone who loved it better. The trees seemed to be marching away across the hill, across the stubble, away from the dusty lanes and the end-of-summer doldrums, trying to escape from the lethargy of the plain. But the craftiness of man and the burden of the baked earth held them bound to their fate.

Loas felt quite sure that the earth was aware of his aims. But a man with two women to fend for, and no beast to help him, couldn't go far. Sometimes you had to wait a month for clouds so that it would be safe to lay the grain in the harrowed soil. And even then you couldn't expect a neighbor to come and help with the sowing before the clods hardened again. In the summer, three consecutive days of settled heat, wind, or storm would beat down the wheatlands, and a farmer couldn't allow the ripe crop to lie at the mercy of rot. So he had to make sure of a friend's help. He must keep hold of Barbaças.

"You seem to be down in the dumps," Loas said sympathetically, changing his tactics, while his clear blue eyes shone with a moist look of affection.

"I'm made like that."

No answer could choke Loas off for long, but at the moment he thought the best thing to do was to take his head between his freckled fingers as though pondering serious matters. Then the next day he came out with something new.

"If you'll promise not to let it go any further, Barbaças. I'll tell you who came to visit me last night."

"I'm listening," the loafer answered curtly.

Disregarding this brazen lack of interest, Loas revealed that his dead mother had spoken to him the previous night. It was, he said, a kind of slow, whining voice, as though it had come floating over woods or as though someone on the other side had been pulling her by the hair.

"She was calling for me, Barbaças!" This weird occurrence

23

would surely strengthen his position, he thought. It would reveal his extraordinary gifts, and show he had influence with supernatural forces. It would bind Barbaças more closely to know Loas for a man who held the dead and the future at his disposal, written in the stars or the lines of the hand.

"And are you going to her?"

"What else is there to do? The wishes of the dead are sacred."

Barbaças felt clusters of needles pricking him in the stomach. He felt really uneasy. Old Loas spoke of the dead and of devils as if they were tavern cronies! He looked at his companion with new interest, scared and attentive at the same time, like someone forced to revise his opinion.

"All right, Ti Loas, in that case I'd better move out tomorrow. To tell you the truth . . ." Barbaças almost blurted out what his intentions were, but then decided to skirt round the point. "If you're going away . . . to where your mother is . . . I can't stay here doing nothing."

Loas saw that he'd made a false move.

"Now, now, you've got it all wrong," he said, then came to a halt, casting round for an idea to save the situation, but could think of nothing. "Now, you just try this," he went on, to gain time, pushing a piece of sausage toward Barbaças. "See whether you like it . . . eat as much as you want—there's more in the house. Now, just get this right, my lad. I didn't mean to say I was going to my mother right now. You have to think over things like that before deciding. Before doing anything at all, I shall have to go to the notary, to make a will. And the women couldn't manage the holding by themselves. So you see?" Here Loas gave the youth a shrewd look. "I can't take the land with me, my lad. It'd be different, of course, if they'd got a couple of strong mules to help them. But without a yoke of beasts, damn it, only the strength of a *man's* arms can keep the land from turning to heath again." Loas took his hat off and scratched his greasy head, giving time for the hint to sink in. Then, slyly, he took the plunge. "I'd be ready to leave you all of it—garden, machine, crops—if you'd promise to take care of my wife and daughter. You're a rascal only when it suits you, I can see that. You've made a fine thing of the holding."

"I dunno about that."

Not a word more. It was really discouraging. He must be pretending he didn't understand. But when Loas took another look at the loafer's blank expression, he saw with amazement that his talk, far from rousing Barbaças' cupidity, was merely sending him to sleep! He was lying down with his head on his cap, trying to snuggle into the shade of the fig tree, his eyes too vague for Loas to believe that he'd been listening properly. And, feeling foolish, Loas walked off.

It was hopeless. Perhaps deep down Barbaças felt flattered by the way the farmer tried to get round him, but the feeling, though pleasant, wasn't strong enough to rouse someone as slack as he was. He wasn't civilized enough to become servile at the beck of a legacy.

So Loas walked away to the water machine. It was lying in an out-of-the-way spot, and its associations were unpleasant, but it was there he liked to go and chew the cud of his own hard luck. The whole thing had been a fiasco, but he never felt humiliated by it. The landscape round him was still bone-dry and bare, the flaming sun licking it dry like a libidinous tongue scorching a defenseless body. But it gave him a feeling of pride. The plain was bare and burned, but imposing. Desolate, but grandiose. And he, too, in his defeat, was not without greatness. A man was born and inherited land, and he had to leave the inheritance entire to those coming after. But the real legacy was not the land, be it small patch or big estate. The real legacy was the measure of love and tenacity he had put into it. Rust had come and corroded the machine. A city dealer held the mortgage of the best part of his holding. There had been bad years. Roads and motorcars had come and robbed him of his mules—but his dream was still intact. He would rise from the ruins; each day he was ready to begin again. In autumn you put the seed in the earth, and before the next autumn you harvested the fruit. Each year and every year the same cycle was repeated, the same joyous miracle of gestation. If only he could manage to make sure of that rascal

Barbaças! If only the money he had put by—heaven alone knew how, but Joana was such a careful contriver she seemed to squeeze it out of the very stones—were enough to buy even a donkey, great days might still come to the holding.

Now Loas was smiling again at the thought of that splendid future. Droves of pigs, pigsties, a fine garden round the house, and, dwarfing everything else, an indolent sea of swaying green, a sea of wheat. Or breezes racing over it like untethered colts, ruffling the tresses of the corn. Gaping at it all, drinking in the rich warm breath of the wheat, Loas felt a wave of lazy well-being and prosperity flush through him. And he, too, fell asleep.

A hundred yards away, Barbaças had probably fallen asleep first. His head had slipped off his cap, and a horsefly stung him so briskly that he hadn't time even to curse. Stuttering with rage, he lifted his hand to swat the creature, when his eyes fell upon a baby field mouse close by. All aquiver, it was nestling in a patch of sunlight—evidently so young and naïve it didn't know Barbaças belonged to a hostile race. And Barbaças was so tickled at the sight that his smothered curse turned into an exclamation of pleasure. Then he saw that Alice was there, too. She was lying on one elbow in the coarse grass, cheek resting on hand, watching the mouse in fascinated silence. Of course, that young mouse was at the mercy of any cat eager to gobble its silky skin and tender bones, and Alice would follow any living thing to the ends of the earth to protect it. But he'd give her something to think about! A nice tasty morsel that mouse would be for Loas's cat. Kitty . . . kitty . . . kitty . . . where the devil was the creature? That would be a lark to see it crushing the soft warm flesh, like crushing a fruit between your teeth so sweet and ripe it sickened you.

"Hey, Alice! Do you want to eat it grilled like ortolans?"

Horrified, the girl shook her head. She rarely spoke, but her eyes and face were so expressive she didn't need words. Her face went red with anxiety, for fear Barbaças might really do what he said. And when he'd forgotten the remark, she was still shaking her head.

All right, since there was to be no fun with the cat, the loafer took the shivering little thing in the palm of his hand. What an exciting sense of power it gave to hold a life at his will, even the life of a little mouse so puny that a single squeeze would suffocate it. But Barbaças wasn't really cruel at heart, and under Alice's watchful eyes he stroked the little captive and put it down again in the patch of sunlight. Then he looked round carelessly for something to feed it with. Crumbs, bits of acorn, snails maybe? What would a mouse of that age like? Corn, lettuce? What a fuss about nothing! Living with Loas must be turning him crazy, too. It was silly to ask himself such questions, and he felt rather ashamed of himself. A good thing Alice didn't talk, because of course she'd sensed his feeling of tenderness and then his shame. She watched people so intently, especially where animals were concerned, and now her eyes were already expressing gratitude at the lad's kind thought. Smiling, she held out her arms for the mouse, begging to hold it in her own hands just for a minute, but Barbaças pretended not to see. Of course, he was going to give it to her later, when he'd indulged his own whim. So, to return to what the creature would like—what could he give it as a great treat? Fresh cheese, crumbs? Searching the depths of his memory, he wrinkled his brow with the effort. Years of living close to the beasts of the field in his vagrancy had clearly not taught him much on this subject. There were gaps in his experience, and once a chap who suspected them had tried to catch him out.

"Where does the starling lay its eggs?" he had asked.

Starling? Now let's see. The starling . . . Barbaças had muttered. Now, where the devil did it lay its eggs? Blushing with shame at finding no answer, he'd had to fall back on bringing out a counterchallenge that would have been quite a feather in his cap, if it had come off.

"I can't remember, so that's that. But you can take me for a bigger brayer than an ass if you can catch me out over anything else. Come on, ask away! Ask anything you like."

"Get away with you, you're bluffing!"

"You just ask, and you'll see."

"Well then, let's see if you know this: Which are the holdings where you can steal rum cherries in September?"

Barbaças had set no limits, and it was a fair question right in his own field, so he couldn't protest. He ransacked his memory, like dragging up buckets of mud and weeds from a well one by one, but even so he overlooked two places. There was really no excuse for it, and for a long time afterward he felt that he had lost face.

And here he was again, just as ignorant about the mouse and the tidbits it might like. Better drop the idea and play with the mouse by snapping his fingers a few inches from its snout. Alice was still smiling, but the startled mouse began to scurry away. Silly little beast. He'd a good mind to call Loas's cat again. Still, why bother? Just let it go. Alice stood up and cautiously followed the mouse's travels, tiptoeing along so as not to startle it again.

That silly little Alice seemed really fascinated. Perhaps it would be interesting to tame a mouse, but it'd take a lot of time and patience. And even if it didn't, neither a tame mouse nor everything Loas promised to leave him in his will could keep him on the holding. He was homesick for the town, for loafing about the place, for the smell of fires burning in the open, and the comradeship of some gang. Life was more pleasant in the small country town. Even monotony was bearable. In fat times or lean times there were always people around. Long days of sultry weather like a warm mattress under your body. Empty taverns where you could lean your elbow on the counter during the hot siesta and fall asleep. Sleep with your nose nuzzled in the heady smell of wine and fried sticklebacks. Long, slow days full of leisurely peace, sleep, and freedom—no obligations. All very well for a chap to be sitting by the roadside, and for a fellow like Loas to come along and talk you into an adventure. But when the adventure turned into daily toil, that was the end!

He'd just have to make up his mind, put a stop to the

farmer's vain hopes, and take himself off. And so, turning it all over in a brain already tired with the effort, he fell asleep again. Mouth open, one knee bent, hands quietly resting on his chest, he let the end of the afternoon, dusk, and nightfall flow over him.

Loas came several times to take a look while he slept. With the flair of a diviner, he suspected Barbaças' intentions, and wanted to prevent them at all costs. When the loafer woke up, his first sensation was of a warm, unpleasant contact on his right hand. Then his eyes fell on the mouse, which, feeling the cool of the evening, and less independent than earlier on, had crept up to the warmth of his hands. And his heart melted at its trust in him.

Sitting on a stone bench, hands clasped on knees and an empty look on his face, Loas watched him wake up.

"Good evening, Barbaças. . . . . You've had a good sleep."

"I didn't notice it was so late."

"I see you've found a little friend," Loas went on, pointing at the mouse. "You could teach it to come and eat out of your hand." He suddenly became very thoughtful. "Sometimes animals make me wonder . . . the intelligence some of them have. Now, when I had those mules . . ."

"Mules! You're always talking about mules!"

But Loas paid no attention to this rudeness.

"I sometimes wonder whether a little creature like that wasn't once a human being. I don't know whether you see what I mean. I'm talking about the mouse. A soul from the other world could pass into an animal and come back to us. If you were to come back, what would you like to be?" At a loss, Barbaças shrugged his shoulders, with no wish to encourage such idle chatter. But the farmer went on unperturbed, weaving the nets of talk in which he hoped to catch the youth. "For my part, when I'm dead, I'd like to come back as a civet cat. And you? Now, Barbaças, just look how that mouse is nuzzling its snout into your fingers. Who knows if it isn't your grandad who's—"

"My grandad my foot!"

"It could very well be. Once, when I was going along the

Aviz road, I saw a man carrying some puppets on his back and some cages of mice. The next day I came across him again at the Cabeção Fair, and the mice were performing. They climbed up a ladder and twined their tails round a trapeze and swung round, really marvelous! Not the sort of tricks you could get an ordinary mouse to do. Mere mice do things like that? Do you believe they could? Upon my soul, you'll never get me to believe that!" (Barbaças shook his head in a vigorous negative.) "It was nighttime, and I'd had a few drinks at the stalls. Then I came to a booth where the puppet man was getting his supper ready, and I heard him talking to those mice as if they were human. Damn me, you can't tame mice that far! And it suddenly came to me that they were the man's kith and kin: one had been a puppet man himself, and another a mason. And they'd come back to this world to help their kinsman."

"That's just rubbish, Uncle Loas!" protested Barbaças in disgust at the farmer's shameless romancing.

"I swear it's true. And that's why I tell you that creature you're holding may very well be your grandad, who was an honest man and a friend of mine. Maybe he finds our company comforting, and likes to see us together. Maybe he'd like to live with us at the homestead. If I were sure of that, damn me, Barbaças, I'd never let you go! You mustn't flout the wishes of the dead, you know!"

Barbaças let his eyelids fall slowly. Now he understood what the old rascal was after.

"Grandad my eye! You're talking rot!" And the coarse lout pinched the mouse's tail just to show he wasn't impressed with talk of ancestors and superstitions. Then he got up, and stood still two steps away to turn and point a warning finger at Loas.

"Understand, I'm going away. I'm sick of the mattock and all your humbug!"

"Now, don't do that to me, Barbaças!" the farmer almost shrieked in alarm. "If you like, I'll call the devil up for you to see!"

The loafer spat with contempt, as though the whole thing

turned his stomach, and took several more strides away, with Loas on his heels.

"Barbaças! Luís! There's just one more thing I want to say!" the farmer exclaimed, clutching at Barbaças, but the latter shook him off, thinking it was only one more tall story. "What I've got to say is the plain truth, I swear it! Don't go away, but just listen to me!"

In aloof determination, Barbaças didn't even turn his head; but then Loas stumbled and fell, his weight knocked Barbaças' legs from under him, and both rolled into a hollow in the coarse grass. But the farmer's voice went on hoarse and pleading, seeming to rise from the very soil.

"You've got to go and buy a donkey for me, Barbaças! I've been yarning to everybody about a pair of mules, but it was because I was too ashamed to own up that I've been saving to buy a donkey. I can speak openly to you, son. Stay with me on the holding, Luís, and this year, with a plow and a donkey, I'm going to fill the threshing floor with wheat. Both of us together, we can turn the holding into the greenest spot of land in these parts!"

With knees barked, Barbaças staggered to his feet, but Loas was still wallowing on the ground, and his voice rose humbly, all blarney gone out of it, begging for the charity of understanding. The loafer was easily moved. Sobbing in a miserable mixture of rage and affection and solemn awareness of the moment, in the end he promised to throw in his lot with the farmer and his dream.

3

While Loas counted out the notes on the kitchen table, there was anxious silence. Old notes of different sizes and values, one of which caught Barbaças' attention. He wasn't an expert in money matters, but it did seem to him that that sort was no longer in use.

"That one there . . ."

But words and gesture were cut short. The master's voice rose irritably a tone higher, because the counting of money is a serious thing that has to be done carefully.

Loas's wife didn't move away from the hearth—a neutral zone of seclusion where she had long been in the habit of hiding from others and from herself. Only Alice took eager part in the family conclave. She had gathered, from talk between her father and Barbaças and from her mother's bewilderment, that something extraordinary was about to happen at the homestead: they were going to buy a donkey. And a donkey is such a big and powerful beast that three or four Alices can jump on its back and ride a long, long way, and it doesn't get tired or unwilling. A donkey to draw the plow or a cart, with teeth strong enough to munch two bundles of hay in a twinkling. She liked to caress small, defenseless creatures like pigeons, ducks, rabbits. But a big animal, strong though humble, that obeys man's behests and—like the tiny ones—can be won by kindness held a special place in Alice's veneration. Often she had heard her father say that a farmer without a couple of mules was less than a beggar, had heard him bemoan his hard luck, but next prophesy wonderful things for the future if . . . She had got really interested, however, only when her father gradually and reluctantly became less ambitious, and talked about a nice, good-tempered donkey. Because a donkey was something that could belong to her too.

"Are we going to have a little donkey, Mam?"

Joana shrugged her shoulders and said just what she usually said, like someone a bit simpleminded:

"I dunno. . . ."

This "I dunno" served all purposes. She had seen that awful man from the city dressed in his blue overalls and champing a cheroot in the corner of his mouth, talking big. And with him had come that fantastic machine her husband had talked about for years, ever since he'd had to give up the cart and mules and had thought of the machine to pin his hopes on. She'd seen it all so many times—enthusiasm, then discouragement, the two so inextricably mixed in his character that she'd understood once and for all that her husband could be happy only in a life where these feelings alternated. After that, she took no share in his illusions and disappointments.

That machine, for instance: maybe it could have improved the holding, but it wasn't the kind of thing that appealed to her. Of course, she liked to see well-tended land round her, but with everything growing from water, manure, and the labor of their hands. People from the north, like herself, had the same homely feeling for the land as for a cradle; they planted their feet on it and set their heart in it. But here in Alentejo your soul and the steps you took were lost in immensity. That machine had promised trees, flowers, land with the odor of fertility; but it hadn't worked, and the rusty monster was only a mockery. Not for her husband, though, who never gave up hope. After the machine, he'd dreamed of a pair of mules, and now it had come down to something more feasible: a donkey.

This time, it might be safe to share his dream. A donkey would free them from want and drudgery. This dream was something real, something useful for their kind of tasks; but Joana had lived through such a lot of this kind of thing that she was now afraid her husband wouldn't be able to persevere in the one down-to-earth struggle. He got carried away with visions, and each time was passionately sincere, but all of a sudden would abandon them. Perhaps these bursts of enthusiasm served to relieve his feelings, because he gave himself up so wholeheartedly to the big and little things of life.

But now Joana and her little girl could be quite sure they were going to have a donkey, because there was the master of the house sorting the wonderful money into different heaps.

"Now, you count it too, Barbaças," he said. "I make it four hundred and sixty escudos that we've got."

That "we've got" was like a stream of milk and honey down the youth's throat, tight with excitement. He felt he'd like to say or do something that would bind him finally to the people round him. He couldn't quite understand what had been going on inside him during the last few days, but it was like what a mangy dog feels when someone holds out a friendly hand.

"I was watching. That's quite right."

He was going to mention that note he'd caught sight of, but then scratched his nose and thought better of it. It wasn't his place to call the farmer's judgment in question.

"Anyway, you count it!" Loas said again, perhaps for the joy of repeating such a pleasant performance.

So Barbaças slowly counted the money over again, in groups of a hundred escudos—"one, two, three . . . and this heap makes fifty"—accompanied by solemn nods of the head from Loas and the womenfolk. He stopped counting from time to time to lick his finger, and during these pauses the farmer wiped his forehead with his handkerchief.

"Well, and what do you say?"

"It's quite correct."

"That isn't what I mean. Will it be enough?" Loas asked the question slowly. You could see he was anxious what the answer would be.

"It's a long time since I've been round the markets," the youth parried.

"Nobody ever bought a donkey that was sound on its legs for that amount!"

All turned in consternation, because it was Joana who had made this blunt remark. She had gathered up all her courage

34

to speak her mind, and stood blushing with surprise at her own temerity, looking as though nothing would ever make her so daring again.

"Maybe you're right," Loas conceded a few seconds later, his spirits much dashed.

Barbaças had been so pleased at the happy feeling pervading the house since the farmer had opened the money box holding their hard-earned savings that he felt impelled to try to shield them from disappointment.

"I promise you'll have a jackass within two months! Give me the money, and next Friday I'll go and have a look round the Brotas Fair."

Loas and his wife exchanged a quick look. They didn't know whether they could trust Barbaças. Could they put money like that into the hands of an idle tramp?

"I think a she-ass would be better," said Loas, avoiding a direct reply. "She-asses are easier to manage."

"A she-ass, then. A jackass or a she-ass makes no odds. What I don't know is whether the fair falls this week or not."

Loas fell to counting on his fingers, muttering and staring at the ceiling with a rapt expression.

"It falls on St. Matthew's Day," he declared, "the eve of St. Gregory."

"Then just you leave it to me."

In his embarrassment Loas began rubbing his hands. It didn't suit him for the youth to put himself forward like this. He wanted to talk the matter over first.

"Well, all right," he stammered. "But tell me, Barbaças, if the fair is Friday this week, what were you getting at when you talked about two months' time?"

"If the money isn't enough, how do you think I could bring a donkey back next Friday? But in two months, a lot of things can happen," Barbaças answered mysteriously. Then he stood biting his lips, and nervously feeling his pocket where he kept the mouse, though the poor creature didn't like its prison at all. And thinking of the mouse, he felt a sudden impulse to be generous.

"Here, Alice, you take it! It's tickling in my pocket."

Laughing with delight, the girl ran and took the mouse from him, and carried it away to a corner of the hearth. The men's talk didn't interest her anymore. Squatting there, she dandled it in her lap.

"To make a purchase like that, you have to keep your eyes open, Barbaças," Loas went on, chewing over his doubts. "Do you know anything about donkeys?"

"Is there anybody in these parts who don't know about donkeys?"

"You're right, there. But, damn me, I was just wondering whether it wouldn't be better for me to go and choose the beast. I've got friends. I might come across somebody who'd sell me one cheap."

"And take you in over it?" Barbaças cut in rudely. Then he saw he'd gone too far, and tried to smooth it over. "You believe everything you're told; any gypsy could fob you off with anything."

At this point, for the second time in this memorable discussion, Loas's wife had something to say. Her face as stiff as a sleepwalker's, she came forward from the hearth and stood at her husband's side. She gathered all the money together into a single heap and, looking at Barbaças, said in a tense voice:

"I dunno.... I didn't know about this money. I thought my man had already spent it.... But putting it in your hands, Luís, is like putting the blood of all of us in your hands."

Choking with amazement, Loas couldn't utter a single word to retrieve the situation, but once the surprise was over, he felt so happy he could cry. His wife's gesture showed there was in all of them a hidden treasure of dream and daring. He felt as though he'd like to cry and gather all of them in a single embrace—wife, daughter, Barbaças, the whole world.

Barbaças had to pass through the town to get to the fair at Brotas. But this time, even if he hadn't got the money sewn into his jacket pocket, he wouldn't feel like letting himself be tempted by the taverns. The purchase of the donkey was now something more than a point of honor. It was a goading ambition as close to his own heart as to Loas's, because he'd become a member of the family, sharing its anxieties, habits, and pleasures. And although the anxieties far outweighed the pleasures, for the first time in his life he felt there was something round him and behind him, that he was a human being who belonged.

In former days Barbaças had walked the streets of the town hundreds of times, light of heart, without responsibilities or problems. He could walk at his own pace, lounge or work according to his mood, or sit on some doorstep the whole day long if he felt so inclined. But this independence isolated him from the common life. Living in the hovel with his brothers, sharing food at times, listening to farmhands in the taverns, playing tricks on farmers—he was never anything but a loafer on the fringe of things. The laughter or complaints his exploits gave rise to formed no part of the real life of the town. The others laughed or complained, and then passed on. Each one of them had a life of his own, but he, Barbaças, was outside it all. His heart, without joy or sorrow, was really full of loneliness. And then, when he was on the point of going back to that empty freedom, Loas had only had to own up to his weaknesses and worries, as man to man, appeal to him to throw in his lot with them, and this had given him a stake in real life.

Loas's wife had got a little packet of food ready for him, and Alice had handed the mouse back to him without a word. From time to time he put his hand to his pocket to feel the warm, living contact, reminding him of the family to which, by such a swift turn of events, he had come to belong.

The Domingas woman was the first person to catch sight of him as he walked up the street. Arms akimbo and a bantering smile on her lips, she stood waiting for him.

"Bless my soul! Look who's here, and see how fat he's got!"

Various heads immediately poked out from doorways, because people were always on the lookout, and a single word was enough to rouse their curiosity.

"Well, well, so he's back again!"

Barbaças, lengthened his stride, and grunted a few greetings without looking to right or left. Vieirinha called out to him from a tavern:

"Do you feel like a drink, Barbaças? Don't be in such a

hurry, man! How's friend Loas getting on?"

Vieirinha, too, belonged to the family circle, as it were, and the lad felt he ought to give some reply.

"They're all well. I'll have a word with you later."

"Tell friend Loas that one of these days I'm coming along to bring him a few melons."

Barbaças strode on, but he'd forgotten to reckon with Dona Quitéria, and when he passed by her window gratings the good lady immediately tapped on the pane and called him, using his proper name. The nickname offended her Christian ears, and she was the only person who always called him Luís. The maid quickly came to open the door while her mistress, with the window open just a crack, kept calling to him.

"Wait a minute, Luís. Wait a minute."

The lad went in with such haste that the maid hadn't time to close all the doors to shut off the draft, so Dona Quitéria took shelter behind a big armchair, pulling her knitted shawl round her to protect her chest. She wore such long, wide shoes that, when she stood still like this, they looked like two pontoons holding her feet to the ground. But she was wonderfully quick in movement, and, thin and stooping, she flitted about the house like an agile puppet. She said her prayers and shouted at the servants all in the same breath; she hobnobbed with the saints and at the same time kept her ears open to pick up any scandal that was going.

"Well, now, is it true that you're at Loas's holding? Does he look after you? Is that machine working yet? Have you seen him talking to Satan?"

Barbaças felt dazed as she shot the questions at him one after the other, crossing herself vigorously at the last one.

"Of course not," muttered Barbaças.

He was sorry he'd come in. He'd put up with her silly questions in other days, in the hope of getting a couple of sausages for his trouble; but he wasn't a beggar now—he was Loas's partner.

"Do you say your prayers, Luís? Does he beat his wife? Does he pray? They say his daughter's a little savage who's never

38

been to church. Does the poor innocent know her catechism, Luís?"

"I don't know anything about that," Barbaças answered, bored with the whole thing.

"Yes, Luís, I know only too well you know nothing about such things. You haven't even paid your debt to Our Lady of Fátima, you young heathen! . . . Close that door, girl!"

And Dona Quitéria went on interspersing orders and sermons as was her wont. It was the normal thing for her to spend the livelong day alternating prayers with the detailed cross-examination of the woman who ran errands for her, or finding fault with the maid. Everybody in the place made fun of her petty-mindedness, her gossiping, and the really offensive nature of the things she said about high and low, because she was quite unaware of the real meaning of words. But of course nobody dared laugh in her face. Dona Quitéria was a lady, "the only lady in the town," as she would often say herself, especially when she was wearing a kind of black cloak with a fur collar, and ladies' boots dating from the time of her grandmother. Just as an example: once when Dona Quitéria had a bout of indigestion from eating too much duck and rice, she had accused her brother-in-law of poisoning her so that he could come into her property sooner. Then, again, when her husband had died with his liver as big as a wineskin, she told the doctor bluntly that *he* had killed him with the castor oil he had prescribed. The doctor, dumbfounded, had swallowed the insult because Farmer Cortes was present and he didn't want to make a scene, but Dona Quitéria had taken his silence as an admission.

Petty and suspicious as she was, her suspiciousness all melted away as soon as a priest knocked at her door to beg alms for the church. Peddlers, marvelously keen on the scent, came from miles away to sell images of saints, and gewgaws and laces that she bought with eyes closed once they said the bishop had recommended them. Dona Quitéria had another characteristic, too, that she was very proud of: she had a very glib tongue. In conversation she always managed to bring in some word remembered from college days, because she thought some dictionary knowledge helped a lot toward proving you were a lady. Among lettered people in the town, the story was told that once, at a reception at the bishop's palace, Dona Quitéria had loudly discussed with another lady the use of *is* and *are;* and at last they came down to concrete examples.

"Well, then, do you say 'There is a number of things' or 'There are a number of things'?"

"'There are a number of things,' of course."

"Then you're wrong. 'Number' is singular."

The bishop, catching the end of this conversation, summed up to the priest with him:

"She's stupid but logical."

And that was the truth in a nutshell.

Barbaças was trying to think up some way of beating a retreat, when Dona Quitéria whispered to the maid:

"Go and fetch the rose-colored rosary!"

Then she drew the folds of her shawl more tightly about her to keep off the draft from the passage, and clutched Barbaças by the arm.

"I'm going to give you a rosary that was blessed last week," she said. "You haven't made up your mind to keep your promise, but at least you can pray to Our Lady to forgive you. I was hoping you'd come to town so that I could give it to you, so promise me you'll pray with it, Luís. Take the rosary, two cheeses, and some slices of ham. That heathen Loas is quite capable of letting you go hungry. . . . Has his wife said any novenas since you've been at the holding? . . . And you can let me know afterward whether you liked the cheeses."

"I don't want cheeses or rosaries."

"You don't want the cheeses or the ham, Luís?"

"I don't need charity!" said the loafer with dignity, savoring his position to the full.

Dona Quitéria couldn't think of anything to say, and the maid burst out laughing at the ragamuffin's retort. Barbaças took the opportunity to open the door quickly and make his escape.

Outside, he drew a deep breath of relief, and for the

hundredth time made sure the notes were still safe in his pocket. Then, with eyes fixed straight ahead, he made for the bypath over the heath that would shorten his way to the fair.

Lost in his own thoughts, it was some time before he noticed he was being followed. It was Noémia, wife of old Peg Leg the tailor, who never got any jackets to make up now. And she'd been following him ever since he reached town. Yes, now he came to think of it, she'd been near the Domingas woman; then she'd been hanging round Dona Quitéria's windows. What the devil did she want?

"What do you want?" he shouted from some way off, then waited for her to catch up with him.

"I don't want anything."

"Going to the fair, then?"

"No, I'm not, and I don't want anything, either."

And she stood there with her sallow face cupped in one hand, looking at him with moist, fascinated, animal-like eyes.

"Do you people at the holding manage to eat?" she suddenly asked in an eager voice.

"Of course we eat."

"Even after harvesting's over?"

"We always have something to eat."

"Enough to eat your fill?"

"Yes, as often as not," Barbaças answered, offhand, not interested in this kind of talk.

"That's what I thought. A farmer's always got something to put on a plate. And this year, for once, I'm going to eat my fill, too. Barbaças, I'm going to sell the old man's sewing machine; then there'll be enough for everybody in the house to eat for a whole week. Just for one whole week I'd like to eat everything I fancy. I dream about it every night, and wake up with such a pain of emptiness in my belly that I have to go and fill it up with a quart of water."

"And when the machine's gone?"

"What does that matter? After that one week, I shan't care if I never eat again. They've been saying in town that Loas lets you die of hunger. Praise be, it isn't true! Nothing but lies they tell. 'That land of his is too poor to grow anything!' they say, and a lot of nonsense like that. . . . Do you think Loas's wife would like to buy the machine?"

"Ask her yourself." Barbaças was pawing the ground, racking his brain for a pretext to get rid of the woman, and suddenly he held out the parcel of food. "I was forgetting this," he said. "Ti Joana sent it for you."

And, a second time having made good his escape, he hurried along the path, determined to keep clear of other obstructions.

Once a year on that open space, hundreds of animals were assembled; beggars and peddlers came; stalls that sold everything—even love—merry-go-rounds and a circus were put up; and a good part of the population from many leagues around gathered to see it all. As Barbaças approached, the languid breeze carried waves of sound to him—sometimes blasts of noise, sometimes just the buzzing of thousands of mingled voices, vendors' cries, laughter. And as it all came to him, drawing him into the clamor, he began to feel anxious, almost afraid. Like any Alentejano, up to then he had always looked forward to the July weeks, when the wakes went the round of the towns, livening them up, deafening them—a whole caravan of marvelous madness and agitation. Showmen came, photographers, hawkers, women; bringing glamour to their uneventful country life, bringing an excitement not to be repeated during all the long, becalmed months, however much they hankered for it. All this activity burgeoned in the ripe atmosphere of the wheatlands—and the fair was like a mighty lung filling with strong breaths of life, then deflating and wrinkling like an empty balloon, only to swell up again with redoubled force, drawing into itself everything that possibly could be drawn in.

In the old days Barbaças never left the fairground. On the eve of the fair he was among the hangers-on who lent a hand raising poles for the circus and the merry-go-rounds or who directed the showmen to the best places for shopping. He used to eat, sleep, and amuse himself near the stalls and huts as though they were his real home. In the whirlpool of activity he just let himself go, enjoying love, wine, and the small amusements that went to his head like wine. In a word, it was the fair at which, throwing thrift overboard, people squandered the money earned during the harvest weeks. And Barbaças wasn't the only one to have his fling—all the lads of the town went off to the fair, for a brief spell sloughed their old skins and flaunted in glory; then went back to their old habits and tasks as though nothing had happened, became taciturn and deliberate once more, withdrawing into the inviolable solitude of the plain.

But this time Barbaças was on his guard. He didn't look upon it as a fair, but as a cattle market. He had money in his pocket, but not to waste on games or on women at the rifle ranges or at the booths. He had come entrusted with the sacred charge of realizing the ambitions of a whole family. Like any respectable farmer, he must show no interest in the paltry gewgaws of the fair. He must study market fluctuations, the prices and qualities of animals, so as not to be taken in by the tricks of gypsies and dealers. Loas, doubtless quite unaware of it, had given him not only a share in the work of the holding but also a sense of the dignity of a farmer's life, notwithstanding its disappointments. He was going to steer clear of the cries and the music, however hard they tried to catch him; and the sacrifice he was going to make gave him a feeling of happiness. His only fear was that the money might not be enough to buy the donkey. He was practically certain this would be the case, but still hoped against hope for some unexpected stroke of luck.

The road from the town to the fairground was a dense jostle of movement. The heavy afternoon air lay like a thick blanket over the low houses, over the fields that bordered them, over the dust. Now and again a breeze wafted the sounds away for a moment, but when it fell the volume of noise came back more than ever. Haughty farmers on horseback made their way through the compact press of womenfolk, farmhands, gangs of youths, and beggars showing crippled limbs and whining the sad tale of their troubles. Barbaças pushed his way quickly through the crowd, like a man with a purpose, having nothing in common with people who had merely left their houses or cottages to come out and enjoy themselves. Sometimes he heard a shout: "Hey, Barbaças, are your feet on fire?" or, "Hey, Barbaças, no need to run; the wine's not giving out yet!" But these shafts of wit had no sting for him. Let them have their fun. Very soon they'd see him leading a fine donkey, like any smallholder with a house and crops, and the responsibility of obtaining animals to make those crops bigger.

In the middle of the fairground a man was bawling into a loudspeaker, inviting people to come and see the wonders he had to show, and his patter carried farther than the echo of a shot. The rhythm of the merry-go-round music was so catchy that, even from a distance, people felt themselves carried away by the urge to let themselves go. Clouds of dust borne on the wind across the plain also brought the sound of the muffled trampling of animals in the coarse grass of the heath, the noise of voices and the hoof-beats of horses in the street. They brought the cries of animals imprisoned in the pens, the clamor of loudspeakers, and the creaking of the merry-go-round machinery. A whole medley of sounds that stirred the senses.

Barbaças skirted the stalls and entered the ground by the tracks coming from the outlying country estates. When he found himself in the thick of the dense crowd of animals, dealers, farmers, he began to doubt his ability to cope with such a tricky business as the purchase of a donkey. He, a fellow who was never at a loss to invent the most unexpected ways of briskly getting over the day's difficulties, felt awkward and unsure of himself now that he was at the fair.

Very soon he found himself in a group gathered round Farmer Cortes, who was sitting on a chair a herdsman had carried from the house. There, as from a throne, one arm leaning on his stick, Farmer Cortes watched the maneuvers of the dealers—a pleasant spectacle for him because, however unexpected the tricks might be, the trumps in the game were always on his side. He would prod his fellow players with provocative smiles. Because he could, if he wanted, forego the yield of half a dozen years of stock farming and not feel the loss, he would keep prospective buyers on tenterhooks. They would bluster, show reserve, cunning, or respect, but in the end they would humbly beg him to accept the price they offered.

"It isn't just a deal, Farmer; a chap likes to get hold of sound stock like yours, so accept my price, Senhor Cortes!"

"You go and try it on someone else. Maybe they'll accept...."

And so, smoking long cheroots and with an eternal smile on his face, he would keep them dangling, till someone less vacillating than the others scratched his head, gave in, and opened his wallet. But Farmer Cortes wouldn't do business with gypsies. He considered it beneath his dignity to haggle with such tricky scum. Very few people knew that years ago he'd been taken in by them when he'd bought two pairs of mules that turned out to be not only worn out but ill-tempered into the bargain; and to the day of his death he'd never forgive the humiliation.

Other important men of the neighborhood gathered round Farmer Cortes. They discussed the prices of wool, the quality of the stock, the yield from the threshing; but a great deal of jealous rivalry lay hidden under the amicable tone of their conversation. Senhor Maldonado of the Brotas District, for instance, considered himself to be the equal of Cortes, and he always felt nettled when some hanger-on sang the praises of Cortes's rams.

"They aren't just rams, Senhor Cortes; they're real stallions!" such a one would say.

"That's right, but they cost a lot to raise."

And Farmer Maldonado would turn away in the nick of time so that the others would think he hadn't heard a word. He was a moody man, changeable as a weathercock, generous or hard without warning at the wrong time. He nearly always wore a cloak, light or heavy according to the season, and this seemed to be an indispensable part of his personality. When he twirled round in a sort of dance step, the skirts of his cloak swayed to the rhythm of his motion, subtly expressing the pride or contempt latent in the movement. At the market or at café doors he had his own personal followers who, of course, avoided any compromising familiarity with Farmer Cortes's suite. There were occasions, however, when their mutual interests required that they meet, as for instance at the cattle markets. Farmer Cortes brought his chair and stick, and Farmer Maldonado donned his light cloak and sometimes brought a black raven (his symbol of power?) his horseboy had tamed by dint of endless patience. Senhor Maldonado felt quite pleased when the great bird croaked at people who came to join the group, now and then giving them such a fright that it made the others laugh. The bird's beady eyes did in fact look cruel enough to make anyone afraid.

Turning away from the oxen and the scamperings of the colts, Barbaças found himself in this group. So far he hadn't come across a single donkey—that lowly sort of creature being more in the gypsies' line of business, and they used the far end of the fairground where there was more space and where it was possible, either by cajolery or the whip, to make any worn-out quadruped put on a sprightly turn of speed. Out of curiosity he stood there, because he always liked to take his place among the poor devils who, at a proper distance, followed the sayings and doings of the big farmers. Maybe he was on a different plane that day, but by force of habit he had to stop and see what was going on, and he stood drinking in the farmers' remarks as though the lonely days on the holding had made him thirsty for the sound of voices.

Several times Senhor Maldonado's sour glance had passed over him as though he were just part of the drab background of flocks and shepherds. Now, Barbaças was used to having his presence noticed in some way, be it only by some jest at his expense. Such banter might sometimes be offensive, but it was notice, tribute paid to his local fame. And so, somewhat nettled, he drew quietly closer and closer to the farmers till he was right under their eyes.

"You still alive, rascal?" said Senhor Maldonado in a bored voice and with a cursory glance, like someone carelessly removing an old rag.

Perhaps Barbaças' stay on Loas's holding as a farmhand had disappointed the townsfolk in some way. Perhaps they thought he was worth kindly notice only so long as he conformed to their idea of him—a shiftless fellow who'd never settle down. He was wounded in his pride, the more so because the farmer's idle remark hadn't even made the others look at him. He felt a sudden impulse to slope off, relieve his feelings by letting himself go at the fair, get drunk, steal if need be—anything to show them he was the same old Barbaças.

Just at that moment someone tugged at the tail of his jacket. It was Vieirinha who stood there, red-cheeked, corpulent, easygoing, beating his baggy trousers with a switch. Vieirinha preferred to keep in the background when he was near the big farmers.

"Hey, rogue!" he hissed. "It's ages since I saw you. And how's friend Loas—is he well? . . . Come on, let's get away from here!"

This interruption was very opportune for Barbaças. At least somebody was aware of his existence, and it also gave him an excuse to withdraw.

"Your pal Loas is getting on all right," he answered.

"And you've filled out, too! I'd already heard you were getting along fine." Here Vieirinha's voice swelled to its normal heartiness. "You're as round as a turnip, Barbaças my lad. It's evident friend Loas keeps a good table. I'll be coming round one of these days—I've got a few melons for him."

"Loas is a good sort."

"That's right. And you're as blooming as a big peach! With a face like that, you can snap your fingers at anybody. . . . Shall we go and have a drink?" Vieirinha was now through with the preliminaries—the real beginning for him was always a glass of wine.

"I can't. I'm not interested in the fair today." Barbaças heard the words come out, as surprised as though someone else had spoken them. Perhaps his conscience was giving him verbal warning of pitfalls to come. No, he wasn't interested in the fair —he had a mission to carry out.

"What's that, Barbaças? Are you doing penance or something? Has friend Loas told you to lay off the drink?"

"Friend Loas don't order me about."

"Well, then, what's the matter? Have you got a bellyache?"

"No, there's a proper reason." And so that Vieirinha shouldn't think there was some silly hindrance, Barbaças confessed the truth: "I've come to buy a donkey."

Vieirinha stood stock still, nibbling the point of his switch, his face redder than ever.

"You've got the money to buy a donkey?" he exclaimed. "Is that the truth?"

"Loas needs a donkey."

By this short reply Barbaças wanted to keep Vieirinha from nosing out the money in his pocket, but Vieirinha had already clutched him by the arm in sudden animation.

"Now, what a good thing you met me! I'll help you buy a really good donkey. I've got a friend, a gypsy from Arraiolos, who'll sell us a fine beast for a reasonable price. How much money have you got?"

On the instant Barbaças slowed down, and Vieirinha, seeing he'd gone too far, didn't press the point.

"Did you know I'm an excellent judge of donkeys?" Vieirinha went on. "Once, when I was in the Amazon . . . But wait a minute! Have you been near the stalls yet? Did you hear they've got some really good wine that'll make you smack your lips? We could go there first, and then tackle the business."

The proposal seemed sensible enough, but then, Vieirinha always knew how to get round you with a show of reason. He'd seen many strange and wonderful things. He'd been to the Amazon. He'd left the town as a lad, made his way across Africa, robbing and killing; gone over to Brazil, and then come back with a bellyful of adventures to live on a legacy left him by a great-uncle who'd been a canon in the diocese of Évora. Vieirinha, then, was a man whose words and gestures told of the wide world and strange experiences. His fellow townsmen, cramped by the narrowness of their own lives, always listened when he told the same tales time after time, feeling the need to believe in them and take part in them. It was quite some time since Vieirinha had retired, but he still hadn't had his fill of drinking and talking in taverns, shops, or simply in the town square with a group of idle laborers or herdsmen round him, whiling away the dead hours when the sun dries up the refuse lying at the doors. Now that the canon's legacy had dwindled till only the house remained, where Vieirinha live alone—and where there were some very nice things, it was said—he had begun to pick up what he could from odd jobs such as penning nicely worded letters, touting for votes in electoral campaigns, repairing damaged motors, and so on, to earn enough to buy food and drink. Sometimes, when crops were ripening, he would act as watchman over some isolated plot, and there he would set up a tent in which to sleep and meditate. He was the kind of man who could live that sort of lonely life for months on end, self-sufficing so long as he had tobacco and a few bottles of wine. Nevertheless, during these lonely spells, he was sometimes caught lurking in thickets, spying on peddler women passing along the road, or following them at a distance with a kind of lukewarm interest. Widows and unmarried women of the district, too, sometimes caught sight of him along some lonely path with his eyes alight and waiting with the wariness of a faun or a thief. But the minute he heard their footsteps, he slipped away in a hurry. Yes, a strange chap, that Vieirinha!

Now the two friends had reached the alley bordered by two rows of booths. Rifle ranges, stalls of cheap jewelry and knick-knacks, the dirty counters of tapsters. And groups of people in from the countryside walked up and down in front of the same stalls time after time, hesitating, comparing, discussing before making a purchase.

"So let's have a glass, Barbaças. It'll be on me, of course."

Barbaças didn't protest. He wasn't going to make free with money that didn't belong to him. Loas's money was sacred. And to excuse himself for yielding to temptation, he told himself that the later he got to the gypsies' site, the readier they'd be to meet his conditions. Then, too, you couldn't snap your fingers at the help of a man like Vieirinha—a chap who'd been half over the world! With experience like that behind him, he might very well get back to the holding leading a donkey bought at their price. And so he ended by convincing himself that Loas's poor savings would be enough to buy a donkey, and a sound one at that.

The stallkeeper served their drinks. Vieirinha passed his fat fingers over his wet moustache, and winked.

"Some pretty girls here, Barbaças! In fact, a fellow could pass some very pleasant days at the fair."

One of the girls in charge of the rifle range smiled in their direction. Vieirinha immediately grew red in the face, and went on nervously tapping his trousers with his switch. Barbaças began to notice that his companion's gestures were getting uncontrolled and incoherent.

"Fine women they are, Barbaças! Absolutely splendid pieces. That one's a real madrigal!"

Barbaças neither knew nor cared what a madrigal was. Vieirinha was always using difficult words picked up in Africa or Brazil or in his uncle's books. He larded his conversation with them, and you couldn't even guess their meaning or even remember them, because he promptly followed them up with others more difficult still. But the words *excellently* and *in fact* held a special place in his vocabulary, because he'd heard them once on the austere lips of a judge who passed through the district and was notorious because he acquitted culprits and put people in prison for perjury. This judge had scattered *excellentlys* and *in facts* so generously about the courtrooms that they had become fixed in Vieirinha's mind once for all.

"Try a shot, love!"

Barbaças crossed his arms in front of him as though warding off the invitation or doubting that it was meant for him. Vieirinha gave a complacent smile that rounded the flesh of his cheeks, and made them ruddier than ever.

"Go on. She'll look after you."

"She meant you."

Vieirinha didn't deny it, and now there was a hint of amused superiority in his smile. Clutching the loafer once more by the arm, he pulled him toward the stall. But it wasn't the grasp of the hand that decided him. Barbaças suddenly felt drawn into the vortex, as though he were the last drop necessary to complete the eddying swirl of the fair. He felt his mind in a whirl, brain and senses melting in a feeling of delicious irresponsibility. Very far away there was still the vague feeling that there was something he ought to be attending to, something to do with a donkey and the gypsies, but the surrounding fun and frolic carried him away into the heart of the whirlpool.

Barbaças accepted the rifle almost without reflection. He took aim at an earthenware pot, then at a tassel by which a rabbit was tied in its hole, but his eyes were really drawn by the red flower pinned to the girl's dress. It was a black dress, silky and flowing, and the red flower was like a splash of blood —a symbol of desperate provocation. Noting the whiteness of the girl's skin, Barbaças couldn't help thinking about the loveliness under the dress, comparing it with the rough flesh of the townswomen. The wish to touch the satiny whiteness became almost unbearable. Perhaps not exactly carnal desire, but a longing for inaccessible pleasures beyond his power to put into words but here personified in a white-skinned girl and desire crystallized in a blood-red flower. More than desire—a lava flow.

Barbaças failed to hit any of his marks, and the girl laughed after each miss. His cheeks were now as red as Vieirinha's, and he felt he'd like to strangle that laugh and possess the girl with savage fury for hours, days . . . spoil the white, intangible loveliness that mocked his pariah flesh. His forehead burning, he had two more tries, while the girl's roving eye wandered invitingly over the rustics standing at the counter, Vieirinha among them, his belly shaking with impatience, waiting his turn to take the rifle and give Barbaças a lesson. Everybody in the town had heard that he'd killed numbers of lions, panthers, elephants, and now they were going to find out for themselves whether he could really smash all the trashy objects on the stall, even with his eyes shut.

"You're like an old woman with your finger trembling on the trigger!" jeered the girl when she took the rifle back from Barbaças.

With a disdainful gesture he tightened the cord round his trouser top, to show he didn't care a hoot whether he shot straight or not, though he was bursting inside with humiliation. Vieirinha pushed him to one side with the butt of the gun, and handed money to the girl.

"Take it from this, my dear. . . . And you, Barbaças, go and have another drink; then come back. You want something to buck you up. . . . Go on, take the money."

"I don't need it."

Barbaças began to suspect Vieirinha's generosity. He'd paid for the wine, paid for the rifle range, and although he liked to show off when women were about, and make believe he was a man of means, his pocket wouldn't take him very far. So Barbaças began to feel vaguely aware that something was amiss. Then there was the humiliation of it all. And now the girl's smile was only for Vieirinha, and this, too, wounded his vanity and was the cause of his next remark.

"I've got money, too, enough for dozens of drinks."

Vieirinha and the girl looked at him as though he'd gone crazy, then paid no more attention. Barbaças didn't budge from his place, and each of Vieirinha's shots shattering the earthenware objects, one after the other and calling forth shouts of admiration from the bystanders, put him still more out of countenance.

"Now, look, Barbaças, that's how you hold a rifle. You put your fingers like this . . . you sight carefully . . . and the shot goes off excellently."

The girl leaned her soft breast against Vieirinha's shoulder, crushing the flower, as though offering herself to him. And when he'd finished shooting, and was leaning triumphantly back against the counter to face the applause of his admirers, she put her arms round his neck. But Vieirinha wasn't the man to let it be seen in public that he could be easily caught. Red as a tomato, he tugged at the ends of his moustache to hide his embarrassment, and winked at Barbaças.

"Let's go and have another glass, and come back later," he said. He gave the girl's cheek a careless pat, but when they were some distance from the stall he couldn't contain himself any longer.

"That wench is a real poem—and ours for the taking. We're going to have such a night!" he exclaimed in a voice hoarse with excitement.

"Ours?"

"Do you want her all to yourself, then?"

Barbaças relaxed and smiled when he grasped the situation. Yes, he'd been to fairs before, and knew all about the girls who served food and drink at the stalls. He knew what they were there for. Farmhands, married and single, squandered the wages of a whole harvesting during the three days of the fair. In the dense atmosphere of the booths—so thick it seemed to have color and body—the men of the town would eat, love, and sleep till they'd spent their last copper. They stayed on till they were drained to the dregs, satisfied or exacerbated as the case might be. In these outbursts there was more than sexual ardor; there was an urge to probe the unexplored sensations of a forbidden world.

Barbaças fell into step with Vieirinha's leisurely pace, screwing up his courage to ask about a point that was worrying him. But he couldn't bring himself to do it. You could ask Vieirinha about things, people, or happenings in the town, or about some piece of roguery, but now he'd seen him treating these city girls in such a masterly way, he felt diffident about broaching what was troubling him.

"What if..." he began.

"Out with it!" said Vieirinha.

"Well, now it's my turn to pay for a glass," he answered, just to say something.

"Nobody's stopping you."

That idea about the drink wasn't a bad one. It'd give him the guts to hold his own with such a man of the world as Vieirinha. And there was no harm in taking a few escudos from Loas's money—it wouldn't affect the purchase of the donkey. The later they left that business, the less demanding the gypsies would be. Nevertheless, when he saw he was having to make excuses for what he was doing, deep down he began to feel uneasy with himself. After all, he'd come to the fair with a single object in view, and any swerving from it was a betrayal of Loas's trust in him, a betrayal of their ambition. Then Vieirinha interrupted his thoughts.

"If only the fair lasted the whole year, Barbaças, I'd come and live here. I shouldn't want anything more. Once, when I was in the Amazon..."

"But we mustn't forget that donkey!" Barbaças objected, pricked by conscience.

"Of course not! I've told you before, I'll look after the whole thing. My friend from Arraiolos must be about somewhere, and he always has the best animals in these parts—quite equal to those in Cuiariba-Pará, where I once killed a dozen blacks all at one go. A kick from a mule there meant one black out of the way."

"But Loas wants a donkey, not a mule."

"That's all right. My friend from Arraiolos has everything. ... But you must see we can't have a lark with those girls if we've got to drag a donkey about with us all the time. There's a proper time for everything."

"And what if she goes off with someone else while we're hanging about here?" Barbaças blurted out, at last showing what was really weighing on his mind.

"Now, you're just an innocent in this kind of thing! You don't have to make yourself cheap, I tell you. I saw straightaway that if you were at the fair like a farmer, to buy a donkey, you must have money in your pocket. Like a farmer, eh, Barbaças? A real bourgeois! I saw that straightaway. Now, what really catches those girls is when a chap comes here, has a few shots at the range, pays up, then remarks as though not interested in them, 'Now it's time for a few drinks!' and goes off and spends his money elsewhere just to play them up. Even if dozens of blockheads come and whisper in their ears now, they won't listen—they'll be thinking about us. That girl's as good as yours, Barbaças! ... How much money did friend Loas give you?"

"One or two notes," the youth replied evasively, at the same time feeling with his arm to make sure the wad was still in his pocket.

"Naturally. To buy a donkey, you do in fact need a good sum."

"And it wouldn't be a bad thing if we went and looked for it now. Then we could come back to the fair with nothing on our minds."

"Nothing on our minds? What, with a donkey snorting at

our heels? You just leave it all to me. Let's go and have that drink, and then we'll see about it. The gypsies won't be leaving the ground yet; it's still early."

The crowd carried them along toward the merry-go-round, and however hard Barbaças craned his neck he couldn't see the girl at the rifle range. Lads were playing on fifes, pipes, or whistles as they made their way through the throng; stallkeepers were dangling their tidbits and cheap trinkets before the eyes of customers; the roars of the merry-go-round man, magnified through the loudspeaker, deafened their ears. The swirl of the crowd carried them farther and farther from the stall. Now they were passing a novel piece of mechanism, an outlandish doll with a turban on its head that shot sparks from its eyes. Behind it, there was a screen with stars and dots and dashes of light flickering over it—real magic. The woman standing by it was explaining that these things showed your fortune. But the countryfolk held back. They wanted to try their luck, but felt shy, and waited for someone else to have a go first. The crowd was so dense that you couldn't breathe. The sky was heavier now, breaking up into dust-laden tatters of cloud under which the hum of the fair gathered itself into one long drone.

Vieirinha made short work of the waverers.

"Here, Barbaças, hand me a copper!" he shouted.

Some people who knew the loafer and his chronic poverty burst out laughing, and Barbaças felt the insult like the cut of a switch. So they challenged him, did they? He'd soon show them whether he'd got money for Vieirinha or not. He pulled his jacket round, ripped open the stitched pocket with a slash of his knife, and took out one of the biggest notes. A murmur of surprise came from the people standing round. The woman in charge of the machine changed the note, and Vieirinha, interpreting what the stars said, told his companion what to do.

"I'm putting the money in for you. Now, close your eyes and concentrate."

"Concentrate?"

"Yes, think hard about something. Close your eyes, and don't think about anything else. That's right. You're doing it excellently."

The machine began to crackle; the doll's eyes sparkled, and the woman handed a little paper to Barbaças.

"Let's see what it says."

Vieirinha's portly stomach rose and fell while he declaimed in a theatrical voice:

> "Your flower is the rose,
> And Rose the name of your girl.
> You'll be a happy man, and rich
> If there's no hole in your purse."

The countryfolk repeated each line solemnly, and Barbaças took the paper back from Vieirinha.

"Rose?" he asked, with an absorbed look in his eyes.

"Rose and flower. 'Your flower is the rose.' You've got her right enough, you rogue!"

Vieirinha absently put the change in his own pocket, and Barbaças thought he'd better be on the lookout for an opportunity to remind him about it. A further disbursement might be a good opportunity.

"Senhor Vieira, let's have another drink, and then we'll go and look for your friend from Arraiolos."

"All right. Do you know what I think? You were born lucky. Even the machine says so. But you can talk of nothing but donkeys, though it's as clear as daylight you were born for another sort of life. In fact, people like ourselves are born for enjoyment. It's true I went off to the wilds and spent some time there, but I never let myself be tied down, no tether round my neck! What I mean is, I always enjoyed whatever I fancied. However, if you want to buy the donkey for Loas, that's all right. He's my friend and a good chap. Come to think of it, he's well up in signs and portents, too. Has he told you your fortune by the moon yet? He has mine. Old Lynx-Eye saw it all excellently!"

At times the jostling of the crowd carried them toward groups of people waiting their turn for the merry-go-round, which circled to the ever-quickening beat of the music. Up and down it went till it made your head swim. Bystanders felt the same twist of the stomach as the people whirling above the thrust of the machine. It was terrifying but fascinating. Some friends clambered onto the back of an ostrich, and stuck there for ride after ride, though the risk of the adventure showed on their faces.

"And what if we took a turn?" Barbaças suggested eagerly.

"That's an amusement for nitwits, Barbaças. The price of a go on that contraption would be enough for two mineral waters and a small glass of brandy."

Barbaças was not slow to seize the opportunity.

"You'll be careful with that money, won't you? Don't lose it in this pushing and shoving!"

"Don't you worry. There's been a lot of money in these pockets. On the plantations in Africa we handled money as though it were ... as though it were ... Anyway, don't worry, Barbaças. It's excellently snug in my pocket."

Vieirinha paid for the drinks from Loas's money, and proposed another visit to the rifle range; but first he tried to set Barbaças' mind at rest.

"The donkey's got to be a good strong one, hasn't it?" he asked with warm interest.

"As good as we can get."

"Well, then, how many notes have you got?"

"Just a few."

"You don't want to tell me, that's plain. So how do you think I can deal with my friend from Arraiolos?"

"Are we going to look for him now?"

"In a bit. But we've got to work the thing out first."

"I've got five notes."

"The devil, that's a bit tight!"

"I mean, there were five before we changed that one."

"Oh, well, we can take that as being part of the reduction my friend'll make. It won't do Loas any harm. And we've got to give something to the girls, that's clear."

"The whole note?"

"Well, no, not all of it. But we've got to do a bit of spending round here, too. To show those girls we aren't penniless. You could offer them a soft drink, for instance. They're mad on orange drinks. Then, later on, when it's nearly twilight, we can take them off to the eucalyptus trees. . . . But we'll have a bit of fun here first. Don't you worry. They won't run away."

"Well, why not buy the donkey now? Then we'd know whether there'd be anything over."

"And take the donkey to the eucalyptus trees, too? That'd be fine! There you'd be with the girl in the bushes, and the donkey braying and rousing the guard. You'd soon have the whole town round and catching you with your pants down. You've really thought the whole thing out excellently!"

Barbaças let himself be convinced. Really, all he wanted was that Vieirinha should finish his drink so that they could go back to the rifle range. He was quite sure he wouldn't miss his mark this time, and the girl with the red flower (Great heavens, "Your flower is the rose"!) would hang round him as she had hung round Vieirinha when he was showing off earlier. And thinking of this, he passed his hands over his ragamuffin's hair, trying to smooth it down. He realized all at once that he must look rough and uncouth, whereas Vieirinha, however tatty his clothes, always had an air of polish about him.

Falling in with his companion's secret wishes, Vieirinha pretended to be interested in some novelties on a Chinaman's stall, and got a good place right opposite the girls. He kept smiling at them, and curling his moustache.

"I've got an idea, Barbaças. With money you can get things —women, for instance. And we've got money. But . . ."

"The money's for the donkey."

"I know, I know," retorted Vieirinha in disgust. "You've already said so a hundred times. But without me, Loas would have to pay out a heap of money. So, if I save him a tidy bit by getting the donkey from my friend, it seems to me I've a right to some little reward. But I'm not referring to money at the moment. Money can buy women, but it can't make them take you, see? It can't make them like you. And just to be with a woman for the sake of having one . . . I mean to say, Barbaças, I've had the deuce of a lot of experience in these things. I've got a plan, and we're going to make the women's heads swim.

Have you ever had a woman who clings to you like a caterpillar to a cabbage?"

Barbaças' eyes became glazed with longing, and his mouth watered at thought of the frantic delights Vieirinha's words suggested. Arms, breasts, hidden pleasures, mysterious rivers in which his senses would plunge for the first time. His mouth was hot with warm springs of desire, while icy shivers swept over muscles and bones. If the girl with the red flower had suddenly risen up near him just then, clinging to his body like a caterpillar to a cabbage, he would probably not have been able to make love at all. Desire had paralyzed him.

"But what are you going to do?" Barbaças mumbled.

"Get away from here."

"For another drink?"

"You still thirsty?"

And without waiting for an answer, Vieirinha pushed his way disdainfully through the crowd and made for the town. Uneasy and bewildered, Barbaças followed him, turning round all the time to see if he could still see the girl between the groups of people obstructing his view. And also to make sure the cattle market wasn't closing down! Nothing but oxen and sheep there! Though, of course, if people weren't interested in donkeys, the few on offer would have to wait till the end of the day to find a buyer. And this thought again lulled his anxiety for the time being.

Vieirinha marched on, flicking horseflies from the back of his neck with his switch. He took a shortcut through Farmer Maldonado's land, which lay in a wide black belt of deep soil round the town, holding it as in a vise. Anybody who wanted to build a house—the rising generation that needed more elbow-room, the cramped township that needed to expand toward the future—all came up against this stubborn wall.

"Would you sell me a bit of that land near the road?"

"What do you want to pay?"

"Name your figure, Farmer."

"My weight in gold. And even that wouldn't pay in full for your presumption in asking."

It was no use; that was the end of it. The farmer wouldn't sell a square inch of what belonged to him. Let the town take a leap over his rich acres where the olive groves were as cool as any in the northern Beira provinces. If laborers would bring children into the world, let the place expand over yonder, on the plain or on the sandy soil of the oakwoods. He had no use for a progressive township. New streets, new houses—all it meant was new families, a monstrous crop of hungry stomachs encroaching on his rights. He wouldn't yield an inch of his soil. When the railway was to be built across the flatlands, like a river cutting a fresh path through arid petrifaction, he thought such a breach opened to progress might encourage the town to entertain the notion of breaking out rebelliously. But there was a man there to stop that hope! The land was his. His the power to avert the danger. And he pushed it as far away as possible. The engineers had to retire into the heart of the heathland, and lay the track and build the station a mile or two from the town, outside the farmer's property.

No doubt about it, though: it was good productive land. However much Barbaças was obsessed with what Vieirinha was planning to do, now that Loas had managed to instill some love of the soil in him, he couldn't walk over these fertile tracts without a surge of admiration. Loas, he thought, would know how to transform such land into gold and greatness. Not gold to feed a man's greed, give him pride of place and power, but gold to be transmuted into more fertility. Loas, cramped on a small fodder patch hardly bigger than his own shadow, so small that the mischance of two bad years was enough to wrest it from him, Loas was still idealistic enough to try to wring the very soul of growth out of a few yards of poor soil. Loas no doubt didn't overexert himself; he didn't harness his muscles to his dreams; but his talk was a spur to those around him, to the land itself, hungry for attention. What wouldn't he make of deep black soil like this! In Loas's loving hands, even a single strip of it, with the help of a donkey . . . A donkey, homely symbol of the farmer's ambition, and now a guilty pang in Barbaças' conscience! One of the notes was being frittered away; Vieirinha didn't look as though he were going to hand back the change, and he himself hadn't the strength of will to resist—the smooth talk mesmerized him.

"Where are you going, senhor?" shouted Barbaças in a desperate attempt to assert himself.

"Home."

"And the fair? And the donkey?" Vieirinha stopped dead. Gone the smiling glow of his cheeks, now livid with anger. He said: "I am in fact going to look for it to hang it round your neck. Take yourself off, you ungrateful scamp! Take yourself off with your tiresome donkey!"

"Aren't you going to help me with the purchase?"

"You can manage on your own. You can manage excellently by yourself."

"But I don't know your friend from Arraiolos. . . ."

Vieirinha curled the ends of his moustache, and slowly the glow of satisfaction came back into his face. He gave a long sigh, like someone controlling his vexation.

"Oh, all right, I don't want to quarrel with you," he said, more in sorrow than in anger, almost with affection. "I'll look after the donkey. But in heaven's name, Barbaças, don't mention it again until it's opportune."

"Opportune?"

"Yes. That means . . . it means . . . the same as if I said 'not till the right time to buy cheap.'"

"Then there'll be enough money?"

"Of course there will. In fact, I'm quite sure there'll be some left over. We could give some to the girls. We'll soften them up first with something I've got at home, but they'll only be really caught when they've had a good smell of our money. See what I mean?"

"And will there be enough left for the donkey?"

"Now, look here, Barbaças," Vieirinha said, his eyes rolling with resentment, "you just listen to me! I've been waiting for months for the fair and the rifle range. I've been a man who's been used to having all the women he wanted half the world over. In the backwoods you just lift a finger, and that finger commands hundreds of women. It isn't just desire; it's the very fire of hell. Can you understand what it is when a man robs and kills for wine? Can you understand what it is when a man who's had women half the world over, drinking them up like glasses of wine, comes back to a place like this where you have to wait months, a year, before you can get one of these girls from the rifle range? These girls have to be paid for, Barbaças! It'd be better if you didn't have to pay, of course, but it's their job, and that's that. Now do you understand? Did you ever see me with money enough to convince a tart in town? There's only the fair, Barbaças, once a year. Just fancy what it'd be for a hard drinker to have to wait a whole year for a couple of glasses of wine. You might object that a man who drinks only a couple of glasses a year isn't a drinker at all. But that's where you're wrong. He's a drinker because every moment of his life he's obsessed with the thought of those two glasses he's going to have when the time comes. I tell you, he's the hardest sort of drinker there is."

These words went whirling through Barbaças' brain, and dazed him. They came in a crazy stream from Vieirinha's lips, and the boy's wits lurched after them in a vain attempt to retain and understand. Vieirinha was gabbling about drunkenness, but it was Barbaças who felt drunk and confused.

"Do you see what I mean?" Vieirinha went on, scarcely stopping to take breath. "Do you see what I mean, Barbaças? For lack of a mere trifle I was going to lose one of the girls from the fair. I need Loas's money. And I need to go to my house to fetch a present. With the money and the present, everything will turn out excellently. Now, have you got it in you to be open with a friend, and tell me exactly how much money you've got?"

Barbaças felt himself being shaken by his friend's trembling hands. But he was afraid neither of the hands nor of the resentment in the last question, nor of the sudden changes of mood in Vieirinha's words and manner. He was just thunderstruck, and his amazement gradually changed to something like weariness.

"It's *Loas's* money that I've got," he said in a tired voice.

"You're so artful you even manage to seem clever in your stupid obstinacy."

Barbaças couldn't understand this cultivated talk, but he didn't ask for an explanation. Dogged and with eyes on the ground, he silently followed in Vieirinha's flurried footsteps.

Very few people in the town could boast they had crossed Vieirinha's doorstep. However hard gossips knocked on the wicket with some plausible pretext to get a swift glance inside, he always so contrived it that the darkness of the house or the quickness of his reply prevented a proper look round. And so the women could let their imagination run riot to describe the wealth of things inherited from the canon or, if they felt that way, the shocking filth of the den.

As soon as Barbaças got inside, he was aware of spiders' webs and a strong, musty smell. He could just make out a variety of strange objects lying in disorder. Vague, distorted shapes loomed slowly in the darkness, drew nearer, and took on volume as though returning to life after a long winter's sleep. To the loafer, it seemed that at any moment a surge of blood or light or air might come and really give life to these things held torpid till then in some mysterious spell. They seemed to be breathing and moving. He could sense their mass, integument, and smell.

Vieirinha was opening trunks and pulling things onto the floor: quilts, old clothing, surplices, gilded cords, laces, their colors bright or dull, like properties for some stage set for a scene of magic, things that Barbaças would never dare to pick up and put back in their places. Vieirinha suddenly stopped his search, thought for a few moments, and then disappeared up the stairs. Barbaças didn't like being left alone in the dark room, with only faint light coming from the chimney opening. He stood there quietly, holding his breath, making himself small in his fright, while the objects round him seemed deformed, as in a distorting mirror.

Vieirinha soon came down again with a triumphant look on his face.

"I've got them, my lad! I'd seen those two fans somewhere in the house a while back, and I thought I'd be able to lay my hands on them. They're in excellent condition. Just take a good look at them, but keep your hands off or you'll get them dirty. Two fans, Barbaças. Two fans in excellent condition. Do you know how much they're worth? Spanish fans that belonged to a great-grandmother of my uncle the canon, silk, and with silver and gold beads on them, too! You can take it from me, friend Loas wouldn't have enough money to pay for one of these fans."

"Are they worth more than a donkey?" Barbaças asked, overwhelmed.

"Now listen here, Barbaças," the other answered, the look on his face changing, "I'd like to know one thing: Does friend Loas talk about donkeys as often as you do? Because if he does, you'll never catch Vieirinha at the holding again, not even if he opened a tap of wine down my throat! Not even if he offered me a dish chock-full of meat! ... Now then, these fans, worth all friend Loas's money put together, are going to be offered as presents by us. Which girl do you want?"

"The one with the red rose."

"Yes, she's a fine wench. She caught my eye, too. As I've already said, you'll find yourself with a very nice piece."

"But she likes you," the youth went on, jealous but honest.

"Nonsense, my lad. They all like any man, once he's given them money and a Spanish fan. And I don't need to choose. All I want is a woman, a woman for the whole night, do you see? Just hand the money over, and I'll look after the rest. Wait for me by the eucalyptus trees. I'll go and fix it all up with the girls. A whole night with the girls! After that, I don't care if I die."

"But I've got to take a donkey to Loas," Barbaças said, looking at Vieirinha in bewilderment.

"That's all right. Wait for me at the eucalyptus trees. I'll bring the donkey along, too."

Barbaças closed his eyes as for a suicidal plunge, and handed over the wallet.

Up by the eucalyptus trees, Barbaças had been waiting a very long time. The slender, lonely trees—their lot to keep eternal watch over the plain, yet having nothing in common with the landscape of their exile—stood firm against the invasion of the flatlands, stood huddled in a closed circle within which wild flowers found protection against the languorous, cruel call of the open. Under the trees the honey-sweet scent of the plants lay gently on the air, though at times the sultriness from the plain made it burn with an almost sensual intensity. It seemed a strange, forbidden world to Barbaças, accustomed only to bare, open landscapes. He hoped it wouldn't be much longer before Vieirinha came.

Of course, he'd have to take one of the more unobtrusive paths up the hill, because it wouldn't do for a person from town to be caught on the road in the company of trollops; so Barbaças had chosen a place from which he could keep an eye on the most discreet exits from the fair. Each time somebody appeared in the distance leading an animal, Barbaças said to himself with relief: There he is. The girls are coming later. . . . But it never turned out to be Vieirinha.

So the lad began to think up reasons for the delay: Perhaps the gypsy friend had been difficult to bring to terms; or maybe the girls were ashamed to leave the stall before dark. And deep down, as though he were thrusting the idea away from him, the suspicion was beginning to work its way through that Vieirinha had made a fool of him, and had run off with the money and the wenches. But, no, that couldn't be true. Vieirinha was Loas's friend; and however depraved he was, surely he wouldn't play a dirty trick like that. But if it did turn out to be true, he'd follow him to the ends of the earth for revenge. Growing more and more anxious, Barbaças glumly watched the cockchafers that settled on his skin, and kept on thinking up reasons for Vieirinha's lateness that angered and relieved him turn and turn about. Light winds came wafting between the trees, and then the shrubs seemed to be shaking their heads at him with surprise, while the topmost leaves whispered that twilight was not far off. The light was no longer hard. It was wrinkling over the sides of the hills, failing, fading away, in search of a covert to hide its death pangs. Time was running on with long strides, and the waiting youth grew more and more impatient.

He was wondering whether he'd been right to trust Vieirinha. To agree to use another note for the girls, seeing that the gypsy friend would allow a good reduction for the

65

donkey; to drink a few more glasses at the stalls—all well and good. But he ought never to have agreed to wait here for the donkey and the women, a long way from the fair, where he couldn't keep an eye on Vieirinha. It was quite plain to him now that the old rascal had just been cozening him with his talk of bringing a woman for a whole night in this dark, lonely place, who would lay open her white body like a flower opening its mysteries in the warm June night. He worked himself into such a rage that, a few minutes more, and he'd have rushed off to the fair to give Vieirinha a thrashing. He champed bitter stalks of grass between his teeth, jabbed at the ground with his boots, spat his anger on all sides, as though spitting at Vieirinha himself.

But Vieirinha was coming. A long way off he signaled his approach with a loud whistling like a nightingale, and of course he was coming from a totally unexpected direction.

Barbaças answered the signal, and with thumping heart set off to meet him. And there he was, portly and eager, still carrying his switch, coming along with the women. Barbaças suddenly stood stockstill, paralyzed by a rush of feeling when he saw the girl with the red flower. Vieirinha had kept his word! For a moment or two he didn't even notice that there was no donkey.

"Well, old chap!" Vieirinha called out, with a girl on each arm. "So you see. A pleasant surprise, eh? You look as if all your insides were in a knot!"

"And the donkey?"

"They were the devil of a price, Barbaças. Couldn't get near one."

"You haven't got one, then?"

"Now, look here, is that the way to welcome these ladies? Two ladies who are quite excellently disposed toward Papa Vieira, two sweet little ladies who deserve dozens of Spanish fans—and all you can talk about is this donkey business! Now, my loves, you're charmed with Papa Vieirinha's little presents, aren't you?"

The girls didn't understand a word of this talk, but they thought there must be a good joke somewhere, and laughed gaily. Barbaças looked at them with awkward disapproval. The other one had a big red mouth in a gash across her face, and hair the color of old gold. There was something shameless and brazen about her. Not like his girl with the red flower.

"You know that Loas, your friend, is waiting for me. I've got to take him a donkey or give him the money back," Barbaças said in a voice he meant to be severe, but which came out in a wretched whine.

"Well, it's up to you. You've got enough money to go back to the fair and buy whatever you like."

Before Barbaças could recover from Vieirinha's offhand effrontery, the girl with the red flower came and stood between them. In the dim light she looked even more slender. Her movements were slow and languorous, a kind of floating among the rustle of the shrubs. The whiteness of her skin was a splash of moonlight against the darkness of her dress. There was a dazed look in Barbaças' eyes—he couldn't believe this woman was there solely for him.

Vieirinha saw that the lad was caught, and slipped off with his own companion. When Barbaças came out of his daze, Vieirinha was already moving away down the hill, the woman's hips clutched tightly to him; and a little later Barbaças heard the sound of hungry kisses and bodies slumping in the bushes.

The girl, looking at him and smiling, lifted an arm somewhat perplexed.

"So what, woolly bear?"

But Barbaças drew back. He couldn't bring himself to touch her. He'd rather run away, and keep the sight of her in his memory forever afterward.

"Are you afraid, stupid?" the girl went on, offended.

What she said didn't penetrate. Her words might be common, her scent nauseating, her flesh prostituted; she might be as slovenly as he was himself, but at that moment she was for him a hallucination, an unattainable desire. She was no better than he was, a casual laborer; and once possessed, the enchantment would be over. Vieirinha had bought her with a Spanish fan and Loas's savings. But Barbaças had a vague feeling that just to be near, without possessing, something that could fill

the fearful emptiness of his existence was worth lifelong remorse.

"Haven't you got anything to say to me, sissy?" And when
finally he drew near to her with bright, hungry eyes fastened
on her flesh, the girl added: "And don't waste time, because I
don't want any trouble with the guards. I'm worried to death
for fear they followed us."

Barbaças sat down, holding her hands in his. With the
coming of night, the scent of ripe grain came and mixed silently
with the smell of bodies.

There was something strangely erotic in the mixture, something heavy with promise that roused his senses. His face grew
pale, nostrils tensed. His hands gripped the woman's hands,
eager to explore further, the white neck, the flower, the warm
flesh. But he couldn't do it. There was a gulf between them, and
he couldn't cross it, much less dominate the inaccessible loveliness. Not for his vagabond's body, not for his pariah desire
had such loveliness been created. He wished he had something
to give her to make her yield, capture her through gratitude. A
Spanish fan or a dress or a handful of Loas's money that that
old fox Vieirinha had squandered on heaven knows what. But
maybe not even a gesture like that could bring their understanding, desire, misfortune, to a common level.

A warm breath coming from the sleeping plain flushed
through vegetation and bodies. It was warm and soft, like blood
from an open vein, and seemed to coagulate on the skin. Barbaças could feel it in the grass, in the night, in the girl's body and
his own. It flooded through him in intoxicating sensuality. But
the more the girl offered her body to him, the stronger became
the taboo in himself. Yet he wanted to possess her. He wanted it
as a man and as a poor wretch. His hands timidly felt for the
rose of blood, and then, in a surge of humiliated rage, hands
and teeth fastened on the girl's flesh, biting, hurting, possessing
in age-old hunger, till she broke the silence of the hill with a
dreadful howl of fear.

4

At that hour when the sun was almost level with the plain, and you had to shade your eyes from its blinding light, Loas made his way up to the cork trees, and scanned the distance. In the heathland sunset was a conflagration. Long after the sun had disappeared from the horizon, which was like a smooth dazzling sea, ruddy drifts and wisps lingered on, foretelling another stifling day for the morrow.

Loas had gone up to the cork trees because he was sure this would be the time of Barbaças' return. More than the actual reckoning up of the hours, his practiced intuition couldn't lead him astray. No, Barbaças wouldn't be long now. He kept on repeating this certainty to himself; he proclaimed it to the stars, to the landscape, to the road along which the lad would come, as though he felt the need to bolster up a confidence that, deep down in himself, was not as firm as he would like.

He had spent the long hours of the day in rather aimless odd jobs, not wanting to show how restless he felt. And each time the thought rose in his mind: Now, will the donkey be sound? Had the money been enough? He ground his teeth. He felt irritated when his wife came out of the house and stood in front of him in mute anxiety, meek but persistent, begging a word of hope. Alice, too, was not her usual self. She was fidgety, and kept dashing about the place for no reason whatever, frightening the hens, stamping over the shrubs. Sometimes she ran to the end of the holding on the lookout for people coming back from the fair.

"There he is!" she shouted, running and jumping down the slope whenever a dark spot came into sight in the distance. Loas caught the fidgets, too, and finished up by keeping a lookout from the same vantage point.

At last, a mysterious voice warned the master of the house that his partner was approaching. He was so sure this revelation was right that, seeing the road was quite empty, he decided to reduce the distance between himself and the donkey by setting out to meet it. Alice ran up to go with him.

"Are you going to the fair to fetch it, Dad?"

"No. They won't be long now."

"Who do you mean by 'they,' Dad?"

"Barbaças and the donkey."

"Can you see them yet?"

"No, I can't see them, but I know they're there."

"Let me come, too."

Loas did not answer. Now that his ambition was almost in his grasp, he gave himself up to the joy of imagining everything that was going to happen during the coming weeks. The morning dew would moisten the soil, and the plow drawn by the donkey would cut through the land in long, fresh furrows. By the end of the autumn, the whole crop would form a carpet of green. Later there should be camomile alongside the wheat, hay and green barley. Then there'd be the hoeing, with the days growing longer under the close-branched cork trees. And always the donkey driving new furrows of growth to renew the life and hope and ward off each season's disappointments. And then the reaping! The reaping that terminated the earth cycle each year, for the stubble to be buried, like dead flesh rotting to give birth to new life.

Absorbed in his dream, Loas didn't even notice that the road was running past and that behind the girl his wife had also put in an appearance, although keeping a proper distance from her husband, and taking cover in the bushes whenever he turned his head.

"Have they got far to come yet?" the girl asked.

The question suddenly brought him down to earth. He stopped, looked up and down the road as though amazed Barbaças wasn't somewhere on it, and this time his wife got no chance to find a hiding place. It was only then he discovered that they'd reached Senhor Maldonado's olive groves.

"Stop asking questions!" he answered sharply, and sat down

by the roadside, chin in hand, to think the matter out.

When Alice suddenly burst into tears, he felt he'd like to slap her face, and his wife annoyed him still more, standing there as still as a statue. Well, there it was: Barbaças was loitering somewhere. Maybe he had such a craving for wine that he'd drunk himself stupid. Very likely the blockhead had stopped at some tavern, and left the donkey outside for any tramp to steal. He ought to have foreseen all these possibilities: drinking bout, theft, some vagabond's dirty trick.

"Damn my eyes! Damn my eyes!" Loas swore to himself. The girl, her face stained with tears, came closer not to miss what he was saying, and then he clasped her to him as though seeking support even from a weak, impressionable child.

But then, coming to a swift decision, he set out along the road again with long, determined strides. Not the strides of a man just stepping out to meet another to lessen the distance between them, but the strides of a man going to search him out through heaven and hell.

"Damn my eyes!"

He went on swearing under his breath, but Alice heard it, at least while she was able to keep up with him. Then, little by little, the distances spaced out between the three members of the family, and Loas reached the slope up to the town long before his wife and daughter got to the eucalyptus trees. Now was the time to ask someone about Barbaças, because a thing like a theft or a drinking bout involving hundred of escudos would certainly be known all over the place. But at nightfall, on a fair day, the town seemed more than empty—it appeared deserted. Loas looked round for signs of an open tavern, and was making his way toward one still showing a drowsy light when he ran into the Domingas woman just coming out of the house to relieve her bladder now all the yards were quiet. She stood stock-still on the doorstep till she recognized him.

"Well, I never, if it isn't the man himself!" she exclaimed. Then she went up to him and said in a condoling voice, "Oh, dear, Ti Loas, what rascals they are!"

"Who did it, woman?"

"Then you don't know?"

"I've come to find out, woman. They won't escape me."

He spoke with a frightening quietness. Mother Domingas could make neither head nor tail of what he meant, and so was at a loss for a reply.

"Tell me who did it," he said again.

"They've already been caught, man. The guard caught them doing what they ought to be ashamed of in the eucalyptus trees. That's what happens to people who go with trollops."

"Then I'll wait for them outside. Devil take me! I won't leave the police station till I get my hands on 'em. The moss can grow under my feet, woman, but I won't budge from the place till they come out. I want my money."

"What do you mean, Ti Loas? Have they stolen it?" asked Mother Domingas, eager but quite mystified.

"They stole it from Barbaças, which amounts to the same thing."

Mother Domingas passed her hand several times over her forehead, as though trying to separate her own thoughts from Loas's incongruous remarks.

"But, sake's alive, it's Barbaças who's in prison!" she managed to get out, though still confused.

"He and Vieirinha. The shameless scamps were wenching among the eucalyptus trees. One of the women screamed— nobody knows why. You never know what beastly men get up to with women of that sort. Poor young chap, though; it must have been that fat pig Vieirinha who led him into it."

Loas's eyes had narrowed as Mother Domingas unfolded her tale. When she finished, his eyes were two slits of darkness, two crevices looking onto an abyss. His brain had been trying to make the woman's news fit in with his own preconceived notion that someone had robbed Barbaças. Then Vieirinha's name had cropped up, and the two things had slipped into place. That scoundrel Vieirinha had led Barbaças astray, and both of them had gone and squandered the donkey money with trollops.

On reaching this dreadfully logical conclusion, Loas leaned back against the wall of Mother Domingas's house and, utterly stunned, let himself slip down till his behind came to rest on a projecting stone.

"What's come over you, man?"

"Nothing. I can't breathe." And with shaking fingers he undid two of his shirt buttons. "I'm too hot."

But it wasn't heat that he felt—it was a cold sweat that beaded his cheeks, lips, and forehead.

"Did you say with trollops?"

"Yes, from a rifle range. One of them screamed. They're both in prison, too, and kicking up such a row. But it's no concern of yours, is it? You just drop that Barbaças; he wasn't good enough for a decent-living man like you. We've all been surprised at you keeping him on at the holding. His life long he's been nothing but an idle scamp."

Footsteps began to sound along the street. Mother Domingas broke off what she was saying to turn her attention to the approaching people.

"Now, tell me, woman, what were the prices at the fair?"

Mother Domingas looked at him in amazement. You always expected some foolishness from Loas's lips, but such a question, so beside the mark at such a time, exceeded all expectations. So she discreetly turned her attention to the street again, to give him time to forget his silly remark. But he persisted.

"Were animals going cheap?"

"I don't buy or sell, man! You must ask farmers that sort of thing. . . . Now, who can this be coming along the street at this time of night?"

"Don't bother about that, woman! Didn't you hear anybody say whether donkeys were cheap or not?"

"Man, you're not yourself! Come inside and rest a bit."

Loas didn't reply. Body and nerves were quite exhausted. The anxious hours of waiting, followed by such a complete disappointment, left him with a feeling of weary indifference. When the woman's words had first brutally opened his eyes to the truth, he felt like running to the square and shouting abuse in front of the prison; then he'd rip Barbaças' heart out. But now, listless melancholy had taken the place of that first furious urge. Even if Barbaças were brought in front of him, or Vieirinha for that matter, he wouldn't receive them with reproaches or blows. If he let his mind run on the dream that had been betrayed, on the years the trickery of these good-for-nothings had deprived him of, there was a sad resignation about such thoughts that was almost pleasant. As though even in frustration there were some kind of morbid satisfaction.

When Mother Domingas at last recognized Alice and her mother in the two people coming up the slope, she hurried toward them.

"Joana, your husband's feeling queer," she said, putting on a commiserating air. "I was just thinking I'd have to take him to the doctor."

"And what about Barbaças?" his wife asked, as though her husband's condition had not been mentioned.

"He's in prison."

At this extraordinary news Alice opened her eyes wide.

"In pris-on?" Joana repeated slowly.

"They caught him with some trollops."

"And what about the donkey?"

Mother Domingas stood there with her mouth open unable to believe her ears. No doubt about it, these folks from the holdings who had dealings with the evil ones were either cracked or bedeviled, all of them. And if you had anything to do with them, they sent you crazy, too.

5

Not far away, behind the bars of the town prison—which was in the lower part of the school building —very different feelings from those that had been troubling Loas were now vexing Vieirinha and Barbaças.

Vieirinha was brooding over all that had happened, and he felt like crying. Not the subdued weeping of quiet yet real repentance—but the loud wailing that clamors for attention. He was a miserable wretch. He longed to transform his disgrace into a beacon of grief so spectacular that the whole town would feel for him, and carry his bitter woe to Loas's ears. He had robbed Loas, sacrificed him to his own lust. It was therefore fitting that his remorse should be so passionate, so tragic, so intense that farmers, peasants, women, and even Loas himself would come to the town square to weep with him, condemn him, pity him, lash him with reproaches, or comfort him, until at last all would unite in a loud chorus of forgiveness.

His eyes were burning with emotion at the thought. Pacing the two yards of the cell, restless, oblivious of the glum presence of Barbaças, Vieirinha wrung his hands as he imagined the circumstances and the characters of the new act in his tragedy. And these imaginings were so vivid that, looking out over the silent, empty square, he could almost see Loas there, in front of a seething crowd. Loas cursed him with a violent gesture of his fist that was really magnificent. The whole town vociferated in a pitiless roar of condemnation. Then he, Vieirinha, center and cynosure of the whole spectacle, would kneel down in his prison den, and with heartrending cries describe his infamy and present affliction; he would beg the town to make it up to Loas with payment of such a vigorous donkey that, compared with it, all others would seem but broken-winded plugs. Finally, Loas would give way and accept the wonderful gift from the town, and they would all embrace one another with tears of pardon. Such a scene it would be that, next year, blind beggars would be singing songs about it at all the fairs.

However, instead of this sublime scene, what actually could now be heard were the crude remarks the women and their companions in misfortune were shouting from the next window in reply to the jeers of youths who came and made fun of them each time the guard was away on the other side of the square. If the youths didn't come up quickly enough, then the women fetched them back with their insults.

"You're all filthier than dung," they shouted, thrusting their heads between the bars. "You're all a lot of snot noses! You and your mothers before you!"

Then all of a sudden they had burst out singing, like crazy creatures, the youths running back from the corner by the clock tower, spitting in the direction of the bars and making rude gestures, till some guard less patient than the others came and shook his fist at them.

"You bitches, just shut your row!"

"Only if you come and take a nip at our tongues! That'll shut us up. Come on, love, and see how nice it is!"

"Where do you think you are, you foul-mouthed sluts?"

"On a dung heap! That's what this place is, a dung heap!"

Vieirinha was tearing his hair in distress. Really, those girls had lost all sense of decency. It was always the same with them; at the first push, there was no holding them back; they rushed down the whole slide. And nothing but talk of dung in their mouths. Yet they had the looks all right, that you couldn't deny. . . . But it was only a poor sort of scene. If only Loas would come, and a dozen or so friends with him!

As the guard couldn't get the women to be quiet, he relieved his feelings by catching one of the youths by the ears.

Meanwhile, there was Barbaças, sunk in his own thoughts, and oblivious of it all, sitting silently in his corner of the cell. The town was ignoring their exploit. The women would be expelled next day, and he, Vieirinha, would go back to the loneliness of his burrow like a wolf on the prowl, dreaming of worlds the others laughed at. The estates, herdsmen, animals, and laborers would go on as before, poor and uncouth, bound to the ups and downs of harvests, incapable of feeling the bitterness of their own frustration.

Vieirinha was, however, grossly misinterpreting Barbaças' silence. He saw him as a dejected lout, a mere brute overwhelmed by events. He despised him for the passive way he'd let himself be drawn on by folk. He even felt indignant because the youth made no gesture of reproach. Vieirinha felt the need of accusation, violence, blasphemy. His big role in the drama of downfall needed to be backed up by the other parts—and the very person who ought to be demanding an explanation was sitting there mute and motionless, like an animal with belly-ache!

But he was very wide of the mark, quite unaware of what was really going on in Barbaças mind. When the guards had appeared suddenly among the trees shouting at the "depraved scoundrels," and had driven them along with the butt ends of their rifles, in the sudden turmoil Barbaças had felt a confused mixture of revolt, fear, that any power could come and interrupt a thing so extraordinary as being with a woman. Loas and his affairs were completely outside this. Neither Loas nor the donkey nor the guard nor the whole township, which was the beginning and end of his world, had any right of presence at that moment when he, seizing the red rose to absorb, possess, crush it, had felt that he was able to taste the full savor of life. He was backward; until then he had been shut up in a refracting crust; this had been ripped open from top to bottom, overwhelming him in a torrent of cruel delight in which life was revealed, unsuspected, terrible. Biting into the flower or the woman, he had wanted only to squeeze the last drop of blood from this revelation. Loas and the donkey were indeed far from all this; but it was only from this distance that he glimpsed their real meaning. These feelings or discoveries were not altogether clear to him, but they made themselves felt in an emotional upheaval, an unrest that, although rebellious, had nothing in common with the primitive rebellion of former days.

Crouching depressed in the darkness of the cell, Barbaças brooded over he knew not what.

News of the imprisonment of the two good-for-nothings, and of the sordidly picturesque reasons that had caused it, only spread through the town much later. Farmers had stayed late at the fair, and it was only after some hours had passed that the corporal of the guard, uncertain of the proper course to take, decided that he'd better go and knock at the door of the farmers' private assembly and, cap in hand, with a solemn face, ask them what they thought he ought to do with the girls.

The same problem came up every year. The notables of the town disagreed on the point. Should, under the guise of peddlers, merry-go-rounds, shows, stalls of ill fame be allowed to come to the fair or not? A lengthy tradition had given them a sort of right, and, all in all, the world was not much worse if the lads had a good time during the week the fair lasted. On the other hand, the brazenness of women of this sort showing themselves off in the streets was an offense to decent people. Farmer Maldonado, who often went to the dance halls in the capital, was amused when other farmers, whose age didn't allow such activities, looked on with secret envy while nobodies went freely in and out of any stall they liked, without fear of scandal. And the others, either because these loose-living folk whipped up the town trade for a few short days, or to see the abbot in a fume, because he became apoplectic at the mere thought that he was denied the right to sweep this evil rabble away with a cudgel—for one reason or another they never arrived at the firm veto, and the trollops came and went away again, and the debate remained in suspense till the following year. Farmer Cortes, however, kept up to the mark by his wife and the abbot, always tapped his thigh with his cane, and declared that it would be the very last fair at which the decent families of the town should be insulted by the presence of women of ill fame. . . .

And so the corporal came in and made a little bow from the doorway. Farmer Maldonado, at whose house they were assembled, turned and half closed his eyes against the lamp-light, to see who the visitor was, and after this pause the gentlemen went on with their game, showing plainly in their looks that the guard had better not disturb them too long.

"Well, what is it, Almeida?" the master of the house asked, when he saw that with the poor cards he'd got the game was not worth playing.

Thus encouraged, the corporal advanced a few steps into the room.

"I've arrested two girls from the fair."

That made them all put their cards down.

"You can put your cap on again, Almeida," Farmer Maldonado said graciously at once. But the corporal preferred to keep it in his hands because it kept them occupied.

"Two of those trollops?"

"Yes, Vieirinha and Barbaças, too. I caught them all in the eucalyptus trees."

Farmer Cortes, the only one who hadn't got his sleeves rolled up, preferring to put up with the heat rather than sacrifice his dignity, seized the opportunity for heavy irony.

"So they were hiding, were they? And quite right, too. Better to carry on among the eucalyptus trees than out in the street!" And so saying, he threw in his cards toward the center of the table. Farmer Maldonado had been waiting for his rival to take up this attitude. Cortes wouldn't miss the opportunity of raising the question of stalls and prostitutes, and forcing the issue in a trial of strength between them. And so he was annoyed at the corporal for being so foolish as to lock the girls up.

"That's what I think, too," he retorted flippantly, turning round to face the lamp again. "And those who like to stick their noses in that sort of thing can always go policing among the eucalyptus trees."

The corporal, who had come precisely to avoid offending the gentlemen by taking any initiative they might disapprove of, felt quite bewildered. But Senhor Cortes, sly dog, came to the rescue.

"Well, just tell us what happened. We all know you have to do your duty. Don't let our jokes upset you!" he said, discreetly carrying his glass of lemonade to his lips.

"The women were screaming about something—I arrested

the whole lot of them, and now I'm wondering whether they ought to be kept in prison for a few days, the women and the men; or whether, to avoid scandal, it wouldn't be better to just expel the women from the district. They're shouting their heads off down there."

"Expel them? I don't see why," remarked Senhor Cortes. "If these gentlemen allow them to come, well, they were just plying their trade, weren't they?" Then, before anyone could get in a counterstroke, and thoroughly enjoying his weather-cock tactics, he bewildered the guard still more by adding: "Well, Almeida, all this is just by the way. I'm sure these gentlemen are of my opinion that you'd better send them about their business right away. There's been too much publicity already."

"But I..."

"I know what you're going to say," the farmer interrupted. "But you can take it from me, next year things will be different."

And he leaned back against the wall in the easy attitude of someone on a comfortable couch, ready to meet any contradiction. Farmer Maldonado, for his part, with angry eyes cast downward, and shuffling his feet, was like a bull waiting the opportunity to rush his assailant. He couldn't think up any telling retort, and he sat there, sweat running down the strong muscles of his arm.

The others felt it expedient to lead the conversation onto less explosive and more impersonal ground; but just as Maldonado picked up his glass of beer, ready to toss his antagonist, it was the corporal himself who unwittingly caused a diversion.

"What is surprising is how quiet those two men are. Vieirinha and Barbaças are so glum they've got nothing to say for themselves. I've got a hunch there's some trouble about money, at the back of it. People saw them drinking and having a good time at the fair. So where did they get the money? Would any trollop follow such scarecrows without getting her money in advance?" he asked, smiling and stuttering over his insinuations. Senhor Cunha, the town clerk, who was passing through the place and staying with Farmer Cortes, felt that the tension had been relieved, and tried to do his bit toward clearing the atmosphere.

"Are they the kind of people who'd be likely to commit theft?"

The others glanced at each other in consultation. It was a somewhat difficult question to answer.

"Well, a fowl or two, or fruit," Farmer Cortes assented at last. "But more than that . . . I don't know. The fact is, you never know what to expect from such rabble."

The corporal thought this a good opportunity to get a lead on the point that interested him.

"Then would it be advisable to release Vieirinha and Barbaças as well as the women?" he asked.

"We ought to overlook a few tricks from Barbaças. . . . He never had anyone to guide him. But as for the other crafty rogue . . ." said Farmer Cortes. His rival, still with a grim look on his face, had taken no part in this exchange, although he'd been itching to ask a question, and at last curiosity got the better of him.

"Do you think the money they've been spending came from Loas's money box?"

"Who is Loas?" the town clerk asked quickly, in polite inquiry, as a mark of deference to these wealthy gentlemen.

"A crackbrain who lives on a holding some way out."

"A farmer?"

Senhor Cortes gave him a look that seemed to say that a question like that was an insult to the assembly.

"He's got a patch of land, heavily mortgaged," he explained coldly. "So long as he's got a square yard left, there'll always be some moneylender dangling money at him. He'll end up by begging, or somebody'll employ him as a day laborer out of charity."

"Then we'll have to foot the bill for old-age pensions for old fogies like that," Farmer Maldonado interrupted, stressing the syllables.

"There are still some people," Cortes went on in a soft voice touched with contempt, "who yet understand that in

81

Alentejo only the landowner worthy of the name can keep going. As for the other sort, one drought ruins them. Barbaças has been working lately for this chap Loas."

The town clerk, his spirits damped again for some reason he couldn't fathom, acknowledged the information with a gesture of thanks.

"There, now, it hadn't struck me that Barbaças came from the holding," the corporal remarked, anxious to get into action, and taking a step toward the door. "I'm going to find out whether Loas has been robbed."

"Keep your head, and don't be too precipitate," said Farmer Maldonado, who had recovered his good humor, in pleasant anticipation that the facts of the case would prove diverting. He drank off his last draft of beer into which a drop of sweat had just fallen, and went on: "As I said, just wait a bit and don't go trudging out there unnecessarily. Why not ask Barbaças first whether he took the money?"

"And will he tell the truth?"

"Even if he doesn't, Loas will be here quick enough if he's been robbed."

"That's so," agreed the guard, surprised that he hadn't thought of this simple solution himself. "I'll go and question them."

"And don't forget to ask the girls if these chaps did in fact pay them for their bit of work," Maldonado added with unexpected jocularity.

"What bit of work?"

"Now, then, Almeida, off with you, and get those details. Don't waste time with questions. . . ." Farmer Cortes interrupted in such an ambiguous tone you couldn't tell for sure whether there was irony as well as command in it.

Farmer Maldonado didn't like the tone at all. Was Cortes poking fun at the corporal's simplemindedness or making a crack at him? Not wanting to look a fool by taking offense if none had been meant, he pretended he hadn't noticed anything. But, looking round cautiously to see what the others felt about it, his eyes fell with displeasure on the town clerk—a stranger to the house and to their circle—an embarrassing witness to his discomfiture. He never liked strangers, and always treated them with a rather supercilious reserve. How else could you treat wretched folk who came from heaven knows where to live at the expense of the southerners, profiting by their wheat and herds, which were, after all, the very foundation of the land? The core of the whole country was their Alentejo with its blessed abundance—a veritable larder for all these dandies, clerks, doctors, notaries, pushing chaps who, presuming on a diploma or two, nibbled the crust the southerners threw to them as though negligently throwing tidbits to hangers-on.

And so, wanting to work off his irritation in some sort of activity, Farmer Maldonado pushed his chair back with a heave of his behind, and dashed after the corporal just in time to catch him in the middle of the street.

"Bring the prisoners back here with you!" he ordered.

By force of habit the corporal immediately stood to attention, but nevertheless demurred.

"It's against regulations, sir."

"Oh, forget all about it. We only want to help you. In my presence, neither of the rogues will dare deny what he's done."

"Yes, that's true."

"And to help you get everything cleared up right now," the farmer went on impatiently, "I'm going to tell my stockman to fetch Loas. He's such a crackbrain that perhaps after all he hasn't noticed the theft yet."

"Yes, I thought of that, too."

"Well, there you are. Go and fetch these fellows."

The Farmer Maldonado went and knocked at the stockman's window, and gave the order.

"Go and fetch Loas, we want to see him tonight. Tell him there's some talk that he's been robbed by his partner."

Ten minutes later the corporal came back with the prisoners. When Vieirinha saw which way they were going, he knew that the great moment had come. This was exactly the kind of audience that suited him. These gentlemen, prevented by wealth from sharing feelings that only an insecure existence could give, would now be the spectators of his self-criticism, his martyrdom of remorse. He would slit through the cuirass that made them hard. Thenceforward, not one among them would ever again make fun of a poor devil like Vieirinha, or scoff at his tales of a world they thought fantastic, a world beyond their hidebound comprehension, even if they had experienced it. Then he noticed Barbaças' stupid dullness again, and felt as though he'd like to shake him out of his mental torpor, rouse him to take part in his proud but tragic triumph. Barbaças, he would like to say, stand by me in the glory of putting these gentlemen to shame! They are so greedy for money, power, command, that they live in a permanent state of indigestion. People who at all times have their belly full can feel nothing but a desire to belch.

Such was Vieirinha's intent. But, by one of those strange contradictions, he was first to make a nice little bow when he came forward to confront the farmers. Smiling in polite attention, his first impulse was to make them think he didn't feel ill at ease in such high society. Barbaças, though, wouldn't budge from the doorstep, and the guard had to push him into the room.

"Barbaças, you might say good evening when you come in," remarked Farmer Maldonado, getting a cigarette ready to put in his mouth, and assuming the lead in the game. "So you two have been misbehaving, have you?"

Vieirinha felt a rush of words surge in his throat—and stick there. The wished-for moment had come, and after all he felt he was going to miss his opportunity. His surroundings intimidated him. The room was small, airless, dimly lit; the gentlemen round the table in their broad-brimmed hats, which seemed specially designed to hide their eyes and sinister designs, looked like a group of conspirators. His tragedy required either blinding sunlight or the solemn darkness of night. These four walls were such a comedown that they cramped his style, turned his tragedy into a farce.

"What's this, Barbaças? I hear you tried to dishonor two virgins."

84

The corporal laughed at the joke, and pushed the loafer a few steps farther forward.

"And you, friend Vieira, you've been leading the lad astray, have you?"

"Yes, Senhor Maldonado. As you say, I am in fact a beast!" And Vieirinha raised his chin haughtily. However, when he saw the mocking look on Senhor Cortes's face, and more especially the irritated surprise that showed in the host's eyes, he hastily corrected his attitude. "We just wanted to offer a Spanish fan to the girls."

The town clerk burst out laughing. Farmer Maldonado, too, had been going to laugh, but when he heard the stranger's outburst he felt obliged to give some support to Vieirinha, who did, after all, belong to the town.

"Well, that wasn't a bad idea, friend Vieira," he remarked.

The town clerk had to tense the muscles of his abdomen, and his eyes watered in a vain attempt to repress his laughter. So Vieirinha thought it advisable to explain his meaning further.

"All women are partial to nice little presents. All women like to be treated like ladies." And he was gratified to note there was a respectful silence all round him.

Farmer Cortes, the only one who sensed that Vieirinha thought he was winning the favor of his audience, began to fidget in his chair. "Do ladies also like you to steal money to pay for their favors?" he asked, putting his stick down on the table.

Vieirinha looked all round, as though searching for the person who deserved this insult, but, meeting with no support, decided to keep quiet.

"Did you steal any money, Barbaças?" the host interrupted, vexed that Cortes had butted in and taken the initiative from him.

Barbaças looked at the guard for an explanation. "The fan belonged to Senhor Vieirinha," he answered. "We didn't steal it from anybody."

"None of your twisting!" shouted the corporal, shaking

the youth by the shoulder. "You know very well what theft we're talking about. Loas'll soon be here to take the stuffing out of you."

"I didn't steal," Barbaças repeated with a decisiveness that implied that the matter was disposed of as far as he was concerned.

"Is friend Loas coming here?" Vieirinha asked anxiously. "Is he coming tonight?"

"The idea doesn't seem to please you," Farmer Cortes hinted.

Vieirinha passed grandly over this coarse insinuation. "There's nothing I'd like better than to talk with my friend Loas!" he exclaimed vehemently. "I want to tell him in the presence of all you gentlemen that I'm ready to go through hell itself to get the money for the donkey!"

"What's the meaning of this gibberish? What are you talking about?"

"I'm not afraid of meeting Loas! Neither afraid nor ashamed. Gentlemen, I'm a filthy beast, and that's a fact! I've played a dirty trick on Barbaças and my friend Loas. A whole year I've been waiting for a woman, and felt ready to rob a saint to get the money to have one. It wasn't Barbaças' fault. I'm the guilty party!" Vieirinha declared, striking his chest with his fist and trying to stand so erect that he seemed to be bending backward. "I want to explain all this to friend Loas! He wanted a donkey to work on his holding, and I, in fact, boozed and frittered his money away, but I'll go through hell to give it back to him!" A thick spittle had gathered at the corners of his mouth, making his words sound pasty, but after spitting it out quickly, he added, "I'll go back to the jungle itself to get it for him!"

The town clerk had listened quite dazed, neck craned forward and eyes staring with a vacant look. But Farmer Maldonado cut short Vieirinha's tirade.

"Let's try to get this thing cleared up, gentlemen—" he said, and turning to Barbaças, "Now, what's this money he's talking about?"

86

"The money Loas gave me to buy a donkey. Senhor Vieirinha told me he knew a gypsy who'd sell him one cheap."

"And you handed the money over to him, of course!" said the corporal. "Oh, no, there are no flies on this friend of yours."

"In fact, that's so," Cortes said, mocking Vieirinha.

Vieirinha's eyes flashed. These blockheads couldn't understand. Never would they be able to understand. But, of course, so far he'd done nothing to make an impression, no word or attitude really crushing. The truth was that so far he'd been nothing but a clown.

"He handed me the money to buy a donkey; that's a fact. And if friend Loas needs a donkey, sooner or later it'll be out there at the holding. Vieirinha never breaks his word. But at that particular moment the money belonged to me because I needed it most. Loas could wait. But I'll see he gets the money for the donkey, because now he's the one who needs it most."

"You're still tipsy, friend Vieira," Farmer Cortes broke in again.

But Vieirinha didn't hear him. He was launched in the level he wanted.

"Now it's friend Loas's turn. I'll turn hell inside out to get the money for him. All's well that end's well, and this'll end in excellent fashion."

"Perhaps a raffle would give good results. . . ." Cortes broke in once more. "You can raffle off a Spanish fan, and raise the money in a trice."

The onlookers applauded this sally; the interruption threw Vieirinha out of his stride, and, before he could get going again, Farmer Maldonado was speaking to Barbaças.

"And you there, you young idiot," he said roughly but with a hint of kindliness, "what have you got to say about all this?"

"The woman was pretty, and so—"

"You don't know how to tell it," Vieirinha interrupted. Spurred on again by what had happened among the eucalyptus trees, his face softened as at delightful memories. "He doesn't know how to express the whole thing. As a matter of fact, the two girls were a real poem, gentlemen! One of them, the one Barbaças had . . ."   .

Barbaças shrugged his shoulders; but suddenly, now that the farmer's question had brought him into the limelight, he began to sob.

This reaction was so incredible, so out of keeping with the jocund tale all had been expecting, that an astonished silence fell upon the gathering. The onlookers felt vaguely that they'd been cheated . . . as though at the height of a pantomime an actor had fired a real shot from a cardboard revolver. It was some moments before they could readjust themselves to the unpleasant turn the spectacle had taken. The town clerk was perhaps the only one who didn't find Barbaças' tears embarrassing, because for some little time he'd been feeling glum. Vieirinha's words had roused a kind of nostalgia in him, a requickening of memories, disappointments, happy days. The upsurge of an emotion the southerners forced you to bury deep down in silent hiding places.

The host, balked of his amusement, roughly opened another bottle of beer; the time had come, he felt, to throw the two men and the corporal out, and let them clear the matter outside.

"Well, Almeida, it seems to me that only Loas can decide the matter. If he considers he's been robbed . . . But as they're all of the same stamp, I suppose they'll end up by coming to some sort of understanding."

"Of the same stamp?" burst out Vieirinha. "You must excuse me, Farmer, but I—"

"Nobody asked your opinion."

From the tone of the reply, it was evident that one word more from Vieirinha, one further protest, and Farmer Maldonado would become as livid as the wall of the room. No one else hazarded a remark because when their host pulled the corners of his mouth down in a half-moon, and made a face that boded no good, not even Farmer Cortes dared put his spoke in.

"Stop that!" The corporal said to Barbaças, who was now sniveling quietly.

"Take them away," said Farmer Cortes at last.

Cast out like dull-witted bumpkins, Vieirinha and Barbaças moved off toward the door, Vieirinha red with indignation, and Barbaças with his eyes unusually wide and shining—giving no inkling of the storm that deep inside was turning him into a changed man.

But before they gained the street, the bulky figure of Maldonado's stockman came into view, bringing Loas with him—Loas so threadbare and scrawny, especially in comparison with the corpulence of his guide, that he looked like some strange excrescence of the herdsman. The latter stuck his head in at the door.

"Good evening, Master. Here's your man!" he said in a downright sort of voice, and set Loas between the corporal and the prisoners, as though setting down some game he'd been asked to deliver; and Loas stood there as confused as the two prisoners. They looked at each other with the wariness of accomplices, at the moment bound only by a feeling of comradeship in face of the common foe. Vieirinha was the first to throw off his embarrassment.

"Friend Loas!"

Loas turned eyes on him that were strangely calm, showing neither censure nor pity—smooth as a lake early on a summer's morning.

"Friend Loas!" Vieirinha said again, though reducing the pathos he had previously put into the words.

"Well, so there you are, Vieirinha! You haven't been to the holding this long while. How are you?"

"In excellent health, friend."

Instead of tearful despair, Vieirinha felt like smiling. His being filled with peace and gentleness, as at those times when after a whole year of gnawing hunger, he finished by possessing a woman.

"What punishment do these men deserve?" Farmer Cortes suddenly asked with a sting in his voice.

Both Loas and the prisoners turned with inquiry at this remark, as though it had been spoken in an unknown tongue. They didn't understand.

"All your life you've been a nitwit, Loas," said the master of the house, taking up the thread. "If these chaps spent a few days in prison, it won't compensate you for the theft, but it'll teach you to be more careful in choosing your friends. . . . What do you want a donkey for? To drive that wonderful gadget of yours?"

Loas made a vague gesture with his hands. Farmer Cortes sensed there was a hint of goodwill in Maldonado's aggressiveness; he could hear the tone that revealed that sentimentality was not far off, so he decided to get in first, and take the wind out of his sails.

"That's all right, Loas," he said. "You can take it that these friends of yours admit they've spent money that should have been used for the purchase of the donkey. They say that someday they'll pay their debt. But as we all rather doubt this . . . well, here's something from me to go on with."

And the farmer, leaning back easily against the wall once more, opened his wallet.

"How much do you need for the donkey?"

Loas looked round the assembly, smiling and clasping his hands. Suddenly his weariness had left him, but he felt so anxious and taken aback that he was tongue-tied.

"A good donkey can be got for eight hundred escudos," said the corporal.

"Pardon me, Senhor Almeida! You couldn't get any sort of animal for that sum," exclaimed Vieirinha, doing his bit toward helping his friend to get the most out of the situation.

The farmer slowly began to lay the notes on the table, enjoying the surprise caused by his generous gesture.

"Will a thousand escudos do it?"

At this point the town clerk, touched by the turn things had taken, wanted to make his contribution.

"If you'll allow me, Senhor Cortes, I'd like to give something, too, so that this poor fellow . . ."

Loas looked at him as though fearing even a friendly word might delay the moment when the money would be in his own hands.

"No, my dear friend. It's really my affair, because I've

got some old accounts to settle with Loas. He's the one who tells me, three years beforehand, what day the pigeons are going to come and settle on the plantation. . . ."

Loas nodded his head triumphantly in agreement, and just at that moment Barbaças ran up to the table as though he'd taken leave of his senses. There was a wild, frenzied look on his face, and suddenly he took the notes and crumpled them in his hands.

"No, Ti Loas! Not with this money, Ti Loas!" he shouted, twisting the notes between his rough fingers as though by so doing he wished to crumple everything the money represented. "I'm the one who has to hand back everything that belongs to you, Ti Loas!"

As Loas stretched out his hand to save the money from Barbaças' crazy onslaught, for an instant he felt that he'd like to strangle the loafer rather than see the miraculous notes made useless. But the next moment a wave of final discouragement and fatalism came over him, and when Barbaças lifted the notes to his teeth and tore them up in frenzy, there was only a look of pity in his eyes. As though, worn out with disappointment and bearing up against it, he could only look on at his own execution with indifference.

Dumbfounded, none of the others had moved; and it was only some moments later that Vieirinha, his red cheeks now copper-colored, announced in a sleepy voice:

"I think I'm going to sleep excellently today. And you, too, friend Loas! You don't need your old Vieirinha anymore. You've got a real man at your side."

PART II

6

When men left their homes in the early
morning, they followed the estate paths in order, day by day,
to watch the growth of the corn. There was a rustling over the
wheatfields, a prolonged murmuring, panting breaths coming
and going across the plain. Even at dawn the sky shone like a
ripe apple. The townsfolk scrutinized the long fine spell, and
asked themselves whether there would be late rains bringing
mildew to the wheat; whether the breeze bore any sign of
storms that might beat the crops to the ground, threshing and
stripping them in a veritable slaughter. And when the air was
hard and heavy, they wondered whether the blazing heat of
the long afternoons would sear the grains to emptiness.

Women and children, expectantly waiting for the harvest
earnings, went out after the men, and lived through the same
anxieties. Farmers spurred their horses to the highest points
on their estates, and turned all this questioning into terms of
bushels of corn, wages, market fluctuations; but even if the
crop should come to grief overnight, they knew that next year
they and the peasants would work through the same round
of sowing, hoeing, and reaping, with all the worries this persistence involved. Whenever they sat round some card table,
or at the door of some shop, whiling away the long, burning
agony of the afternoons, however hard they tried to get away
from it, in the end they always came back to the one theme:
soil that was too hard or too soft to receive the grain; rain
that made the weeds multiply, but lay in pools round the roots
of crops, and rotted them; the ravage caused when the June
sun dried up blades that were still tender; fertilizers; wages;
the inroads of clandestine flocks. Some small thing that, ever
feared, ever expected, might in one hour destroy the work

of months. And, leaving the card tables and the stagnant afternoons in the townships, any man who possessed land, whether
a small patch or a vast extent, or who merely took part in its
life, would go out once more to have a look at the crops, pick
out places where the wheat had not come up so well, and, by
dint of staring at them, try to urge the sap up the stems and
stimulate growth.

Clouds had often passed on the horizon, dense and pur-
plish as though blown from some fire, but all they brought and
left behind was a vague hope—and the portending flight of
vultures and crows. The gravelly soil was split with wide cracks
of thirst.

Loas would stand on the bank by the roadside for hours
on end, as though, perched up there, he were expecting some
event to be revealed to him.

"When you left town, did you happen to see any clouds?"
he asked a farmhand who happened to pass by.

"No, nothing at all."

"But yesterday the sun had a hazy look about it. . . ."

"Well, maybe the clouds'll be coming along soon."

Nevertheless, Loas went off and picked up a bucket of
water to throw over the dry garden. The farmhand, who hadn't
seen him for some time, thought he'd grown very thin, less
talkative than before, and there were white threads in his hair.

One afternoon the bus from the city passed the bank where
Loas was standing, set down a passenger, and then roared off
again, filling the air with the smell of burnt gas. When the
mudguards throbbed and the monster vibrated like an angry
beast, Loas felt stifled. Then, suddenly, there was a mist before
his eyes; he began running after this enemy that had driven the
mules off the road, and pelted it with all the stones he could
find—as though chasing off all the obscure causes that had
submerged his life's ambition to conquer the plain. But soon
the monster could only be sensed through dust and distance,
dust and fumes that left Loas stifled and mocked. . . .

At last the wheat was ripe. Like a full, heavy womb it
undulated gently in the wind, and men were gathering in
the town squares or at farmers' gates, silently waiting to be

assigned to the various reaping gangs and estates.

Barbaças was among the first to offer his services. For weeks past he had been seen on enclosed land, cutting rock roses and furze as though he were trying to get back in the shortest possible time that skill with the sickle which folk in those parts learn from childhood but which he had lost through idleness. Of course, some people laughed at him for this belated whim to take up activities that required continuity and trained muscles. But there were others who would venture no comment on his inconsistencies. As a matter of fact, people could no longer understand Barbaças. Since he'd given up his priceless freedom and living by odd jobs to go and have part and lot in Loas's crackbrained schemes; since he'd been caught in the company of trollops and accused of squandering a sum of money that was more than sufficient for dozens of adventures of that sort; since he'd ripped between his teeth the fistful of notes that had been offered to compensate for this breach of trust—since all these doings, far too peculiar in an ordinary chap like Barbaças, people's judgment had naturally been disturbed. So he was definitely going to give up loafing for a regular job, was he? Well, then, let him get on with it! they said in united derision and encouragement.

However that might be, Barbaças' efforts to find work were not very promising. "Hey, there, good-for-nothing, what have you come for?"

"To reap," came the curt and scowling reply from Loas's ex-partner.

"To reap my money or just corn? Now be off with you!"

Probably the township had put up with Barbaças' waywardness and idleness because it was his nature to be obstreperous, lazy, and so unimpressed by the established course that he had even given death the slip. To do as others did was to lose his reputation for the unusual and lay himself open to being measured by the common yardstick, thus disappointing those people who liked to talk about the doings of their village black sheep. Then, again, reaping was a very serious thing, requiring careful consideration; farmers couldn't view it lightly, like some passing frolic. "Since hobnobbing with the devil on

Loas's holding, you've gone quite crazy," they said. "What are you up to with this new fancy for grabbing at a sickle?" And Barbaças went on to the next, neither replying nor humbling himself. He wasn't the sort to persuade people with mealy-mouthed words. Somehow he couldn't get his lips to speak them. He just went from one farmer to another, one estate to another, until only one door remained—Farmer Cortes's, the one he'd been avoiding from the first.

Reaping had been in progress for a week when Barbaças walked into the farmer's yard one night. Combing his hair back, and this time with a look of proper submission, he called out, "If you need another man for the harvest, sir . . ."

"What man is it?"

Barbaças scraped his feet on the ground. He wouldn't ask again. After this vexation, the only thing left was to go to some other district, where he wasn't known. But then, unexpectedly, the farmer gave a little smile, though it wasn't easy to catch what it meant.

"Do you think you can stand up to the work?" he asked.

"Yes, sir."

"All right. But no mice-breeding on my lands, eh? I've heard tell you carry them about in your pockets and in cages."

Barbaças looked down at the cobbles.

"So, no mice, then. My man says you've got one with a fluffy coat that you're always showing people—"

"Yes, sir. But that's the only one I've got. The rest's just talk. . . ."

"Well, come along tomorrow and see my headman. And you can bring the one mouse."

At daybreak Barbaças was at the estate before the gang-master and immediately to work with a will. Then the gangs that had come down from the north for the harvest appeared on the scene, silent and humble, week-old beards on faces lead-colored with sweat and dust. The local hands bandied a few whispered gibes or rude remarks, and then all bent over their task again, merged in the sea of wheat. Behind them lay swathes of corn, and stubble—a stretch of plundered land.

The sun, rising and flaming in the sky, made Barbaças'

dark skin burn; his eyes were feverish and bloodshot; and although the others, in a spirit of rivalry, did their utmost to keep up with the mad rhythm of his reaping, it was the loafer who kept well ahead, the wedge point driving into the heart of the crop. The men went more and more frequently to get a drink of brackish water from the water carrier, meanwhile sheltering for a few moments in the thin shade of the oak trees; and at midday they all knocked off for a rest. Sitting quietly with their hands between their knees, as though waiting for something to happen, at first they hadn't the energy to crack a joke or talk of other things. They just sat with a heavy, absorbed look. All round them, silence like sleep lay over the countryside; trees, men, wheatland and furzeland were so open to the sun, so motionless in time, that all seemed eternal.

Then, when they felt a bit rested, the young ones got together and tried to stir up the girls with light mockery, until the whole gang was drawn into it.

One of the older men, who liked a change of woman whenever he felt like it, was trying to get closer to a dark girl with eyes like a snake's. A companion from Vimieiro egged him on.

"It seems to me you won't lose by the change, so get on with it Ti Cesar!"

"Maybe, but nobody wants anything from me but talk now! Some light the oven and others put in the bread."

"Don't you believe it, Ti Cesar. If Ti Rita walks out on you, you can tie up with this one!"

"That's the way to talk. There's only sense like that in Vimieiro. Over here at Brotas there's not a rascal with heart enough to give good advice like that. What do you say to it, lass?"

An old man who didn't like Ti Cesar's silly nonsense and who had been sitting chin on breast, now lifted his head and looked at a high purplish-colored cloud tinged here and there with white.

"The master's got wonderful corn," he said.

"A wonderful estate, you might say," put in one of his companions. "It'll grow anything you put in it. It's real good loam. Well looked after, it'd support a dozen families."

"It'd be still better if it'd been sown earlier," another man put in. "That's what I told the headman at the time."

"Maybe you're right," the old man agreed slowly.

And they all gave another appraising look at the smooth plain stretching away into the distance, and breathed in the smell of ripe wheat saturating the summer air. These comments, and appraisal of eyes and nose, reflected the pride of a subconscious desire to possess that had been frustrated.

During the rest period, Barbaças lay outstretched in the sun, eyes closed, unsociable. But as soon as work began again, he went in the same mad rhythm. Barbaças must be in a hurry about something. What could it be? If not, all this feverish activity was just a further example of his lack of balance. When the farmer came to have a look at them, the gangmaster could no other than tell him that the loafer was like a fire kindling the crafty slackness of the other reapers. Barbaças didn't try to wangle any rests: he ran straight to the water pitcher (which toward the end of the afternoon was as warm and dust-laden as a lava wave of sunlight), splashed his face and lips—and then got straight back on the job. In this mad desire to get heaven knows where, Barbaças seemed determined to protect the farmer's pocket. Once his hand met another man's just as it was taking the pitcher by the handle; the other man, with a challenging look, offered water to everybody, and when they had all drunk their fill, emptied the last thick drops on the ground, where the dust drank them up with the sound of an ember hissing in water.

Days later, there was a lurking animosity round him, ready to burst out at any moment. But at dusk, when the reapers were dawdling about the corn wains, nibbling stale bread that smelled like leather, word went round that Barbaças was off across the plain to Loas's homestead to help with the poor harvest there.

And so it was. One evening, when Loas had at last settled that it was time to get the corn in, and was waiting for friend Vieirinha, who had promised to come, to decide with him which corner was the best starting place, Barbaças turned up, covered with dust, arms and face stiff with anxiety, as though he were expecting nothing but hard words. For Loas, however, it was just an unexpected visit. And a visit was always cause for rejoicing. Whoever it was, tramp or relation, beggar or farmer, the person who came from anywhere, choosing this lonely holding from all the places in the province, was warmly welcomed as bringing a feeling of human companionship into Loas's wilderness.

But however hearty Loas's hospitality was, such visits were not frequent. Their host might give up the last inch of sausage in the house, offer his bed, and anything else that might tempt a guest—but they also knew they would have to put up with endless hours of endless talk.

"Now then, eat!" he would spur them on with a hospitable smile, like a cannibal who is fattening up a prisoner to make the coming banquet more succulent. And it wasn't only a smile of the lips; eyes, cheeks, gestures, all smiled, in a slow and patient pleasure, sure that in his turn the time would come for enjoying his companion's goodwill.

And so, after weeks of absence, he found himself face to face with Barbaças.

"If it isn't friend Barbaças!" he burst out in surprise.

"Well! Bless my soul!" and his eager welcome soon took all the stiffness out of the youth.

"Have you begun reaping?" he asked quickly, before Loas could swamp him in a stream of words.

"I'm going to start one of these days. Vieirinha has promised to give me a hand. We've discussed it and decided that it'll be best to begin over yonder, at the end of the strip. You see what it is, Barbaças; it's backbreaking carrying the swathes! You see? Dammit, but we could do with a donkey here! So it's better to start off farthest away, while your back's still strong. But it's the last year we'll have to do it. Vieirinha says it's the last time. He says he's going to get me a donkey from somewhere, even if he has to go to hell for it. He's a real friend, and no brag about him, dammit!" The farmer sighed, and his look expressed deep satisfaction. "Dammit! Vieirinha and I have had such good times, talking it over and nibbling at sausage, that we've put the reaping off for a few days. That's why I'd like to get some animals on this place again. They solve all these problems in a twinkling, and there's still time left for a chap to have a bit of talk with friends. Did you know I'm still thinking of getting that donkey?"

Loas wasn't joking or cruelly hinting at the unfortunate past. Quite simply, in the joy of conversation and the ideas that conversation brought up, he'd forgotten that Barbaças had been one of the principal actors in his misfortune. But all of a sudden his wrinkled face looked sad and thoughtful, and he fell silent, turning his eyes away from the youth. He'd suddenly remembered, and was looking round for something to say, to make them friends again.

"Would you like a bit of something to eat?"

"No, thanks."

"Have a bit of supper with us."

"No, thanks. I came to ask if you'd let me help with the reaping."

"That's all right. I'm always glad to see you here. Whenever you want to join me again, we'll do really big things. Have you noticed those olive cuttings we planted out? Just look at them!"

"When do you want us to begin the reaping?"

"All in good time," Loas answered vaguely, still looking with moist, affectionate eyes at the sun-baked olive cuttings. "Tomorrow, or some other day when it suits you. Friend Vieirinha's coming to help, too. And we'd better start off right over there, so that the last patches to be done are near the house. How much do you think there is?" he added craftily.

Barbaças listened impatiently.

"Does Vieirinha know how to reap?" he asked.

"Look, now, if a man wants to help a friend, he always knows everything. If he cuts a finger or two, I've got herbs to heal everything. And I've found some other herbs, too, which kill the germ in carbuncles. But dammit all, Barbaças, stop and have a bite with us!"

"No, thanks. If you like, we can start reaping tomorrow. I'll be here a bit after sunset, about the same time as now."

"The same time as now? Oh, you young scamp, so you're afraid of working with the sun grilling your back. . . ."

"No, it isn't that. I'm working for Farmer Cortes."

"You're working! . . . Now, blast me, Barbaças! After that, let's go and eat a nice slice of ham."

And he took the youth firmly by the arm. He was breathless with curiosity to hear Barbaças explain everything at length. Alice came out of the back door, smiling at him and waving her hand in shy greeting. She looked all round, as though searching for something to bind him to the holding, and finally pointed to a tree. Barbaças went nearer, but he couldn't see anything special about it.

"There's a wagtail making its nest here."

"It's still early for wagtails to make nests."

The girl pouted with disappointment, so Barbaças tried to put things right again.

"There are years when they begin building earlier, though."

Loas, eager, almost vexed at this delay, tugged at his arm again. But while the master of the house followed him about, asking questions, and making much of him, Barbaças went off into the kitchen to look for the implements they would need next day; he cleaned them, greased them, and asked for a sharp knife so that he could make a new haft for the sickle. And it was only after finishing these preparations that, still awkward and silent when face to face with Loas, he agreed to sit down and eat.

Alice sat down near him on a basket, and quietly pushed it along till she could touch his shoulders. Joana signed to her to come out, and so Alice looked round for some excuse to stay in the kitchen, and set about washing dishes. Her mother, hard-faced, went on waiting for her to move, and, seeing she was lingering there on purpose, with arms dangling idly in the bowl, she remarked, "You'll have frogs growing in your hands before you know where you are." And went out.

Barbaças swallowed his bread and soup without looking at anyone. He answered Loas's questions with quick nods of the head, and drew away from the little shoves that the girl, now free of her mother's vigilance, kept giving at his arm. He had seen that Loas's wife had gone out into the garden to avoid him, and this took all pleasure from the meal. He had kept the bit of ham for the end, to enjoy it slowly once his hunger had been satisfied—but even this tidbit lost its appeal. Loas was disappointed, too, and went outside and stood there waiting for the youth.

Alice thought this was a good opportunity to push her hands into Barbaças' pockets.

"What are you looking for?" he growled, annoyed. "Leave me alone." But when he saw the pained surprise on the girl's face, and was afraid she'd start sniveling, he drew her to him. "What are you looking for in my pockets, love? Do you want a piece of twine?"

"No," she answered, her little chin trembling. "I wanted to have a look at the mouse."

"Then you should have said so right off. I keep it in a cage now."

"A cage the same as for birds?"

"A cage made with reeds. The poor little thing was just stifled in my pocket. But when it gets cooler, I'll carry it about with me again."

"And grasshoppers, too?"

"Yes, of course, Alice," he answered falling in with her enthusiasm. "I've come across dozens of them, and wonderful singers!" Barbaças, being wild himself, was quick to see and enter into the habits and feelings of wild things.

"Singers! And you never brought me one!"

"I'll bring you one sometime, you'll see."

Dreamy and pleased, the girl lay her head on his shoulder, and closed her eyes. Barbaças could feel the soft rhythm of her breathing, and this trusting contact made him feel happy and full of affection. He liked Alice—he said to himself, pleased as though at a sudden revelation. To be near her was like coming back to something good, something good to remember and preserve, but he wasn't sure himself whether the moment had been really lived or only imagined.

Soon afterward Alice sat up.

"My mother doesn't like you," she said. "She says we haven't got a donkey because of you. But I don't believe it."

Barbaças felt the muscles of his throat tighten so much that he couldn't speak. When he did get the words out, they were jerky and gruff.

"We're going to have a donkey; I promise. You know I wanted to bring the donkey, don't you, Alice?"

She nodded Yes, and in his emotion Barbaças could only show his thanks by squeezing her hands.

The girl lay her head on his shoulder again, as though his promise was enough to set her mind at rest. Then, gazing dreamily at the hearth, she said:

"It'll be a nice little donkey with a white star on its forehead. . . . And we're going to have kittens. Our gray cat looks very fat." Then her look suddenly grew preoccupied, and, staring at her companion, she went on: "Have you ever noticed that when animals get fat, there are always kittens, puppies, and lambs soon afterward? What if everybody grew fat? If I ate a lot and got fat, and you, and Mam and Dad, there'd soon be a lot of little uns in the house. What do you have to do to get fat?"

"Don't talk such nonsense."

"Wouldn't you like to get fat?"

"No."

And not feeling able to face any further questions, Barbaças suddenly jumped up.

"I'll come back tomorrow."

"With the donkey?"

"When the harvest's finished, then the donkey'll turn up."

Next day, Barbaças found Loas and Vieirinha already there, both sitting under a tree. Loas looked delighted, and shouted to Barbaças when he was still a hundred yards away.

"Ah, Vieirinha, here he comes! Bless me if this harvest isn't going to be the best we've had years back! I'd rather see three friends working together, just the three of them, than a gang of men who've got nothing to say to each other. Aren't I right? Come on over here, Barbaças!"

Vieirinha daren't risk a greeting. He heaved himself up

stiffly, not being able to bend the layers of fat on his belly, and looked about him, trying to make Barbaças think that he'd already been busy in connection with the task that had brought them all together. Barbaças lost no time. Without waiting for any assistance, he carried off all the implements, and when the other two reached the end of the strip, he was already cutting swathes.

"It's a real joy to see how that lad works," said Loas, delighted.

Vieirinha felt rather down in the mouth, and vaguely annoyed. His belly prevented him from getting his sickle well down to the ground, and in his wake the stubble was so high that it didn't look as though it had been cut. By the end of half an hour his face was swollen, and as wet as an apple in the dew of a summer's morning.

Loas very soon got drawn into the swing of the work. He didn't want Barbaças to get too far ahead of him, but as Vieirinha was falling pitifully behind, and was soon quite lost in the corn, and as Barbaças' rhythm got more and more furious, it finally came about that he was alone, with nobody to listen to him. He had to remain silent, and he was very disappointed.

The air was warm, full, almost sensual, with a womanish smell about it—the smell of corn. Loas's nostrils drank it in greedily. The panting breath of the plain came up at them, too, rising and falling like a soft belly that, in the distance, seemed to be transmitting a huge batrachian pulsation to the atmosphere. It was a strange call that urged Loas on to work. Reaping, at such a time, was to take part in the magic wonder of the plain.

When night began to fall, Vieirinha was worn out, and he made it an excuse to knock off.

"My eyes begin to burn at this time of day. My sight isn't as good as it was when I was twenty."

He brushed his clothes down carefully, keeping his eyes away from a rent here and there, and then sat with his back against the trunk of the only oak tree that broke the bareness of the wheatfield. Loas quite saw his friend's point, and thought it only polite to join him for a spell.

Sitting where they could see Barbaças, and look with approval on his activity, they both felt that their mere presence was helping him on in the good work. Loas was so happy at the sight of this idle fellow transformed into such an industrious worker that he felt lifted above all bitterness.

"People say Barbaças played me a dirty trick with that trollop affair," he exclaimed. "But I think he's a good lad. Don't you think so, too? I certainly needed a donkey very badly here, but I wouldn't exchange Barbaças' friendship for all the donkeys in the parish."

Vieirinha gave a vague growl of assent, not liking the subject of conversation; but very quickly the look on Loas's face changed again, as though some new problem were puzzling him.

"And people've been saying something else, too, Vieirinha. They say he was a silly fool to give so much money to the trollops. He could've managed with a great deal less."

"I was the guilty party!" exclaimed Vieirinha, unable to contain himself any longer, the words bursting from his chest. He couldn't make out whether Loas was discreetly setting him outside the unfortunate incident out of politeness or whether it was a subtle way of torturing him. "Don't put the blame on Barbaças, friend Loas! We only meant to spend a bit of the money—but you see, when you're with a woman you just forget everything. A woman deserves all the money a man's got with him. The money burns you like a fire till you've given it to them."

Loas began to scratch the thick rough joints of his fingers.

"Dammit all, you're right there, my friend," he said. And without daring to look his friend in the face, he went on in a low voice: "And they were . . . you know what I mean, Vieira . . . nice breasts and nice . . ."

But Loas's gestures to show what he meant were so awkward and inadequate that Vieirinha interrupted him indignantly.

"They were two fine women, my friend! Excellent forms. Excellent. From top to toe you couldn't find anything to quarrel with. I'd go back to the jungle and face serpents and lions to have two women like them! And they smelled good, Loas. Have you ever been in the woods in spring when rosemary comes into bud? You whole body is intoxicated, a lovely intoxication as though you'd got your head stuck in a pitcher of wine. That's how the women smelled."

Loas sat there with his eyes alight, and strangely absorbed. Vieirinha's talk transported him to a wonderful world. The suggestion of lovely women being only a pretext, isolating him so completely from the gross, concrete things of life that his senses no longer accepted the crude reality of Barbaças, bending under a shock of nearby corn.... Barbaças violating the earth. What was the purpose of this barbarous desire to gather everything the earth produced? Whenever and wherever the bare earth gave forth fruits, when the sandy places became covered with whin bushes, when rosemary bloomed in the thickets, it was beautiful. Men could collaborate in this fertility, but never exhaust it. The earth was as sensuous and capricious as a woman, and only those whose hearts were pure and senses tranquil could truly love it.

"I've still got the scent of them in my nostrils, Loas," Vieirinha went on, his nostrils quivering. "It's as though it had penetrated my very flesh."

"You must think a lot of the women, my friend. Dammit, I bet you'd rather have a woman than a fine estate with mules, oxen, pigs, and everything! Why don't you get married?"

"I, get married? Everybody talks to me about getting married. Get married, Vieirinha, they say; get married! But have you ever heard me say I don't want to? Where could I find a woman to marry me?"

Loas was unpleasantly struck by the implacable logic of this question. There was his friend Vieirinha with a dramatic problem eating him up, and he was sadly admitting to himself that it was impossible to solve it there and then, when he suddenly opened his eyes wide.

"What we've got to do is consult the book of St. Ciprian, which treats of such things," he solemnly pronounced, his prophetic finger pointing at his friend's ruddy nose.

Barbaças, as before bent under the weight of a heavy shock of corn, was passing near the two talkers for the fourth time. Each time he'd given them a surly look as he passed, but this time he expressed his utter disgust by spitting at their feet. Of course, he'd suspected from the beginning that he'd have to do the cutting and gathering practically alone, but this brazen idleness was too much. He felt really vexed.

When he got to the barn to put in the final shock of corn for that day, the mistress of the house was waiting for him at last. There was no hostility left in her expression, only reserve. She held a packet out to him, and when he hesitated, she in-sisted.

"Take it. It's your food for tomorrow."

And Barbaças felt that Joana, too, had forgiven him.

The day they finished the reaping at the holding, Loas wanted to have a bit of a celebration. He'd been to town to borrow some money from the schoolmaster, signing a paper on the sale of the crop, and on his way back he bought a big flagon of wine, some beer, and a kid ready flayed. Barbaças didn't feel like joining them. Sitting in the middle of the stubble field, sullen and brooding over foolish thoughts, he could hear Vieir-inha laughing away, and Loas talking away, and it all got on his nerves. Twilight was coming down from the hills; the earth was darkening in sudden death—the kind of moment when melancholy looks round and sees its own reflection.

Ti Joana was moving about the holding on her endless tasks. When she passed through the garden she would finger some flower or cabbage; or, taking Alice's little watering can, she would give a sprinkle to leaves that sun and dust were turning yellow, to make them look greener. At times her stifled lungs drew in long breaths of air from some nonexistent breeze. No matter how long she lived on the plain, she'd never get used to it. Even if she were there for centuries—the flat baked horizons would always stifle her.

Vieirinha was telling Loas how one fine day the farmers had taken their men to the city in a bus to cheer some important person.

"They said to the men: 'Now cheer!' The men all cheered, my friend Loas, without knowing why."

"And what about you, Vieirinha?"

"I went, too . . . and cheered."

"Bless my soul! Whatever for?"

"It's nice to take a trip to the city, my friend. You have an excellent time there."

Loas felt quite perplexed at talk like this.

"We cheer," Vieirinha went on, "like the blacks used to shout in the jungle, when I ordered them to shout and whipped them to it. It's nice to let off fireworks at fairs and on feast days, and it's nice to cheer when we're taken to the city where there's wine and women. It's just having a good time away from the family."

"Oh. And who was the important person?"

"Somebody high up in the city."

"Do you think he'd know anything about motors, Vieirinha? I'd still like to see that damned machine of mine working. That other chap who came from the city . . ."

"I don't think so, Loas. Gentlemen like that don't need to know about motors or anything else."

"How do you know?"

"Because in the jungle I was a gentleman myself."

Loas became thoughtful. That kind of talk didn't interest him, and so he cast about for another subject. His eyes searched keenly beyond the hillocks. What could they chat about more to his liking? In the distance, in front of Farmer Maldonado's olive groves, he caught sight of the wild olives gnarled and twisted with age, like ropes coming out of a coil. And beyond them were fine cork trees, the color of red ocher.

"Now, just look over there at that plantation, Vieirinha. The acorns are as big as your fist."

"Better not look too often, my friend. It's the same sort of thing as if you kept looking at a woman who already had a lord and master."

These unpleasant words put a damper on Loas, but he didn't feel like giving way to an attitude of resignation. . . . And now Vieirinha in his turn looked thoughtful. The coming of evening encouraged melancholy, and so he began to talk quite wildly.

"Have you ever noticed? There are some places . . ."

"Noticed what?"

"These flatlands, Loas. There are some places that make a man feel small. Have you ever seen the sea? When you're out at sea, you know you're just nothing at all. And it's the same on this heathland. It just swallows you up on all sides. A man's worth nothing. Can you remember that chap Barao who hung himself? He went off and bought a rope from Justino, and hung himself on a tree. And when he went off with the rope, we all knew what he meant to do. Here, a man's just nothing."

By this time, the wine was beginning to make it difficult to get the words out, and Loas pulled himself together to throw off the sad impression made by this dreary tale. The best thing to do was to go over to Barbaças and make him join in, and with Vieirinha helping, he carried the big flagon and the pan of kid stew to where the youth was sitting.

"Have a drink, Barbaças! Dammit all, we deserve a good drink of wine. We've worked like the devil the last few days. Isn't that so, friend Vieira? It's a good job done!"

Vieirinha nodded in agreement. The wine had begun to make him feel sleepy. His eyelids felt so heavy they were closing even while their host spoke.

The smell of the stew treacherously crept up Barbaças' nostrils, and sent pride to the devil. For a long time now his stomach hadn't been near anything with the flavor of proper cooking, and certainly nothing so savory and well cooked as this. Suddenly he threw himself on the pan in a rage of hunger, yet angry with himself because he couldn't resist. Sauce dripped from his lips and fingers, and the pieces of meat, which he swallowed almost whole, dropped into his stomach like stones. Vieirinha felt nauseated. Really, it was a disgusting sight. And when the uncouth fellow pushed his fingers right to the bottom of the pan to soak a piece of bread, Vieirinha felt quite sick. To avoid this, he looked the other way, closing his eyes and mind against the coarseness of his surroundings.

"Clean it all up, Barbaças!" Loas encouraged him, delighted. "You helped us quite a bit with the harvest, you know, and I don't want to make merry and you not get something to eat! Isn't that so, friend Vieira?"

But Vieirinha had closed his mind to such purpose that he was fast asleep. His head had dropped down toward his globe of a stomach. Earlier on, he'd unbuttoned his trousers to give him more room, and his belly bulged out grotesquely like a huge gourd. Alice had come up, and was fascinated by the sight. She stood there such a long time with her mouth open that Barbaças went to have a closer look, too.

"What are you looking at, lass?"

She blushed, as though she'd been caught doing something wrong. Then, putting her mouth to Barbaças ear, she whispered, "Ti Vieirinha's got such a fat belly. Both he and the cat are going to have little uns."

Barbaças was just swallowing the last piece of bread. He choked with such noise that Vieirinha woke up. Loas set to thumping him on the back.

"That bread's stuck in your throttle, my lad. Don't guzzle it so. . . ."

7

Now that the harvesting was over, the bare earth, ribbed with furrows where the plow had passed, was visible again, but so rough that it hurt feet and eyes. Gangs of seasonal laborers were coming down from the farms, for the last time that summer, in a slow, heavy ebb tide. In the empty fields, red and porous under late sunset, the breeze winnowed the dust, but without disturbing the silence that lay over everything. For weeks past the plain had been silent, but always with the soft rustling of wheat. Now it was one of those complete silences that hang round ruins. There was still some corn stubble here and there, scattered ears, dried-up camomile plants, remnants that lay still and spectral.

At night, Farmer Cortes gathered the gangs of reapers in the courtyard of his house and, with a few condescending remarks, paid out the last wages. On that day it was the accepted thing to ask small favors of the landed gentry. Tradition compelled them to show generosity. Assembled by the score in the courtyard, with dour, wrinkled faces, like masks of wood, the men made a forbidding picture. The farmers, for some reason they couldn't formulate, didn't like to see them gathered together like this. During the long winters, when work was short, the sight of a somber crowd was enough to give the landowners an unpleasant feeling. Deep down, they sensed the mysterious strength and dignity of the oppressed. And when they were arrogant, when they gave vent to egoism or brutality, they did it in some shabby way. Their power was fragile.

One of the oldest men present opened the session of requests and favors.

"Master, there's a dry bough on one of the cork trees in the wood. Can I go and get it?"

"This winter I'm thinking of fattening up a young pig. Will you give me a backward one from one of your farrows, Master?"

"Go and get one," the farmer consented with the emphatic generosity of a feudal lord. "And tell the stockman to pick out a good one."

One of the women was very anxious to get her turn, but her voice didn't betray her anxiety. "My old man thinks he could act as guard," she said quietly, in almost a wheedling tone.

"Well, now, if young men, even, can't keep folk out, what'd happen with your husband? All the thieves in the parish would take advantage. What he needs, my good woman, is a pension!"

"He's had an allowance, Master."

"And a good one, they say...."

"It might be worse. But that isn't what he wants, Master. Folk prefer to work. My old man..."

"I suppose what he wants is a job fit for a man in his thirties!"

And nobody knew whether to laugh or not.

The gangs would hang about the courtyard as though they wanted to make these days, when the whole family had work and food assured, last as long as possible. Except, of course, the gangs from the north. These took their wages and went off as though afraid of trouble. They felt insecure, out of place among these reserved, taciturn companions. They went off to some other place to carry on the struggle, but the following summer would see them back again like laborious birds. They lived through a cycle of migration. But the gangs from the south had lived all their lives in the heart of the plain. They lived like trees or stones—so part and parcel of the landscape that they couldn't be transplanted.

The farmer asked them what they intended to do after the harvest. He had kept an eye on the best of them, and wanted to arrange with some of them for other work. He noted that Barbaças was sitting on a wall, counting his money.

"This time it's a holding you're going to buy," he said to him. "How the devil did you manage to keep all that money?" And he pulled the notes from Barbaças' hands, and began to count them. "Do you mean to say you've managed to keep all your earnings for the whole season?" And Barbaças followed the counting, repeating the movements of the farmer's lips, and watching, as though afraid he might filch one of the notes. "Two more weeks of harvesting, and you'd have enough money to go to America. . . ."

"No, sir."

"Do you know how much money you've got here?"

Some of the laborers came up to enjoy the scene, but Barbaças paid no attention to them.

"I hadn't finished counting," he answered.

"Well, you've got eight notes."

"Eight!" exclaimed one of the men.

"Eight, and a few coins over to buy a beer or two. . . . But you're not a man who needs money! Do you remember how you tore up those notes with your teeth?"

At that moment Barbaças was in no mood for joking. He quickly put the notes in his pocket, and then glanced at the men standing near with a trusting, friendly look, which reassured they understood his satisfaction, and shared in it.

"Master, have you noticed that our young friend has turned into one of Loas's apparitions? Working out there like a real champion, like a diligent head of a family."

"No, I hadn't noticed it. He's got you all whacked, though! And what's more, it wasn't for love of the money." The farmer, drawn into the pleasure of talking, was more familiar than was his wont, and this was a source of anxiety rather than surprise to some of the onlookers. "If he'd guarantee that he's going to be a good worker for the rest of his life, I'd even he ready to take him on permanently in my house."

Barbaças was still smiling and heedless. The crowd round them increased. The farmer went on enjoying his own banter, but a little edgy, not quite in tune with his pose as a provincial aristocrat. Suddenly, his pale cheeks coloring slightly, he turned on the group.

"Did you ever hear that Barbaças chewed up a couple of notes I wanted to give to Loas? . . . Remember, Barbaças?"

The expression on Barbaças' face changed. His animal instinct warned him of some menace. He wanted to get up from the stone bench, but the firm hand of the farmer held him in place. He steeled himself to look straight into the master's face, and saw a glint of keen, impatient cruelty in his eyes. The group drew still closer round the farmer, and Barbaças began to feel trapped in his hole, at the mercy of the ferret's teeth.

"Are you going to tear this money up, too, Barbaças?"

"No, sir."

The farmer's eyes came down on him, angry and predatory, tightening the circle round him. He wouldn't be able to escape. He saw in a troubled, confused way that the farmer had never forgotten the scene at the club and that, come what might, he never would forget it. He had taken him on for the reaping just to get him into his hands. And Barbaças' primitive mind began to stumble on strange thoughts. He began to compare Loas's attitude—the donkey episode hadn't roused his resentment against anyone—and the farmer's long memory. What Barbaças needed at that moment was to be able to sit on a lonely hillock where he could work out questions and answers on many mysteries that he hadn't been aware of till then.

"Then what is the money for? Trollops?"

"No, sir."

"So you don't need money for anything at all. You even rip it up!"

The farmer's eyes were drawing closer, and he was savoring the words as though they left a pleasant sharpness in his mouth. "And even if you did need money, you could always steal it from Loas, isn't that so, Barbaças?"

Barbaças felt himself dwindling into a small, fearful soul. The other laborers were not laughing, either. There was a closed-up expression on their faces. They suspected such unusual things had happened between Barbaças and Senhor Cortes that the farmer had become unrecognizable. Never until now had the farmer shown himself so ruffled in this common way. He had always been a man who in all circumstances liked to keep a gentlemanly attitude.

"Answer me, good-for-nothing! Have you lost your tongue?

Now, look here, there's something else I want to know. What's become of that silky mouse of yours?"

Barbaças found himself compelled to answer.

"I've got it in my bag."

"Then we're going to see what a mouse can do. A mouse like that, if it hasn't got legs, can be torn up like a piece of paper. A nice little mouse in a raven's talons can be ripped up more quickly than you tore up my notes with your teeth. Did you know that ravens like nice little mice?"

Anxious sweat was running down Barbaças' forehead.

"Yes, sir," he answered in a voice that didn't seem to belong to him.

"Well, you're going to see it again."

And the farmer's strong, unyielding hand grasped the youth by the arm and forced it to pull the bag round.

"You, there, João Mira! Go inside and tell Lucia to bring the raven on to the veranda."

After giving this order, the farmer rapidly untied the bag, which held a medley of mouse, catapults, pocketknives, and placed the mouse on top of the wall, stroking it as it trembled.

"As soft as it's furry, Barbaças. A nice little bit of tender flesh. It'll make a nice little tidbit, don't you think?"

"Give me the mouse, Master."

And Barbaças got up, looking quite determined to take back what belonged to him, but the farmer held him off with one arm, meanwhile watching the veranda on the first floor. In next to no time the housemaid came out with a black, beady-eyed raven that flapped its wings halfheartedly and perched on the iron railing.

The men withdrew to the wall on the other side of the courtyard, and watched with anxious curiosity. Barbaças had turned pale, and again tried to push past the farmer, but he was now convinced that, however strong was the urge to stand up to him, he'd never manage it. Once again he was discovering with dismay that there were unyielding forces and that even if he went on being a loafer outside the sphere of employers, he'd still be up against them. And by some strange turn of feeling he found himself thinking of all those people he had not understood and loved enough, with whom he had not sympathized as much as he now wished; Loas, for instance, Vieirinha, and all those brothers-in-toil who were retreating to the far wall as though to watch the execution but have no part in it.

The raven had been watching with suspicious, predatory eyes what was going on under the veranda. Suddenly its eyes clouded with surprise and greed, focused on a small circle the center of which was the mouse. The movements of its neck and wings became jerkier. It walked here and there, as though trying to dissimulate its purpose from the men, then swooped on its prey in one swift flight. The onlookers scarcely had time to see that the mouse was no longer on the wall under Barbaças' anxious eyes, but was fast in the beak of the dusky bird, which carried it up to the stable roof, looking for a place to eat undisturbed. Then the raven made a short inspection of the cubbyhole of the dove tower, and finally decided to go back to the veranda.

Nobody, not even the farmer, had uttered any word of encouragement or protest. The look on the farmer's face might have been savage pleasure or alarm or nervy expectation. He turned toward the men and saw them all so still that they looked like one compact mass. He stared at them as though trying to find the reason for this silence, this huge immobility that made them seem numerous and to be feared. Looking them in the eyes, he seemed to be defying them to speak out either in approval or indignation.

Because everybody's eyes had been fixed on the movements of the loathsome bird, nobody saw Barbaças take one of the catapults from his bag and aim it at the raven's head. The onlookers became aware of this only when the bird suddenly crashed dead on the flagstones of the courtyard, as it dropped the soft, crushed corpse of its prey. Barbaças felt liberated, too. Even during his years of loafing, when he had drunk great drafts of life, sun, and poverty, never had he experienced such an incomparable sensation of freedom, of having broken through the webs of ignorance and oppression.

8

Such were the main events in which Barbaças was involved till he went back to Loas's holding. But the day he went back, he was a changed man. At any rate, he was carrying in his jacket pocket, fastened with a pin he'd borrowed from Dona Quitéria's housemaid, a small wad of notes that were really his own. Not even Loas himself grasped the purpose of the words he heard when the loafer came through the kitchen door.

"Here's the money for the donkey. It's my wages."

And he sat down with the assured air of someone coming home after a day's work.

"You must be tired, Barbaças. Sit down and take it easy," Loas said, to gain time and to ponder what the words could mean.

"Count the money. If Ti Vieirinha was telling the truth, and his gypsy friend'll sell a donkey cheap, by St. Michael's Day you'll be going over the holding with a donkey at the plow."

"Bless my soul! Barbaças, my lad, you don't mean to tell me—"

"All the money's in this pile, as much as you gave me to go to the fair with."

Loas could doubt his ears no longer. He turned pale, and his eyes, limpid as a seabird's, looked at Barbaças with incredulous affection. He fingered the notes one by one, but found when he got to the end that he was none the wiser because of the blur that clouded his eyes. He counted them again, smiling and nodding his head, as though to indicate that it was quite right, quite in accordance with what he'd expected. Then his face went stiff. He turned on Barbaças with a long, cold, suspicious look as though facing a stranger. He could neither smile nor weep nor count the money again. He folded the notes up slowly, put them in his pocket, and went out into the garden.

Barbaças saw him go and lean against an olive tree; then he sat down on a bag, lifting his hands to his unbuttoned shirt to lay neck and chest more open in the sultry atmosphere. At last he got up and made his way with slow, thoughtful strides through the dry shrubs till he was out of sight on the stubble.

For the next few days nobody at the house mentioned the matter of the donkey. Loas seemed to be buoyed up by redoubled energy and enthusiasm, putting his hands to everything from morning till night, as though getting ready for a celebration. By nightfall, he was tired out; but now it was real solid fatigue made up of peace and satisfaction, not feverish weariness without cause or purpose. His eyes alight like a young man's, he felt sudden waves of tenderness for people, plants, and even for Alice's dog, which formerly she'd had to keep out of his way. But at other times he looked absentminded and far away, and this showed that some deep incubation was in progress.

Joana, for her part, looked after Barbaças with quiet but careful attention. She followed the two men about as they set things to rights, and directed their efforts with a competence that was beyond them. Finally, Loas got a tin of whitewash ready, and, while his wife was given the task of whitewashing the little thatched stable, he set about fixing up a new manger inside. All he would allow Barbaças to do, though, was to hold the hammer and nails. This work, he thought, required such delicate attention that he couldn't trust anyone else. When the task was finished, they drank a pitcher of wine and, when Loas was alone with the youth, he said to him, blushing:

"You know, that talk about the will was all lies."

"What will?"

"Remember I told you I was going to the notary to leave the holding to you when I died. It was all a lie, dammit."

"I don't want any holding," Barbaças answered, feeling hurt without knowing why.

"We don't always understand people properly. Now, listen, Barbaças," and Loas's eyes became so anxious that the youth was afraid of what was coming, and felt he'd like to stop the words. "Listen, my lad, even without the will, you aren't going to leave me, are you?"

"But you don't need me anymore. The donkey'll help with the work."

"A real friend's never unwelcome. Didn't you see how you and Vieirinha helped with the harvest? If I had two or three friends like you on the holding, I'd count myself richer than if I possessed Farmer Cortes's estates."

"Would you let me work with the donkey?" Barbaças went on, adding humbly, "I'm beginning to look forward myself to seeing a donkey on the holding."

"Now, bless my soul, Barbaças! The donkey's yours, isn't it? Who earned the money? Perhaps I can't leave the holding to you by will; maybe I didn't even want to; but the donkey, Barbaças, must be set down in writing as yours, even after my death. And if anybody should try to take it from you by force or by law, I'll be there, ready to come back from the other side to return it to its rightful owner. And you know what a spirit from the dead can do!" Loas sat there rubbing his knees with his hands. Little by little his movements became gentler, and his voice was a dreamy monotone. "It'll be your job to feed the donkey, change its straw, and rub it down on Sundays. And when it needs clipping, my friend Bernadino is the man to do it. He's the finest hand there is for leaving a nice little tuft at the end of the tail."

Barbaças had another matter on his mind, and wasn't giving these last words his full attention. Several times he'd thought up a remark sufficiently plain for Loas not to misunderstand, and at the same time sufficiently wrapped up not to bother his host, who was so warmly hospitable.

"Ti Loas . . ." he drawled, in the vague hope that the other would help him out, "Ti Loas . . ."

"If you don't agree about having my friend Bernadino, speak up; it's your donkey."

To hear Loas talk, the donkey wasn't merely a promise, a

craving, a hope. It was a reality so evident that the senses could see and touch it in all its parts.

"That isn't what I mean," Barbaças put it. "Just listen to me for a minute. . . . I'd like you to tell me if those things, you know, about talking with the devil, are really true."

Loas fell silent. His face expressed panic, pain, and dignity, one after the other. But he didn't hesitate long.

"I've felt his hooves as cold as a dead body. But I couldn't see the rest for smoke," he declared.

Then he moved off to the useless water machine that lay rotting away with rust in the weeds. He leaned on the arm of the pump; and suddenly, as though he had to vent his ill-humor on something, he began kicking at the inert mass of rickety iron.

"Vieirinha said those city men don't know anything at all about machines," he remarked, but his eyes were vague, anxious, and his chest heaved as though shaken with silent sobs. Evidently, he was in no mood to talk about machines. "Now, listen, Barbaças, I couldn't see the rest for smoke. That, you can believe. But, dammit all, I'd like to know myself whether it was true or not."

Not until after the evening meal, in the long warm summer evening, did Loas return to the subject of the donkey. The four of them were sitting outside, the mellow silence of nature all around them, feeling rather weary but content, when Alice whispered to Barbaças that there was a nest of grasshoppers not far away. They came out to drink the dew at the side of the hole, so if you piddled near it, perhaps . . .

"We should catch them all! Will you come with me and piddle on the holes?"

"Leave Barbaças alone!" Loas said, scolding her for being such a nuisance. "He wants a rest." Then he leaned back against an old cask that had at times been used for preparing sulfate, and looked round the threshing floor still covered with glinting straw. "Just remember," he said solemnly, "that Barbaças has brought us the money for the donkey."

It was an unnecessary remark, because they all knew or had guessed it. Nevertheless, the announcement in so many

122

words by the master of the house gave it positive and solemn confirmation. Barbaças felt the eyes of all three resting on him with reverence. The sudden emotion he felt seemed to cause an unbearable itching on the sides of his nose. He began to scratch with such vigor that he scraped off a layer of sweat and dust so hard and scablike that the skin beneath it bled. Loas saw that the youth was concerned at the filth that had come away in his nails and, giving him a close inspection, said affectionately:

"You'll need to wash your face one of these days. And perhaps your legs, too. This business of harvest leaves folk really smothered in dirt."

Barbaças eyed himself from head to foot, turned his feet round to inspect his shins and heels.

"Yes, sir, it is necessary," he answered.

Joana got up there and then. Nobody asked her what she was going to do, but Alice followed close behind her. Some time later they came back with an earthenware bowl, hot water, and a linen towel. Barbaças was on the point of turning his trousers up to dip his feet in the bowl, but Loas stopped him.

"No, Barbaças. Your face first."

Then Joana, with the care of a mother looking after her son, helped him to scrub off those scabs of dirt that were the hardest to get at and the hardest to move. Barbaças seeing her bent at his feet in humble service, showing in this way all her gratitude and affection, thought he'd have to swear or do something to relieve the whacking happiness he felt.

9

Although Loas kept the money for the donkey in the inside pocket of his waistcoat, and due preparation had been made to receive the new inhabitant on the holding; although the barn, house, and land were all in order to begin a new cycle of tasks, the master of the house couldn't decide which market to try or whether he should start inquiries in the vicinity about a good donkey going for a price worth considering. But it was evident that Loas had something on his mind. Every morning he made some excuse to get the family all together in the garden, and leaning against the upright of the water machine as though leaning against a tree, he would bite his fingers and scratch his face, and then end up by having nothing to say.

Barbaças couldn't understand his attitude at all, and as no one suggested any kind of work, he spent the days with Alice looking for nests or catching small lizards. He would cut off their tails and make them twist and turn like mad. Alice covered her eyes so as not to see the torture, and ran off, squealing with nervous laughter, in search of anthills where she placed bread crumbs near the holes to see the ants get into a frenzy and lug them inside to the hoard. She was quite capable of spending hours on end watching them. There was no doubt that all the members of the household were impatiently asking themselves the same very natural question: "Well, after all, when's that donkey going to be bought?" but each had personal reasons for not saying it aloud. Until at last one evening, after the siesta and the evening soup, Loas exclaimed, stretching out his arms like someone on a cross:

"You're a good lad, Barbaças! Damn me if you're not a good lad!"

Barbaças crossed his legs, which were comfortably stretched

out on the hay, and had the feeling that this opening gambit, however sincere, hid some ulterior motive.

"At times I've even wondered," Loas went on, "what a lad like you'd be like if you'd been born a farmer's son. You don't look too bad, either, Barbaças. And you're a good lad. People didn't really understand you." Barbaças looked at himself curiously, as though Loas were talking about some stranger, and noted with surprise that his arms did in fact look daintier since Joana had scrubbed them. "Yes, that's what it is. They used to say things about you, but that's all finished now. If you'd been born the son of a farmer or of a teacher or of any sort of fellow who could've done something for you . . . Yes, that's what it is. If you put a seed in the ground, and there's no sun, no hoeing, no manure, no water, what can you expect? Nothing but a sickly plant, of course. But if you choose a nice place that suits it, and look after it with fertilizer, and give it all the water it needs . . . that's how fine properties are built up. Of course, you need to be lucky with machines, too. Bless my soul, talking of machines, one of these days . . . I've been thinking that what's his name from the city . . ." Loas was now well launched, but Joana cleared her throat to such effect that the master of the house immediately curbed his fancy. "Well, what I was saying was that you're a good lad, but until now nobody cared whether you were born twisted or straight, and all those good-for-nothings thought it was a great joke to see you taking the bad road. It meant being friendly to laugh at your tricks. That Barbaças, what a rascal he is! they'd say, but they were glad you were, and did their best for you to go on being a rascal, so they could have their fun cheap."

The monologue was so long drawn out that Barbaças lost interest. He began to move his hands in the air as though knocking mosquitoes down, or airy wings, and then watched them as though following the distant flight of some angel. Alice, openmouthed, was trying to catch sight of the invisible insects he was stalking, and in the end she thought she could see thousands of supernatural creatures floating in the nebulous air. How clever Barbaças was to have discovered them so soon!

But Loas had not yet said his say.

"Damn me if you won't make the best farmhand in these

parts! You only have to see what you did this summer. And when we've got the donkey on the holding, we'll show them what we can raise on this stone heap! We've got to buy that donkey, Barbaças."

Loas lifted his hat to scratch his head, and at the same time wrinkled his forehead till it looked ribbed with furrows.

"You know, this time I don't want Vieirinha to have anything to do with it."

Joana had caught her husband's roundabout drift, and she lowered her eyes. She didn't want to hurt the youth's feelings, either, but the truth was they couldn't risk it a second time. There was nothing else for it but tell Barbaças plainly that it was the master's place to go and buy the donkey so that there wouldn't be any further temptations or so they wouldn't have to rely on him to keep out of mischief. Before her husband could go on, she announced:

"I've already asked if anybody has a donkey for sale. Folk say there's someone over at Malhadas with a donkey, a five-year-old gray, well treated, that has already been taken to market. They say it's so gentle . . . even a child like Alice could manage it."

Loas wasn't pleased to hear that someone in his household, with no help from him, had come into possession of such important information. He couldn't hide his vexation.

"That's just silliness," he retorted. "If it were true, I should've heard something about it."

"Well, you can take it from me it's true."

This was such a long speech for Joana that she immediately got up and took refuge in the kitchen.

Loas cleared his throat, and went on coughing till he'd thought up an honorable way out of the humiliation.

"I just said that," he remarked, "because I've never been able to trust those people at Malhadas."

"Do you know them, then?" Barbaças asked with a provoking smile.

"Yes, I think so," the master of the house answered in a lofty, negligent tone.

126

"But it's a good-tempered donkey, Dad," Alice put in.

Loas raised his eyes to the wispy clouds as though watching the approach of a storm.

"All right," he said, "the best thing is for each of us to begin looking round and find out what's going. You can go over to Malarranha, Barbaças, and I'll take a turn through the outlying farms, until we come across an animal to suit us. Then we'll decide. But mind this, Barbaças, not a word to Vieirinha. Vieirinha's no good. He's a pleasant chap, and knows things about the backwoods, but he's capable of jumping out on us and laying a snare. Dammit all, he's such a womanizer he'd succeed in convincing us he could buy a dozen donkeys with the money we've got for one! I only want to see Vieirinha again once we've got the animal safe inside the stable. You look round on one side; I'll look round on the other; then, when we come across something likely, I'll go and fix the business. It's always to the good for the master to go and settle the price."

At these last words, blood rushed to the nape of his neck and flushed all round. Alice was tugging lustily at his trousers, trying to interrupt him.

"But Mam said the donkey they've got at Malhadas would be all right for me. Buy that one, Dad."

Loas pushed the little girl aside with his knee.

"This isn't your business, my girl."

"But Mam said it; that's what Mam said," the girl went on, tears rising to her eyes. Then she ran to Barbaças for support, clambering over his slim legs. "You go to Malhadas and bring the donkey back for Dad to see."

"That's all right," the youth whispered to her, stroking her hair with shy fingers. "I'll go to Malhadas."

The following day, very early, both men set out along the macadam road. After the violent clarity of endless summer days, the light was becoming misty and languid, but it still picked out red patches on the branches, and the clouds of dust that rose on the road carried the smell of organic matter decomposing on the deserted fields.

When they got to the clumps of aloes, Loas decided that

127

each should now go his own way. Barbaças went off without a word of farewell, but Loas screwed up his courage to shout a warning from some distance away.

"Now, don't have anything to do with Vieirinha. For heaven's sake, don't take up with any idle scamps or go into taverns!" Then it struck him that the money was safe in his own pocket and not at the mercy of the lad's callowness, so he added, "Unless, of course, you want a quick glass of something."

Barbaças didn't turn round again, but went off lengthening his ungainly stride so as to feel free and alone as soon as possible. In spite of all the incidents in his life, he couldn't help feeling excited whenever he approached the town. This time he wouldn't even enter the main street or waste any time chatting with any comrade he might meet on the way. The mere fact of skirting the outer walls of the town put him into a flutter, but he must resist the temptation. He wanted to make sure that he'd have the satisfaction of finding a good donkey and that it'd be the one Alice wanted. Loas, of course, if he happened across anyone with time and breath to spare for an hour's talk, wouldn't get any farther than the first farm he visited. And so Barbaças was certain he'd be the one to make the purchase. It wasn't enough for him to have given back the money; now that so many things had taken place inside him, he wanted to carry his effort and common cause with Loas to their very furthest conclusion. If they'd let him, he'd lead the donkey through the town streets, bidding defiance to farmers, gossips, and all belonging to the past that it now pained him to think of. And hadn't Loas assured him that the donkey would still belong to him? And this matter of the donkey, wasn't it one of the things of life that meeting up with the people on the holding had revealed to him? Yes, he was going to have a liking for the donkey, produce, crops, all the holding stood for, be capable of understanding and taking part in Loas's dreams and disappointments; he was going to let himself sink into that kind of life, just as in former days he used to let himself slide into the stream to feel the sappiness of the reeds and the coolness of the water.

Spurred on by these pleasant thoughts, he reached Malhadas while it was still early. It was an isolated farmstead, with a high-growing vine hanging like a porch over the door to protect it from the sun on blazing summer afternoons. There was only a bristling dog to welcome him, but it soon stopped barking after close inspection of the intruder. All his life Barbaças had possessed the knack of making himself agreeable to dogs, just with a simple gesture of his hands. This gift had facilitated many an attack on hencoops—though of course there was no magic in the gesture, only some latent affinity in him that animals quickly sensed. Near the cottage was a stack of straw and a small pigsty, with two young pigs in it, grunting with annoyance at being forgotten by the farm people. In other days, Barbaças would certainly not have despised the opportunity of carrying one of them off—the fatter of the two of course—nibbling away under his jacket; but now this idea only caused a rather prim smile. Because now he understood the meaning of a simple creature, and a piece of land, in a man's life—things that become engraved in the flesh like tattoo marks.

Barbaças knocked twice on the cottage door. No one answered, so he sat down on a stone bench outside. Very likely the people had gone out to the garden, which he could see some way off, lying green along the bank of a sandy stream between patches of yellowing cane reeds. But he didn't mind waiting for a quarter of an hour or so; his legs were tired and, what was more important, he wanted to think out a plan of campaign. In a blind hurry to get there early, he'd forgotten it would be necessary to draw out in a roundabout way what the intentions of these people were, before they found out that he was eager to buy the donkey. . . . This was a kind of game, with tricks and laying of snares, that he'd seen played whenever there was some deal in view. It was known and foreseen by all concerned, but it formed part of a ritual no one would think of disregarding. Also, he would like to know what the donkey was like before he spoke to the owners, so as to be sure up to what point he could carry a show of disdain. He didn't really feel up to carrying on a duel in words. Now, Loas, when he talked, could flummox almost anybody with the conviction, or lack of interest, he put into his talk. But Barbaças felt his best plan was, through silence and obstinacy, to compel these people to try to convince him, and so give him a good opening. Barbaças was used to the tricks of the chase, in which the lie of the land, hunter and hunted are bound together in a web of intuitions, ruses, and baits. And he felt all these natural instincts wake up in him now. He needed to be able to weigh up the donkey by himself, with no one to disturb his judgment. And at this time of day, if it hadn't been taken off to the garden, it would be wandering about somewhere near in search of blades of green barley. Barbaças got up, stretching his legs, which had grown numb from sitting, and looked around. The dog, which had got used to his being there, was lying with its nose on its front paws, watching him with a friendly eye; and when Barbaças moved far enough to make it think he was going altogether, it gave a little bark, almost a whine, of disappointment.

Barbaças began to search the holding from its boundary by the roadside, and when he got as far as the garden he unexpectedly encountered the farmer's wife. She was carrying a basket of greens. She was dressed in dark clothes, and her hair was so smooth and shining it looked as though it had been oiled. Coming upon a stranger, she compressed her lips, which were naturally so dour and thin that they then seemed to have no flesh on them at all. One hand, swinging at her side, suddenly fell still. Behind her, pushing its way out of a clump of canes, came the donkey, and a thin bareheaded man, with gray, docile eyes, who was supporting the load on the donkey's back. Barbaças scarcely noticed that the woman stopped still with surprise and that the man immediately followed suit. All his attention was concentrated on the donkey, in a mixture of bashfulness and fright. He felt as though, after years of talk about something, it had suddenly taken on form and substance, and any encounter with reality would inevitably result in disappointment. But the donkey looked all right. It wasn't white, as Alice wanted; it hadn't any very precise color; but its haunches were well covered with gleaming coat, and its muzzle looked sensitive, which was all to the good.

"What do you want?" the woman asked in a disagreeable voice.

"I've heard you're selling this donkey—"

"How do you know it's this one?"

"Why, have you got another?" Barbaças asked eagerly, as though her question implied that the white donkey with the star on its forehead that Alice wanted might be somewhere in reserve nearby, waiting for what was preordained to come about.

"We've only got this one," the woman said in an indifferent tone of voice. She turned to the man, and added: "Let's move on so that he can see the donkey. Let it walk by itself, so that this . . . gentleman can have a good look at it."

The man had stood there quite still and impassive, just letting his glance fall on Barbaças now and again with an uninterested look. Then he sent the donkey forward, so that it could walk unimpeded and fully visible.

A grayish cloud lay over the township, unmoved by the light wind that, after the wheat had been harvested, wandered over the plain in a mournful whisper, making the warm ground crepitate as it passed.

"What do you want the donkey for?" Suspicious all of a sudden, the woman took another look at Barbaças' doubtful appearance, and couldn't see anything of a buyer about him. He looked more like some shady fellow from a gypsy camp, so she went forward and took the lead, as though to enclose the stranger between herself and her husband.

The donkey's pace was firm and nimble, but more than that, Barbaças liked the appearance of its thick, healthy-looking coat and its plump haunches. And there was something quite human about it. There was a moist light in its big round eyes that seemed to express resignation or compassion. It was really a fine donkey, and, judging by appearance, as gentle as Alice's mother had said it was. Quite surprising they wanted to sell it. He'd have to look into that point.

When they reached the cottage, the woman took the basket inside, and then, out of patience with Barbaças' silent examination, prodded him on to some more definite reaction.

"Well, you can't get anywhere with just looking at it. Does it suit you?"

"What's the price?"

"You should have asked that before," she answered severely. "The price is twelve hundred escudos."

"Twelve hundred!"

"Did you want it for nothing? People round here haven't stolen what they've got, so they value it at its proper worth." And she looked straight at him with hostility and disdain.

All the crafty tricks that Barbaças thought he could play fell to pieces in an instant. He had got so used to the thought that the money he'd earned during the harvest was the exact sum required for a donkey that, on hearing this high price, he felt cheated. He didn't know what to answer. He made jerky movements with his arms, scratched the thin beard on his chin, and finally declared his decision.

"If that's the case, I'd better go."

But this final-seeming statement hid the hope that the owners would think again. And so he kept his place near the donkey, looking first at the man, then at the woman. In the man's eyes, which were shortsighted and therefore vague and absent-looking, he thought he could glimpse a hint of sympathy, as if he understood Barbaças was hoping with all his heart to get another answer.

"Do you think the animal isn't worth the money?" the man said, as though this were the most suitable remark for picking up negotiations again. And he passed his hand over the donkey's back, white with dust. The donkey thanked him by shaking its mane, then laid its neck against its master's body for him to repeat the caress.

"I don't know much about donkeys. I only came to find out what it was like," Barbaças said in a disappointed voice. The man sat down and took a cigarette paper from his pocket.

"She's a pretty creature. I'll be sorry to lose her."

"Not so much chatter, and let's get on!" his wife ordered. And, seeming to consider the matter closed, she began gathering together a layer of maize that was drying in the sun.

The man got up slowly from the stone bench, picked up the donkey's halter, and, making sure that only the visitor could hear, whispered, "Just sit and rest a bit before setting off again. I've got some oranges inside."

"But can't you give me a better price?"

"That's her business," the man replied, nodding in the direction of his wife, who had disappeared to show it was useless to prolong the discussion, or to signify to the stranger that he could consider himself dismissed. "She'll be sorry to lose the animal, too. I know that." By this time he had finished rolling his cigarette, and it was now hanging from his mouth. "People come after the donkey and offer their price, but she insists on twelve hundred. She doesn't want to let it go; that's what it is."

"She won't sell it, then."

"We've got our reasons." And the man closed up in stubborn silence; but, before turning the corner of the house, still leading the donkey by the halter, he tried to make sure the visitor would wait till he came back. "I shan't be long; just rest there a bit."

Barbaças sat down, lost in thought, his hands gripped between his knees. He didn't like the idea of having to look for a donkey elsewhere; very likely he'd have to go to a lot of places before he found anyone willing to take eight hundred. His first surprise over, he had the feeling that the donkey they all wanted, and that the holding was waiting for, was the one from Malhadas, and that he must make an effort to get it by hook or by crook. If they bought some other animal, maybe it would be capable of plowing end to end, but nothing more. It would never be the donkey they had all dreamed about so intensely that they could see it standing before their eyes. But the next harvest was so far ahead, he couldn't hope to get the money before Loas wearied of his own dream.

The man came back with a handful of oranges and, sitting down beside Barbaças, shared them out.

"These oranges are from down there," he said, pointing to the far end of the garden. "I planted the trees myself. I like oranges. Where do you come from?"

"From town."

"Oh, from town. There are a lot of people in town. But not here. Nobody passes here. It's a dreary place, really. Some time back, farmhands used to come and fill their water pitchers with our water, but not now since . . ." Then he bit quickly into the peel of his orange as though to bite off a remark it was better to keep to himself, and Barbaças noticed that he reddened with embarrassment. "Do you want the donkey for some trade?"

"It isn't for myself."

"I thought you might be a peddler of haberdashery."

"I'd better be off now."

"Don't go yet!" the master of the house exclaimed, with a look of alarm on his face. "Eat some more oranges."

"I don't want any more."

"Well, rest a bit longer. I'd like to ask you to wait for a meal, but . . ."

"I've brought a packet of food with me. I'll have to go and have a look around somewhere else. Do you know if there's any donkey for sale in these parts?"

"There's mine. And upon my word, I'd have liked to sell it to you. You can tell right off who's likely to treat a beast well."

"The donkey isn't for me, but I've promised to get one for a friend who has a holding."

"Oh, I see. . . . So you come from town. I'd like to live there. I'd give up this cottage for a place in town any day. You just burst with loneliness here. Sometimes I go as far as the road, and sit down, waiting for someone to pass. But now you never see mules or herds or people. Only trucks. And they rush by at such a rate you don't even have time to wish them good-bye. . . . Take the rest of the oranges with you, and look us up from time to time."

Barbaças went down the hill without looking back, afraid the man might still try to keep him a bit longer. People like that just stuck to you like a caterpillar. People who lived in lonely places, and spent their time thinking of this and that, treated you as though you were meat and drink to them. But he couldn't waste time over that at the moment. With next harvest so far ahead, he must look around for some swifter means of getting the rest of the money. If only that blackguard Vieirinha had helped a bit. But his good intentions, though loudly expressed and maybe sincere at the time, didn't last long. For him, a promise or a plan changed beyond all recognition within twenty-four hours, and each morning Vieirinha woke up washed clean of the shadows of the day before. His sincerity was valid only at the moment it was voiced, being so ardent that it soon burned itself to ashes. He threw himself ruthlessly and wholeheartedly into the flames, then rose completely renewed with the same rapidity.

To the devil with Vieirinha! No use counting on him. But despite that, Barbaças couldn't find it in his heart to dislike him. He would always associate him with the revelation that had come through the woman with a red flower on her black dress. So the devil with Vieirinha! As he wasn't to be relied on, it was imperative to find some other means of raising the money. Three or four hundred escudos, though, wasn't a sum you could just go and borrow from a friend. Nor could you earn it by touting for a few errands at Justino's door.

The certainty that it was impossible was written in the savage look on Barbaças' face. Anyone catching sight of his hard staring eyes and the bitter smile that twisted his lips would have thought that someone or other had maliciously sprung his poaching traps. And in truth, Barbaças was in such a turmoil of revolt that he felt like rushing blindly off and flinging in the face of some farmer: "You, sir, who, closefisted, possess hundreds of pigs, lambs, mules, and who have such vast possessions that your heart and life will never be enough to love them properly and suffer for them, just give up what really belongs to Loas!"

A poor man is satisfied with little. Loas wanted nothing more than a donkey; that alone would give him the sensation of being master of estates and pairs of mules. Barbaças himself was even less demanding; all he asked was to be allowed to contribute toward Loas's dream. But the earth wouldn't open in a cataclysm and give all men the opportunity to be happy. Happy! That was the point to start from. What did a man need to feel happy? The town was crowded with people who were born and died with empty hands, while others were born and died in such permanent abundance there was nothing left to wish for. Take Dona Quitéria, for instance. Could church-going make up for avarice? Could a lot of praying redeem malice, harmful gossiping, envy? Ah, that Dona Quitéria, dammit all! Why hadn't he thought of digging that pious vein before? Barbaças' slow wits leaped into sudden keenness to work out the details of his brainwave. By donations, novenas, indulgences, she was acquiring the right to a place near St. Peter, at the same time as acquiring the corner in church most sheltered from north winds. Surely she wouldn't refuse to subsidize a pious pilgrimage to Our Lady of Fátima. And three or four hundred escudos wouldn't be too much to ask for a journey like that. If she was so interested to see him make his peace with the saints, then let her buy the outfit necessary to tramp such a distance. Of course, that was it. A blanket, a pair of boots, and at least a couple of shirts so that he wouldn't look like a beggar when he got to Cova da Iria. Roughly, all that would about equal the amount still needed to buy the donkey. And the saints would surely understand better than the old girl that the money would be more usefully employed on Loas's donkey than on saying half a dozen litanies during the pilgrimage. After all, he could just as well say the prayers in their town church, on some saint's day, explaining the whole problem to Our Lady of Fátima, with the reasons that had compelled him to deceive the old girl. This explanation would be given in all sincerity, because, although Barbaças was not given to churchgoing, he respected the saints, and feared the wrath of God whenever thunderstorms broke over the town. "Our Lady of Fátima: Loas and Alice want a donkey; and one day I went to the fair to buy it, and then that Vieirinha stopped me on the way, with those girls from the rifle range." And so on. Explain everything properly, though of course in decent terms. And last of all he would say that now he was just as interested in the donkey as Loas and Alice themselves, because the donkey was going to link him with a world it had taken him a very long time to discover.

136

Absorbed in these thoughts Barbaças, without having noticed where he was going, found himself in the square where Dona Quitéria lived. He looked round cautiously, just as he used to look round when following someone to beg or offer his services as guide, and, turning a deaf ear to a quip shouted from Arturinho's tavern, made straight for Dona Quitéria's door. A curtain that had been pulled aside fell quickly back over the window, as though the modesty of the peeping person had been affronted, and before Barbaças could touch the knob the door opened.

"Come in," the housemaid said. "My mistress wants to speak to you."

Dona Quitéria was waiting for him in her sitting room, arms folded on her bony chest, silent, black as an old plucked bird. When her visitor was someone of consequence, she would first incline her head, and then put on her usual martyred expression, composing herself to listen in penance to the world's harsh doings. But with Barbaças, there was no need for this decent interval before indulging in gossip.

"What were you doing at the harvests?" she asked him point-blank, looking at him with a veiled stare, her eyes narrowed like a cat's.

"Well, harvesting."

"And why?"

Evidently, even the old lady was displeased because he hadn't stuck to his vagabond's privileges.

"I want to be more reasonable."

The servants listening at the door let out a few smothered giggles, and Barbaças turned on them, ready to give them a bit of his mind. But their mistress forestalled him.

"What are you doing there? Be off with you!" Then, turning back to Barbaças again: "Now, there's something under all this. That Loas is enticing your soul to hell! He'll be the ruin of you, Luís! He has dealing with the devil, son!"

"I didn't go reaping with Loas."

"But he led you on to it!"

"No, it wasn't Loas." And Barbaças, with a stroke of genius, went on humbly: "I wanted to get the money for the promise. I'm going to Fátima."

Dona Quitéria leaned for support on the arms of the chair, then had to sit down. She went hot. Her heart seemed to have stopped beating suddenly, and only slowly recovered its normal regular rhythm.

"My dear lad, why didn't you come and tell me about it? Our Lord would be so pleased for you to offer your sacrifice. You've lost so many years of indulgences!"

"I don't know anything about that. All I know is I made a promise and needed money for the journey."

"But we both made the promise, God be praised! I'd like to pray with you Luís!"

And Dona Quitéria allowed herself to stretch out her arm and stroke Barbaças. She looked lovingly at his unkempt hair and heathenish dirty face. She felt she'd like to imitate the handmaids of the Lord and wipe the filth from his body, now that his soul was on the path to purification.

"Have you had anything to eat, my lad?"

"I didn't have time."

"You don't get enough to eat: that's what it is! That Loas is wearing you out, soul and body. You just come with me to the kitchen."

While Barbaças chose what he wanted from the larder, Dona Quitéria watched him with rapture, and murmured a prayer. The glory of this regeneration was her work. And although the saints might have foreknowledge of mortal intentions, Dona Quitéria provided against any forgetfulness on their part by thanking them for Barbaças' conversation, at the same time giving them a subtle hint of her role in the miracle.

Once his stomach was full, Barbaças pushed his plate away and let out a loud belch. He had gulped the food down in next to no time, like someone launching an attack, spilling it, and very often missing his mouth in his eagerness to fill it quickly. But not for a moment did Dona Quitéria feel disgusted at such wolfish manners. The lad was hungry; very likely he hadn't known the taste of good soup and well-cooked meat this many a long day. Let him eat and belch as much as he liked, poor soul!

Barbaças was leaning forward in his chair, chin almost touching his neck, so heavy and drowsy he felt. He was waiting for the old girl to throw him the bait.

"And what next, Luís?"

"I'm going to get things ready for the journey."

"So you're really going, Luís! Does Loas give you anything to eat? How do those heretics live over there?"

"I don't know anything about that. They talk."

"What about, Luís?"

"They talk of this and that. People don't talk about the same thing all the time." And disappointed with the turn the conversation had taken, he reminded her bluntly. "I was speaking about the journey to our Lady of Fátima. The money I earned is enough for a bit of food and somewhere to sleep. But it's the rest that's the trouble. . . ."

"What do you mean, 'the rest'?"

"Well, a chap needs blankets, shirts, footwear. . . ."

"But I've got them. I can give you things like that. I've got a cupboard full of clothes and boots that belonged to my husband, God rest his soul."

Dona Quitéria cast her eyes to that point of the ceiling where the divine presence seemed most real to her, and so she didn't catch Barbaças' evil look. The loafer felt cheated in his calculations. Now that his stomach had no room even to wish for anything else, it seemed to him that the meal had been a useless sacrifice. A trick played on him by Dona Quitéria.

"I don't want to wear dead men's clothes!" he declared, and got up, offended, but at the same time he felt relieved he hadn't got to go on with the pantomime.

"But they're good quality, Luís. All my husband's shirts were linen."

"I don't want his linen shirts."

And Barbaças put such conviction into it that he seemed to have forgotten the story of the boots and shirts was only a stratagem.

139

Very shaken at this turn of events, Dona Quitéria sat down in her usual attitude: hands on lap, body bent forward, eyes resigned in martyrdom—just as she always did after lustily reprimanding the servants, when they thought proper to answer back.

Barbaças made for the door into the passage. His plan had failed. He'd still got a lot to learn from Vieirinha in the art of persuasion. But at the door he turned for a final remark.

"I don't want linen shirts. People'd call me altar boy."

"And what if they did, Luís?" the old woman whimpered, ready for a reconciliation. "What harm would there be in that? . . . You could always say they were my husband's shirts, God rest his soul."

"I don't want to hear anything about that. Let's drop the whole business. I won't go to Fátima; that's all."

"Now, don't say that, Luís!" Dona Quitéria begged in a panic. "You're living in mortal sin so long as you don't fulfill your promise. How I've prayed for you, son!"

"I don't want to hear any more about it."

"But I promised Our Lady that you'd go."

"Without a shirt? Without boots? . . ."

And Barbaças tugged at the foul rag that covered the nakedness of his chest, and thrust out a half-shod foot, showing off his sordid poverty with something like pride.

"No, you can't go like that. But you won't take my husband's things, though they'd do very well. Tell me, Luís"— and Dona Quitéria gave way in a voice of tortured resignation —"how much do you need to buy the things?"

Barbaças looked at the housemaids in dismay. Now that he'd got the better of Dona Quitéria's closeness, he felt a kind of disappointment. As though it were not really what he'd wanted. The servants were ready to help him. They were the first to encourage tricksters who came a long way to try to cheat the mistrustful old woman over some so-called bargain; they were disinterested accomplices in the petty thieving of the washerwoman, and of a small host of pietistical women, gossips, odd-jobbers who played up to her liking for gossip. Dona Quitéria often snubbed her servants, and this was their revenge.

"How much, Luís?" Dona Quitéria repeated her question in a suffering voice.

Barbaças was biting his fingers, eyeing the two housemaids turn and turn about.

"Maybe two hundred escudos," he suddenly blurted out.

"That's just the price of the boots. What about the rest?" one of the girls put in, trying to make up for the youth's lack of boldness.

"I'll manage with that," Barbaças insisted, as though trying to quiet his conscience by milking the old lady as little as possible.

Dona Quitéria put her hand to her pocket thoughtfully—the pocket where she kept her keys in a thick bunch that made the side of her dress sag. It was her habit to lock everything up. Drawers and cupboards were carefully classified according to their use, and carefully closed against the servants' acquisitive instincts. In some instances, keys for certain places were kept inside mysterious caskets that in their turn were locked up in other hiding places, and so the old lady herself lost track of them.

Dona Quitéria took her bunch of keys and went into the sitting room, closing the door behind her so that no one should see what drawer she went to. The housemaids quickly turned on the youth, egging him on.

"Get as much as you can out of the old girl, you nitwit!"

But Barbaças didn't feel easy. He felt he'd like to slip away before the old lady came back, race off through the fields to wash his soul in pure heathland sun, get back to the holding, and hear what Loas had to say. Loas would be able to find some honest, marvelous way of getting the rest of the money. And they could spend the remainder of the day talking about the future of the holding, the two of them sitting outside the cottage door, in the open air, their hearts at peace, the sun's warmth running softly through their veins. Where he was, he felt guilty and weighed down, as though in a sacristy.

"You said two hundred, didn't you?" Dona Quitéria called out before opening the door. "Here you are, then, and fifty escudos more. That's for my husband's soul. You won't take his shirts and boots, but in this way my sainted husband will also be present when you offer your sacrifice to Our Lady of Fátima. Pray for us, Luís."

Barbaças took the notes reluctantly. He said nothing, although the good lady was waiting for his thanks.

"When are you going?"

"I don't know."

"I'd like to give you a chicken for the journey, but I've killed them all. They're a lot of heretics—like that man Loas who was leading you astray." Dona Quitéria's livid lips became flecked with foam, and the wrinkled skin of her face quivered with indignation. "I miss them, of course, because if you keep hens you've always got new-laid eggs in the house, but I couldn't go on eating eggs from such heretics. Don't you know what happened? Has anybody told you?"

Barbaças, his head hanging, was folding and refolding the notes, still hesitating, and he shook his head in reply, not very interested.

"I was out in the garden, threading the beads of a rosary onto a silver chain, and the rosary had already been blessed by His Reverence the Bishop, and I hadn't noticed that some of the beads had fallen onto the ground. And they ate the beads, Luís! Those fowls ate more than half my beads, and they'd already been blessed! Ah, but I had my own back! I killed them all with a hatchet. The only pity is that we don't get the eggs now. If I'd still got that rosary, I'd give it to you to take with you. Those I've got in the house for children who're learning their catechism haven't been blessed yet. When are you coming here again?"

"Would you like some eggs, lady?"

"Well, they're not very good for my liver, but I feel a bit weak without an egg flip now and again. Come back later and show me your boots and shirt. And if anyone asks who gave you the money, say it's for my husband's soul. Don't say much about me, but you'll have to say something, or they'll think you've stolen it. . . ."

"Stolen it?" exclaimed Barbaças, as though jerked out of himself, and he rushed out without further leave-taking.

He felt surprised at himself. In former days, this successful trick played on the old lady would have given him infinite satisfaction, and he'd have gone off full of self-conceit to boast about it to his comrades. But not now, not now!

Such strange impulses were coming over him all the time. He'd rejected the farmer's money. Like a lunatic, he'd prevented Loas from accepting it, just because it was charity. Yet he hadn't hesitated to play this trick on Dona Quitéria. But wasn't it the same sort of thing? Wouldn't they be getting the donkey in the same way, with money that didn't belong to him? It was as though he hadn't properly paid off his debt to Loas, as though the donkey would remain for ever bound to those who had been deceived, and not belong entirely to himself, to Loas, to the holding, to Alice. No, he didn't want to have anything to do with the old girl. The two hundred and fifty escudos would be better spent on some huge spree, which he still sometimes felt he could do with, but not toward helping to pay for Loas's donkey. And yet ... and yet, couldn't he use the old girl's money provisionally, knowing that, sooner or later, he could pay it back in some honest way that would finally give him the right to full ownership of the donkey? And although this solution didn't completely satisfy him, the knowledge that it could be carried out relieved his mind for the time being.

When Barbaças got back to the holding, Loas had not yet returned, and as he didn't feel in the mood to answer a lot of questions, he shook Alice off and also refused Joana's invitation to eat a plateful of bread salad. Surly, and keeping himself to himself, he remained lost in thought while mother and daughter, eager for news, and disappointed, kept watch on him. In her husband's absence Joana hadn't the courage to refer to the subject, and Alice was too timid to brave Barbaças' dogged silence.

A fresh wind foretelling the approach of autumn was shaking the leaves on the juniper tree, though the sun still drew warm scent from the bugloss. If Barbaças stretched out an arm or a leg, it was like holding it out to the pleasant warmth of a hearth.

143

As Loas still hadn't come back, Joana tried again.

"Won't you have an egg, at least?"

"An egg?" Barbaças asked, as though speaking in a dream. "Have you got many eggs?"

"Yes, I've got some. I've got a dozen or two to sell. I'm expecting Joaquina Engracia to come and buy them. But I'm keeping a few for us."

"I'll buy them," shouted Barbaças abruptly. "Take this money, and give me all the eggs you get till the money's used up."

Quite breathlessly Joana looked at the wad of notes the youth handed to her. The whole thing, money and what he was saying, was too fantastic and farfetched to be true. Where did this money come from? What were the eggs wanted for? And though she was used to her husband's oddities and the strange things they caused, Barbaças' attitude was even stranger than what she was accustomed to.

"Put them all in a basket and give them to me."

And the lad began striding restlessly back and forth, until the woman—the habit of unquestioning obedience ingrained in her—brought him the basket. He immediately set off for town and got there in record time, panting and so exhausted that people stopped to look at him. As soon as Dona Quitéria's servants opened the door, he pushed past them and made straight for their mistress's stronghold.

"What's all this?" the old lady shouted.

"Here's some eggs for you," answered the youth. "I don't want money from anyone. Neither for Our Lady of Fátima nor for anything else. Maybe I shan't even go. I'm going to pay it all back in eggs."

And he strode out again before the old lady could recover her wits. He felt as though he'd thrown off a nightmare. Now let Loas go and buy the donkey. Let the hens go on laying eggs. It wasn't his business anymore. Let the days and nights go on renewing the hunger of the earth that absorbed seeds, fertilizer, sun and rain, everything, and the muscles and brains of men who live with and for the earth. Now it was all straight.

He stopped at a place where two pine trees, standing away

from the road, held back the sandy soil of a hillock, and chose a patch of shade to lie down in. This long while he hadn't felt the joy of letting himself go like this for hours on end. But gradually he felt disturbed by pervasive presences. From the bare heathland came an insidious solicitation, as though wheat had always been there. The slow echo of its voice rose and fell, undulating in the atmosphere like the voice of a river, at times becoming clearer and sharper in tone, and turning into a lament. And many other voices came and joined in with it: voices of the earth, of trees, of distant people, mysterious voices that answered and implored, charged with sweet perfidy. They wouldn't let him rest.

10

Without asking any questions, Loas heard the news that there was a donkey at Malhadas that would suit them; nor did he show any surprise that Barbaças had come back with enough money to buy it. He didn't say anything, either, about what had happened to him during the long day spent wandering about the farms. Had he come across anyone interested in selling a donkey? Loas seemed to have forgotten the reason that had taken him out to the holdings and cottages in the neighborhood. When he did feel ready to talk, the only thing he said was that it had been a nice day, that it had.

"Dammit all, Barbaças," he kept saying in a weary voice, "it's many a long day since I met such good friends to have a chat with. Vieirinha, the old cuss, let us drop because he was ashamed. And, I must admit, I've missed him."

As nobody paid any attention to him, he laid his hands to his back, aching from the long walk, and put on a face of nostalgic regret. This indifference toward talk made the events of the day and the people he'd met, people who listened with interest, seem even more pleasant in retrospect.

"Damn me if it hasn't been a nice day!" he exclaimed, shaking his head, disgruntled and regretful.

"You can go and fetch the donkey tomorrow," Barbaças put in.

"Yes, of course! And look here, Alice, what'd you say if I let you lead the donkey by the halter?"

"All the way, Dad?" she asked anxiously.

"Yes, maybe all the way," he agreed solemnly. Then, turning to Barbaças: "It'll be better for you to stay here. If you came with me to Malhadas they might think we were just bursting to get the donkey. A chap has to outsmart them, don't you see? I turn up there with the girl as though not specially interested, talk for a while about animals, and it's almost a sure thing they'll push the donkey under my nose. Then I begin to find fault with it, and before they know where they are, they're offering it me for a song. There'll be enough money over to buy a new packsaddle, I tell you.... Now, Alice, remember, not a word about wanting a donkey, do you hear?"

Barbaças suspected there was some other purpose behind this, but he couldn't make out what; for some reason or other, Loas didn't want his company. But Joana knew what lay behind her husband's wiles: He liked to open his wallet with a flourish and look flush; most certainly he wouldn't haggle over the price, because, if he did, they might think he hadn't brought enough money with him. Barbaças would be an unwelcome witness to his swagger; and, more than that, his presence might cause those folk to take her husband for a good-for-nothing sort of chap, a rascal of the sort the lad's appearance would lead you to expect. A companion like Barbaças, already known at Malhadas, would be no credit to anyone.

Alice didn't give her father any peace till she saw him throw his jacket over his bony shoulders.

"Let's go, Dad. Let's go."

Barbaças didn't answer Loas when he said good-bye. He was just sick of all this hanky-panky. At the moment, he felt he didn't care whether they got the donkey or whether they didn't. He was tired, fed up with it all. What he wanted was for the matter of the donkey to be settled one way or another. What was necessary was for something conclusive to take place —one way or the other, it would bring peace. And what he wanted was sheer animal peace.

However, as time wore on after Loas and the girl had set out, that cursed unrest came over him again. Was it possible that Loas was able to cast spells over people? If so, he'd better clear out for good. All Loas wanted was a slave at his orders, a willing slave not exacting as to wages. Oh, no! He'd better clear out before Loas got his witch's hooks into him, before it was too late. He'd like to be there, though, for the arrival of the donkey. He'd never attached much importance to such passive creatures as donkeys (now, bulls and horses, they were something like!) , but the donkey from Malhadas, Alice's donkey, yes, even Loas's donkey, that was different. . . . To hell with it, why should that donkey be different from any others? It was almost un-Christian to be thinking about an animal in that way, as though it were a person, as though it were somebody in the family. Yet something very like it was happening to him; that he couldn't deny.

He grew more and more restless. He jumped from one task to another, trying to cheat his stupid anxiety about what was happening at Malhadas. And as though instinctively working the gnawing restlessness out in some concrete action, he went inside, took a piece of bread from the drawer, and set about munching it slowly.

Joana seemed nervy, too. For no reason at all, she came up to him, adding her anxious impatience to his, then wandered away again only to return soon afterward, until at last she made up her mind to ask the question that was troubling her.

"Now it's all over . . . Luís, now that . . . Do you feel like telling me where you got the rest of the money from?" she asked in a shaky voice.

"Somebody lent it to me," he answered, after a moment's hesitation.

"There's no need to tell lies, Luís."

"I'm not telling lies. I'll pay it all back in eggs."

She stood there with staring eyes, as though sifting her thoughts.

"Ah, now I see. . . . That's lifted a weight from here, lad." Joana put her hands to her chest, and her austere face took on a happy, almost childlike, look.

"I'll raise a few more hens, lad. You shall have all the eggs you need."

She bent over to smell a flower, then went off, her cheeks rosy with relief.

When Loas and his daughter got near the holding, you could hear them quite some distance away, because Alice was shouting at the top of her voice. But neither Barbaças nor Joana went out to meet them: They seemed paralyzed with nervousness. Alice came along bending forward, pulling at the halter with all her might, yet unable to stir the donkey with any of her impatience to get there quickly.

"Eh! Mother! Eh! Barbaças! Here we are!"

Loas was smiling with pleasure. His jacket was hanging from one shoulder, and his eyes were shining with delight. The muscles of his face worked spasmodically; he laughed and cried, turn and turn about. He wiped his forehead vigorously and blew his nose into his big red handkerchief with a mighty trumpeting. Little wafts of wind blew from the west and eddied away over the heath, and when the air fell still it was voluptuously soft, like a cat's smooth coat. Alice kept on stroking the donkey's neck, at the same time eagerly watching what her mother and the youth would feel about it. But neither of them spoke. They seemed to have worn out all capacity for feeling, and their silence finished even by discouraging Loas, who sat down on the stone bench and wiped his damp forehead once again.

"Well, now," he said, "that was a good bit of business! Bless my soul, Barbaças, if that girl of ours didn't keep on at the woman till she ended up by letting us have the donkey for two hundred escudos less. They're nice folk, after all. And the man, you saw him, didn't you Barbaças? kept wanting to make us stay a bit longer. He gave Alice so many oranges she's sure to have a bellyache. . . . We talked quite a bit, and I soon saw they were decent folk. You see, Barbaças, you wouldn't have managed to get it so cheap!"

And Loas, cock-a-hoop, touched his jacket as though to signify there was good money in his pocket. Joana gave Barbaças a meaning look. Like this, it wouldn't be necessary to take any more eggs to Dona Quitéria. But the master of the house soon scotched this possibility.

"The money'll come in very handy to buy fertilizers. Now there'll be work to do, eh, Barbaças, eh, handyman!"

Then, he began to think again over what he'd just said.

Oh, no, that idea wasn't quite the thing. Flies stinging the nape of his neck were worrying him, too, and he began to flip them off with his sweaty handkerchief.

"It's still a bit early for fertilizers, perhaps," he went on, looking a bit put out. "The best thing now would be to get a nice new packsaddle for the donkey."

Without answering, Barbaças led the donkey off to the stable. He gave it water and flung another armful of hay into the manger. Alice had gone with him.

"Are we going to leave her all by herself already?" she asked, when he was about to close the door.

"She won't be afraid."

Alice thought Barbaças was sulky about something, but, having stroked the donkey's rough short coat a last time, she resigned herself to following him out.

"Aren't you tired? It's been such a long tramp for you!" he said, taking her hand.

"Oh, no. I'm not tired. I should've liked to have stopped a bit longer to watch the donkey eat."

"Never mind! You'll be able to watch it tomorrow *and* the next day!"

11

For the whole of the following week everybody at the holding had a great deal to do. Loas, with a mattress needle and an awl, took upon himself to make good the harness and packsaddle, while Barbaças cleaned down the donkey with a brush that Alice had found in one of the holes in the kitchen wall. Alice, too, was eager to find out the donkey's preferences with regard to straw, hay, maize, and green barley, until her father had to put a stop to such waste of fodder. Sometimes Loas would give the animal a noisy slap on the rump and make it take a good run over the holding. He also spent a lot of time examining its teeth with such persistence that Alice, when she happened to find herself alone with the donkey, took the opportunity to examine all the crannies in its mouth, to find out what her dad was looking for. Only Joana seemed detached from all this activity.

When they had come to the end of all the possible ways of attending to the animal's appearance and well-being, Loas and his family glanced at one another, rather at a loss, waiting for someone to suggest something else to do. Then Joana looked at the motionless clouds in the sad-looking sky, stared so fixedly that it made her husband sniff at the air noisily, as if there were some obstruction in his nose. Yes, there was certainly a change in the weather. The light was not so vigorous. Houses, trees, and clouds were taking on a melancholy, autumnal look that breathed mildness and peace but also ushered in the sadness of days about to die. Loas picked up a handful of dry soil.

"Bless my soul, it looks as though it might rain one of these days," he said. "It wouldn't be a bad thing if we plowed over the holding. What do you say, Barbaças? Shall we try late wheat or early wheat this year?"

"You're the one who knows all about that."

"Well, the early comes on better so long as it's dry. But what if it's a wet year?"

"I don't know anything about that."

"You just wait here and I'll go and look it up."

And he went inside to fetch an old book that forecast when rain would fall for a long time ahead; it was infallible, he told Barbaças, because weather and events obey a predetermined cycle of storms, fine weather, and catastrophes.

"It's all written in the book, my friend."

He wiped it lovingly on his shirt sleeve, then held it some distance away the better to see, and finally declared, "We can sow early wheat."

Next day they began to plow furrows across the dry earth, and as the days went by each person fell into his own routine. Barbaças looked after the fodder. He kept an eye on the manger, and sometimes, with Alice always at his heels, led the donkey off to higher ground where it could graze with a certain freedom. He filled the bucket of water twice a day, and was as happy as the girl to watch the donkey as it drank thirstily. The animal seemed to understand the affection that surrounded it; its lids would droop over the moist protuberant eyes, and it would close them sometimes as though veiling its gratitude.

Loas reserved the more important occupations for himself, such as harnessing the donkey to the plow, and urging it on with almost guttural cries. When it couldn't manage to cleave the summer-baked ground, then Barbaças came to its help, by pushing the plow or the donkey's flanks.

On the journey home, Alice was allowed to ride on the donkey's back, and when she urged it forward it put up with it with a great deal of understanding. And at twilight, all work finished for the day, she always found some reason or other for going back to the stable to say good night again. She thought the donkey might still be a bit thirsty or a bit hungry, or want to be stroked just one last time. Loas and Barbaças would linger at the cottage door while the breeze ruffled the shrouded out-lines of the trees, and then one of them would notice that the girl didn't show any signs of coming back.

"Alice! You naughty girl!"

"She's in a dream; she can't believe it's true," Loas explained rather mysteriously, as though only his senses had miraculous power of divination.

One day when violent sun and the effort of labor covered the animal's flanks with gleaming sweat, Alice forced her father to stop work, so desperately anxious did she look. Loas felt like laughing at her; then he wanted to swear; but finally he gave her a look of uneasy disapproval and did as she wanted. But he was thoughtful for the rest of the afternoon.

By nighttime, Loas's muscles ached, but he seemed fairly happy. When he pushed his wide-brimmed hat back on his neck, it made a dark band of shadow across his forehead, barred with furrows and red as a cockerel's wattle. Then he would roll a cigarette, talking meanwhile in his usual way about this, that, and the other. But sometimes his eyes would become fixed, staring at the deep sky where a few wisps of cloud floated like shadows mirrored in a lake. Joana and Barbaças knew that he wasn't absolutely satisfied. He always felt the need to plan new and extraordinary things. He had really wanted the donkey and to work up the holding; but the price he had to pay was a stiff one: monotony, perseverance, months and years of unbroken effort, wheat sown, wheat ripe, and a calm steadiness that wasn't in his blood. Now that he had the donkey, he'd go on and struggle to get the holding well fertilized, but he did need these flights of fancy toward tempting mirages. Then, again, he felt humiliated by the sneaking suspicion that, a mile or two beyond the confines of the holding, no one would be impressed by the fact that he possessed a donkey. Maybe some people would say: "For a man who once had a pair of mules and lost everything, of course, it's a step in the right direction to start off again with a donkey. But he wanted more than that. He had a right to more than that. Each day he used to hope that some ruined smallholder or boastful farmer would pass that way and say:

"That Loas has the devil's own luck! Now he's got a sound beast, the man's capable of making good." But neither the one sort nor the other seemed impressed by the event.

When he had given up all hope of a visit, Loas decided to go out and seek comment. For a whole day he went visiting the town and outlying farms. But when he came back he was lost in thought, and looked older.

"I didn't find any suitable fertilizer," he said. "But, blast me, Barbaças, we two'll turn this bit of land to good account! You with the donkey, which is yours, and me with the rest, damn me if we won't turn the holding into a real garden. In two years' time, we'll have enough money for a couple of mules, and to plant some vines. That'll make those jackanapes in town open their eyes!"

"So you went to look for fertilizer, did you?" Barbaças asked with a hint of mischief.

"Yes, but I didn't see what I wanted in the shops."

"Well, if you like, I can get you some."

But Loas quickly put him off: "I've got the promise of some."

"Where will you plant the vines?" Joana broke in, with such emphasis it seemed she'd been holding it in her mind this long while, waiting for an opportunity to bring it out.

"Oh, we'll find a spot somewhere or other," her husband answered, offhand.

"Well, just let me choose the plants. I'll have them sent from home," Joana persisted, bringing it all out in one breath, as though she had to be quick to get it out before her courage failed her. Her husband looked at her listlessly, then closed his eyes as though to shut out people and words.

Then the first rains came. Suddenly in the silky sky dense clouds rolled up, toppling one above the other; the thunderstorm burst, then stopped with the same suddenness with which it had begun. Heavy drops of rain spattered on the burning ground, and left scars smelling of burnt flesh. Then the atmosphere resigned itself to the inevitable; rain fell again, but this time softly and persistently. Streams ran down all the gullies of the slope, slipping over the hard earth without penetrating

154

it, and only losing impetus on the lower levels of the holding.

Stagnant muddy pools remained that lazily reflected the movements of men waiting for action.

During these days the master of the house went the round of the neighboring holdings, and Barbaças and Alice used to sit at the stable door, watching the donkey and the rain. The girl would look at the creature a long time, and then come out of her cogitations with some question or other. For instance, a donkey ought to have a name. ("Can you give a donkey the name of a person, Barbaças?") Or, wouldn't it be better to put a cushion of hay under its head, so that it's neck wouldn't be twisted? Or she'd notice that its flanks were dirty again from lying on the hard layer of dung, and she'd go and get a brush, wet it in the rain that had gathered in puddles near the doorstep, and rub down the warm rough coat. Barbaças, too, liked to hold the can of water till the donkey had drunk its fill, and give it handfuls of straw or feed. He liked the moist touch— like a caress—of the donkey's lips as it delicately took hold of the grain on his hand. Once Loas caught him at it, and wasn't pleased.

"You'd better not forget to wash your hands before eating. You'll be sleeping with the donkey, next, nuzzling your face in its tail."

But next moment he tried to wipe the disagreeableness away by giving the donkey an affectionate slap on the rump.

When the rains stopped, the holding emerged with a covering of lush vegetation that seemed to grow from hour to hour. The donkey lifted up its head and drank in, with dilated nostrils, this fragrance of new life, then brayed with eagerness. Suddenly it pushed through the stable gate and galloped away over the holding like a child let out of school. Alice ran after it in dismay and came up with it a long way away, munching at purple and yellow wild flowers; then it galloped off again, and she had to lie down in the thick grass, tired out.

But Barbaças didn't let this madcap freedom go on too long. He harnessed the donkey to the plow again, and set about breaking up the rest of the land still waiting to be tilled.

Now that it had plenty of green pasturage, the donkey's

coat was glossy, and good strong muscles rippled on its flanks. Loas, full of admiration, saw that he'd got a donkey fit to be the envy of all the other small farmers in the parish, and he fitted it out the best he could with the mended packsaddle, filled the saddlebags with garden produce, and went to town to show off. He chose a Sunday, the day when people sit at tavern doors or lean against the bandstand railings, wearing broad-brimmed hats, talking at leisure—all of them looking as though they're going to hang about like that till the end of time. Masking his pride with a show of indifference, he made his way through the streets without looking straight at anyone.

"Eh there, chaps! Come and have a look at Loas! Here he comes with a donkey loaded with cabbages!"

Or: "Here comes Loas with the devil disguised as a four-footed nag!"

Or: "I've heard tell as how you're getting on in the world, Loas! Come over here and let's have a squint at this gem of a donkey!"

Loas smiled fatuously, though these remarks weren't as flattering as the donkey really deserved. Nevertheless, he smiled, looking as though he'd go on smiling with satisfaction for the rest of his life. However hard he tried to hold the muscles of his face still, however firmly he set his teeth, to keep up his brave show of indifference, he had to smile when he heard such tributes to his success.

When he got to the top of the street and found himself facing the church that marked the limit of the township, and where there was no further possibility of continuing his parade, he set his cabbages down against the wall in the church square and waited for customers to come up for a closer view of both donkey and cabbages. But they didn't seem in any hurry. What was the matter with them? Wasn't the sight fine enough to make anybody want to stop lounging in the town square, or in taverns, and come up to the church? Or hadn't anybody noticed the sound, glistening appearance of the animal? The people who finally showed up were the lads of the place, and two women. One of these tried the weight of the cabbages, and, not thinking much of them, offered half the price asked.

Loas wouldn't agree, and so the other one chipped in.

"Are you selling them so expensive because they've been watered with donkey's stale?"

And the low-down brats hanging round, on the lookout for a jolly rallying cry, all burst out in chorus, "Who wants cabbages watered with donkey's stale?"

The cry quickly made its way down the street, and when some fellow right at the bottom made a megaphone with his hands and shouted back: "Eh, Loas, what's that? Have you come here to sell donkey's stale?" Loas chucked his cabbages down, stamped them underfoot in a rage, and set off for the holding by the back ways.

He was sadly disappointed, but had to admit he'd laid himself open to ridicule. He was a farmer, not a peddler of cabbages. Cabbages, indeed! However had such a silly notion come into his head? He, a grower of corn, a man of ideas, who could manage pairs of mules! However could he have felt so proud of owning a wretched donkey? At that moment, it became the symbol of his defeat, and he hated it. He'd made himself look small by showing off with it.

He slowed down, letting the donkey get well ahead, as though putting as much distance as possible between himself and the humiliation it had brought on him. When all was said and done, though, what had the donkey got to do with him? It didn't even belong to him. The best thing would be to put it back into Barbaças' hands—its real master, and such a ragamuffin that even being seen with a donkey couldn't disgrace him. Then, on his own, he would take up once more the road of mighty vistas. He would again become a farmer, with pairs of mules, and copse land that mechanical devices would transform into market gardens.

They were approaching the bridge when the flow of Loas's thoughts was interrupted. The donkey, well ahead, had begun to climb the slope, its head nodding over its knees in dejected, measured rhythm. At that moment, it looked round, and Loas took this movement to be a last appeal to his generosity. But he remained where he was, unmoved. The creature rubbed its neck against the ragged packsaddle, and went on alone.

157

Loas felt as though a knife had cut him to the heart. Who was he, a poor droll whose ambitions had been crushed in life's hazards, to despise those who came to share humbly in his poor dream? What matter wide estates, vast herds, pairs of mules, if they were not touched with the love of earth's presence? What was he thinking of to let himself be cast down by the mockery of people whose hearts were closed to the true greatness of the plain?

Suddenly, he ran up the slope, anxious to catch up with the donkey and hug it to him, show his affection and repentance; but the donkey, startled, set off crazily along the road, kicking in all directions, making any attempt at reconciliation impossible.

Quite disheartened, Loas sat down by the roadside, waiting for something, but he himself didn't know what.

12

Barbaças noticed that from that day onward, Loas was more affectionate toward the donkey. In addition, his enthusiasm for the holding began to show itself in the concrete form of methodical effort. As the days wore on and the gray winter weeks came nearer, the land grew greener from end to end. Loas religiously gauged the growth of wheat crop and pasture; he spent whole days bent over the young sheaths of corn, cleansing them from any corroding blight. For the first time, he made use of all the manure the holding could produce, from donkey dung to kitchen waste. He gathered everything together in a heap: rags, urine, dry leaves, dung, everything that could later be used to improve the soil. Loas said to his daughter, so that all could hear: "From today on, don't go making heaps in any odd corner; here's the manure sump for that kind of thing." And they all understood it was an order for everyone in the house. Later on, however, when Loas, in a hurry, had to hang about holding his trousers up while Barbaças finished off a lengthy session, he added a rider: "Everybody to the manure heap except when you've got a pain and can't wait." The donkey, too, had to abide by the regulation. Sometimes Loas even walked behind it with a shovel, patiently gathering up all the dung in a wooden bucket.

"Others have got money to buy fertilizers, Barbaças, but fertilizers are evil dusts that consume the earth. It's the same as making a twig fire under a weary beast—it gets up, takes two good steps forward, it's true, but then falls down and can't move again. Dung, live dung, that's what you want. It helps the soil without eating it up."

And when he saw the healthy, jocund growth of his fields, he would call his family round him, give the donkey a slap, and smile happily without saying a word.

Barbaças had filled out, too, though the look of him was somewhat spoiled by his wild-animal appearance. Frankly, he was really filthy. Nobody had ever taught him that he needed a barber's services and a change of clothes. And there was no doubt that, if he persisted in this self-neglect, he would disgust any visitor to the holding, though Loas and his family were so used to him they didn't notice it. One day, however, when he went to town with a basket of eggs, his one-time companions gave him a pitying look, and wouldn't have anything to do with him. Dona Quitéria was so nauseated that she had long since forbidden him to come into her house. So Loas, one Sunday—that being the day when he always began to think about a tub of water and a change of linen—became aware of a strange discomfort when the youth came near him.

"Don't keep so close to the donkey, Barbaças," he said. "You're getting a very funny smell." Then he took a good look at the youth's clothes and head, and added: "I'll have to trim that mop today. Dammit all, I ought to have done it before."

He went and fetched a collection of scissors, then set about lopping off the hair with some pruning scissors, talking as he sheared.

"It's a real shame to go about like this, Barbaças. If you happened to go to town for an outing, people would think we were a scurvy lot out here. They'd just look down on you."

Barbaças, neck twisted from the position he was in, and hair dangling over his eyes, remarked in a strained voice, "Yes, that did happen the other day."

"There you are, what did I say?" shouted Loas in triumph, lifting the scissors like a stick. Simultaneously, the implication of what Barbaças had said came to him, and his expression became crafty. Oh, so Barbaças had felt put out at being given the cold shoulder! So much the better. Like that, he'd think twice before running away from the holding. His resentment would turn into loyalty toward the humble, hospitable world that had given him shelter. The holding would finish by being his home for good and all, his refuge, his own world.

Loas didn't finish cutting the hair. He thought it better to leave Barbaças with something of the unkempt appearance that had disgusted the town.

All this, however, served to underline the need of giving some attention to appearances. Sometimes Loas thought the nonsuccess of his visit to town was due to the fact that he hadn't been able to fit the donkey up with a decent saddle. He'd done his best to repair it, but it was still only fit for a beggar's nag.

"Have you heard of any saddler in these parts, Barbaças?"

"No, I haven't."

"Those fly-by-nights call only when we don't want them. You'd better keep a look out for one."

"What for?"

"Bless my soul! Can't you see what the animal needs?"

A few days later it came about that Joana, passing by the tavern that stood halfway along the road between the holding and the eucalyptus trees, where she had called to ask the price of some young pigs, saw a saddlemaker at the door. She couldn't make up her mind to speak to him, and it was only when she saw him putting his tools into his bag, ready to go, that she took the plunge.

"Are you going to be in these parts for a bit?"

"I was just getting ready to leave."

"Oh . . ." and she stood there hesitating. She didn't know whether she ought to take the man back to the holding so that her husband could come to some arrangement with him, or whether to order the packsaddle from him there and then. She was ready to sacrifice the young pigs once more, put off the planting of the vines to a later date, and use the money for a surprise for her husband, Alice, and Barbaças. And she wouldn't mind seeing the donkey spick-and-span herself.

"Why, do you need anything?"

"Yes, a packsaddle. Do you make packsaddles?"

The man smiled from under his beard, a smile of indulgence rather than vanity, as he stood staring calmly at Joana.

"I'll show you what a real packsaddle should be like," he answered, and fell to opening the bag again.

"Not right now," Joana said hurriedly, afraid she'd gone too far, and trying to find excuses to put a brake on too great haste. "I want a packsaddle made of good straw, new straw."

"And what else besides that?" the man asked in a tone of patient irony.

"And the canvas well reinforced."

"I know all about that. You'll see what a real pack-saddle is."

After repeating this remark, he spat into the road, rubbed his hands as though he were cold, and began to set his tools out. His eyebrows were so long, thick, and disheveled that they hung down from his brow. His hair and full gray beard and the calmness of his face made up a steady, reliable, prepossessing whole. Joana couldn't say No.

"It's going to be the best packsaddle I've ever made in my life."

As she had not the courage either to gainsay him or leave the tavern door, the old saddlemaker looked up and said:

"You can be off, lady. The order's settled. Come back here in three days' time."

Some hours later Joana, back at the holding, was measuring the magnitude of her impulsive decision. She was anxious for Loas to mention the matter again, so that she could somehow or other make it look as though he'd done it all. Of course, he'd been the first to think of a new packsaddle, but he wouldn't take kindly that someone else had stolen a march on him to get the plan executed. Joana took the halter off the donkey, looked at it with disapproval, and made a remark calculated to rouse her husband to further enthusiasm.

"Now, just look at this! It isn't only a packsaddle the donkey needs!"

"Bless my soul, Barbaças," he exclaimed on the instant, turning to the youth. "Can't you dig up a saddlemaker anywhere in the parish?"

"I don't know of one."

"I came across one this afternoon at the tavern door," Joana put in, relieved.

"And didn't you say anything to him?"

"Yes, I did mention it."

Loas seemed satisfied, but then his keen eyes focused on a distant point in search of inspiration. People on the holding had reason to be wary of this gaze staring over and beyond the heathland, leaving near concrete things behind and losing itself in a world from which they were barred.

"What did you say to him?" he went on a few minutes later.

"I spoke to him about the packsaddle." Then she went on hurriedly: "But nothing was settled. I was waiting for you to go and order it."

"You did right."

"If you like, I'll go back tomorrow. Or we could send a message."

"Just leave it to me," said Loas. "Look here, Barbaças, have you ever seen a packsaddle with bells?"

"No, I haven't."

"Well, ours . . . Bless my soul, I think we'll have bells!" He was so taken up with what he was saying that he didn't notice he'd stepped into a puddle.

Two days later Loas agreed that his wife should go back to the tavern to give a firm order for a packsaddle and a halter. Joana got there in next to no time, but the shop was closed. She had to wait till the tavernkeeper came back from whatever business had taken him out.

"What's become of the man who was working here?"

"I think he's gone."

"Gone away? Has he left the district? And what about the packsaddle?"

"What packsaddle? Oh, yes, I seem to remember he was carrying something of the sort on his back. Was it yours?"

"Yes, I ordered it."

"Well, I just can't say."

163

Joana had to go back and tell her husband all about it. Loas pushed his wide-brimmed hat back till it was perched at an awkward angle on his unkempt hair.

"Is there any mother's son of that sort thinks he can make a fool of me?" he exclaimed.

He hurriedly got into his waistcoat and set off down the road. Where could he go looking for the saddlemaker, and in such a taking as though the man had stolen something belonging to him? Nobody knew. He didn't know himself, unless the devil had whispered some idea to him. But the fact of the matter was that the craftsman, going off with the pack-saddle, intended for their donkey, became associated in his mind with all those envious, cheating, misguided folk who had ever belittled him—and Loas didn't intend that anyone else should make light of him. The man must be somewhere, most likely at the counter of some low tavern, and Loas swore to himself not to return to the holding without the saddle.

To give some method to this indefinite kind of search, he took the shortcut to the nearest farms. The trees, already damp with chilly autumn, were swaying gently in the evening breeze; a rustling ran over the leaves, and reached the ears as a light shiver. Loas opened his nostrils to the smell of damp grass, sap rising from the earth that seemed full with the fullness of a fertile womb. At times, Loas forgot all about his indignation.

Nothing was known at the farms. A saddlemaker? Nobody had heard of him. And anyway, these days, whoever wanted to make a donkey look smart? Saddlers had disappeared from the heathland. And as soon as Loas turned his back, they shook their heads and said it was a pity he was so odd and peculiar.

Disappointed, Loas finished his round at the tavern where the saddlemaker previously had taken up his quarters. He'd spend the night there, if necessary.

"Will he come back, Master?"

"Who can tell? There's no relying on such folk."

"But dammit all, the saddle was ready."

"Maybe it was." And the tavernkeeper put an end to the

exchange, bored with the whole thing.

Early next morning, Loas set out for the interior of the heathland, where sandy scrub with broom, shoulder-high in places, isolated the houses from the rest of the world. Who knows, maybe the saddlemaker had betaken himself there? The peasants looked out from half-open doors or from the darkness of closed porches, when Loas with angry gait, defying their barking dogs, came up through the brambles. A saddlemaker? Yes, a man had been that way with a saddle on his back, showing it to everybody, but he hadn't looked like a thief.

"Did he—was he trying to get away on the sly?"

"On the contrary, he came up to the doors, and insisted on showing the saddle."

And that was how Loas picked up the trail. But the man had several miles' start, and had zigzagged all over the place, and so Loas found himself back at the tavern a good hour after the saddlemaker had returned there.

And he was such a quiet, steady sort of chap that Loas, feeling unable to make a fuss, gulped back the explosion waiting to burst out, and silently they weighed each other up. The saddler, very leisurely, passed his fingers over his shaggy brows, and then went and leaned against the packsaddle, preparing for a quiet smoke. Loas tried to look detached, calm, and disinterested, but couldn't hide his vexation.

"So you're the owner of the donkey. . . ." remarked the saddler.

There was no irony in his words, only an unavowed bitterness. His fingers trembled as they wandered over the edges of the saddle, as though stroking a human body.

"You've been following behind me, so people said."

"Yes, but that packsaddle . . ."

"I promised the saddle'd be the best one I've ever made in my life. And it's turned out what I promised. Here it is." But he made no movement to hand it over. "Now, look here, my friend," he went on, "it's a saddle the like of which you never saw in your life before. I couldn't let it go without showing it at least to a few people. Yes, I've been showing it round for the masterpiece it is. We all feel a bit of pride in what we've made with our own hands. So hadn't I the right to do it?"

Loas nodded his head in agreement, somewhat crestfallen. Then the saddlemaker went up to the counter with a swagger quite out of keeping with his usual manner.

"Fill up two glasses," he called to the tavernkeeper. "And to the devil with the saddle!"

PART III

13

After the uncertain autumn days, scattered clouds raced from all points of the horizon, closing the sky in a final layer of heavy gray. Then rain fell for weeks on end. At times it dwindled into a mist, a damp haze; at others it fell in torrents, washing soil down the ridges. In the early morning the fallow land was covered with rime, and Barbaças was one of those who went catching hares (in their burrows, numb with cold).

Loas, pent between the four walls of the cottage, had fallen into a melancholy frame of mind. Whenever a blue patch opened in the sky, he would go out into the garden and wander among pools of muddy water, or further afield to the house of some friend where they could shake their heads and complain that such a hard winter would end by rotting the plain. Wheatland required sun, Loas said. Ripe wheat was the color of the sun, and the flatland was wheat. He limited himself to such maxims, but what also lay heavy on his heart was that, during the rainy weeks, there was no hope of anybody's making the effort to cover a league or so to gossip with him.

Sometimes he would be caught in a storm on the way back, and then, standing almost naked by the hearth to dry his wet clothes, he would again voice loud complaints about the foul weather. But on Joana's face there was a quiet, happy smile. She liked the rain. It reminded her of the long winters of her own part of the country, wind whistling in the mountains, distaff and spindle, peaceful indoor tasks. And so she smiled. The rain made up for the tranced suffocation of summer.

One morning Barbaças discovered that the roof tiles over the donkey's stable had slipped during the night, and it was raining almost as hard there as outside.

"And how's the packsaddle?" asked Loas.

"I shouldn't be surprised if it wasn't full of mold."

Loas looked round as though for an immediate remedy against all mishaps, and, vigorously scratching his head, with Alice watching anxiously, he gave the order: "Bring the animal in here. And the saddle, too."

Whenever he had occasion to mention the packsaddle, he couldn't help thinking about the man at the tavern. Now, there was a good chap for you, an artist in his craft, who attached value to things, and had his feelings in the right place. If he'd been a man apt for husbandry, he'd have invited him to come and join them on the holding. Perhaps he would've been able to learn to love land or animals the same as he loved the craft that came from his rough hands like magic.

"Yes, bring the animal here. It's flesh and blood like ourselves."

And so the donkey had its bed near the hearth. The whole house then took on a strong, sensual stable smell.

Till one morning, the sky appeared clear and warm once more. Leaves on the trees and the hills glittering in the tepid light. People came out of their houses so hungry for sun and fresh air that, when night came, they didn't even want to go in for a few hours' sleep. Loas took to plowing just anywhere, and nobody had the heart to ask what for.

Vieirinha, whom they hadn't seen this long while, turned up one afternoon when they all looked very busy. He came up red-faced and in a hurry, nervy, and with such an important question on the tip of his tongue that he blurted it out without any greeting.

"Have you seen a woman pass by here?"

"What woman?" Loas inquired.

"A dirty slut of a strumpet . . . A fine woman, in fact, but as intractable as a nanny goat. She ran away from me, the sly bitch."

"We haven't seen any woman. Isn't that so, Barbaças?"

Barbaças shook his head in corroboration.

Vieirinha, with anxious, unbelieving eyes, searched carefully on all sides, as though Loas had in fact hidden the woman from him.

"She ran away from me along this road," he burst out. "I could still see her in the distance, and it seemed to me that she cut off by the path to your holding."

"We haven't seen any woman here, friend. Dammit all, it's years since anybody passed this way. It's done nothing but rain and rain. Who was the woman, Vieirinha?"

"She came with that group of laborers who're working up at the barrage. She caught some disease or other, and I used to see her every day at the doctor's door. She was a fine woman, good at the job women are meant for, but, as I said, as intractable as a goat. I had her with me for two weeks. And I swear it was three months since I'd touched a woman! God, I'd forgotten what a woman was like!" Vieirinha didn't take his hands from his face, because he hadn't shaved and the white bristles made him look terribly old. "I can't understand how she could have got away so quickly, with her bad legs."

"Bad legs?"

"Her legs weren't too good. She had to walk with them so far apart that she looked like a frog. In every other respect, though, she was a fine figure of a woman."

Vieirinha's voice had taken on such a pitiful, plaintive tone that Loas felt he must try and console him somehow.

"Well, friend Vieirinha, perhaps you could . . . You know, there are lots of other women round here. . . ."

"That's so. But they already belong to someone. I don't know how it is, but all women already seem to belong to someone. And even if there does happen to be one still free, how can a man invite her into the broom clumps when in every nook, behind every stone, near every hole, there's always somebody about? You can't even manage to whisper a word in their ears!"

"Not so loud, Vieirinha. There are women on this holding."

Joana had walked past the two men, her eyes on the ground, unfriendly.

Just at that moment, the south wind carried the sound of the train to them as it rumbled over the heath. It carried the shrill sound of the engine whistle, too. Vieirinha gave a start. He forgot all about keeping his beard hidden, and the puffy wrinkled redness of his cheeks made him look like an old man.

"Don't you feel well, Vieirinha?"

"I can't hear a train whistle without thinking of the jungle. In the forest, the whistle seemed to come blowing up all the dust in the village and around it. There were only two white people there. Myself and a fur trader. People just died off in that hell of dust, heat, and mosquitoes. And whichever way you turned, all round, the jungle was waiting only half a mile away."

"But you've always said the jungle—"

"Well, you know, people don't always tell the truth. In that district, it was nothing but dust, and all round there was nothing but trees and more trees, and when you were shut in like that, the dust gnawed away your bones. It was nothing but a prison, Loas. We had a garden round the houses, and the clouds just rained down dust on it."

"Dust?"

"Yes, dust. And not one white woman in the place. Not one woman who didn't reek of dust and the jungle."

"Is that what they smelled of?"

But Vieirinha didn't hear the question. He was far away.

". . . And once, my friend, they called me up to the governor, and I thought at last they were going to do what I'd often applied for—send me somewhere else."

"And did they?"

"No, and all because of a dog. That's the truth. The governor was there, sitting behind a huge table, big enough to carve up two or three pigs without inconvenience, and when I mentioned what I wanted, he became very stiff and haughty, very difficult, and maybe he was just going to say Yes, when a dog came running in. 'What's this?' he shrieked, leaping up in a rage. Can you imagine it, my friend, a dog there, in those rooms, on those carpets, making light of a governor!"

"What's a governor, Vieirinha?"

172

"A governor's a man about this size. This governor was short and fat. But let me tell my story my own way, and don't interrupt with questions like that, Loas. So when the governor looked at me and saw I was amazed that a dog should enter a governor's rooms, he began to shout for the orderly."

"What's an orderly?"

"Don't you know what an orderly is, either? What do you know, man?"

"Well, the jungle isn't my line...." Loas was beginning to lose patience with the good-for-nothing's pretentious talk, and so he went on angrily: "All right, I know what an orderly is. Go on with your tale."

"Very, well, my friend. So you know what an orderly is. All right. Now, the orderly bowed down almost to his knees (an orderly's a human being the same as a governor, as you know), so, as I was saying, he bowed before coming in at the door, and when he saw the dog he turned even whiter than the governor. A dog was quite out of place there, quite against the rules, my friend. The governor saw he must pass off the irregularity in some way, and he said to me: "This isn't the usual thing here. It's the very first time it's happened." And he was so angry, he didn't have me transferred to some other place. All my life, things have always gone against me."

Loas cleared his throat to no purpose. Whatever could you say to a man like Vieirinha?

Vieirinha seemed to understand. He got up and moved away from his friend, giving him more elbow room. His feverish eyes wandered over the myriads of green blades springing from the damp earth. He was still breathing heavily, biting his lips as though biting on his own humiliation. Loas didn't feel at ease, either. His friend's presence made him feel uncomfortable. With growing impatience, all he wanted was for Vieirinha to go away. Let all those who were strangers to life on the holding go away. He wanted to be alone with the donkey and Barbaças and the womenfolk, and show them all the affection he now fully realized they were worthy of. He felt such a strong impulse to get his hand on the plow and get on with his work, win back the rhythm of his own life, threatened by

173

Vieirinha's private tortuous world, that, if his friend stayed too long, he wouldn't be able to contain himself. Trampling his feet on the soft earth, he suddenly said in a peremptory sort of voice:

"I've already told you the woman hasn't passed this way. Strumpets don't come here. We're working folk."

"I know, my friend. I know you're getting on very well. You've got a donkey now."

"Who told you?" Loas asked, his face suddenly brightening.

"People are talking of it hereabouts. A fine donkey... Well, we've had a nice chat, friend Loas. I'll be seeing you again one of these days. I must be off now to look for that ungrateful woman."

"You just wait, Vieirinha. When a woman runs away, she really runs away. They're like goats. Only sheep come back to the fold. But, dammit all, at such times a man ought to show what he's made of, and not go running after them."

"Do you think she'll come back, then?" Vieirinha asked, craving a crumb of hope.

"Do you mean the donkey?"

"No, man! I mean the bitch who's run away from me."

"Oh, I thought you might be wondering whether the donkey had run away from us. . . . Are people talking about it?"

"About the woman?"

"No, about the donkey, hang it!"

"Now, look here, friend Loas, I'm talking about a woman. Just get it into your head once and for all that I'm talking about a woman."

"All right, all right," Loas answered, falling in with him, though a bit vexed. "As for that, if you've given her some presents, and still have something left in the house to give her, she'll come back all right."

"Yes, I've still got some lace things, a surplice, and embroidered purses."

"Then she'll come back."

Loas was feeling easier in mind. He was hoping their talk would still give him a chance of finding out what people were saying about the donkey, and he felt better able to put up with Vieirinha.

"Now, listen, Loas. I want to talk about something I'm a bit ashamed of." Vieirinha drew his friend away toward a more private spot. "You mustn't laugh at me. You know I've traveled the backwoods. I've read some books and am a plain, straightforward sort of chap who's got eyes in his head. I've never believed in charms and spells and all those silly old-wives' tales. Don't take offense, my friend. I like to say straight out what I mean."

"Well, what is it?" asked Loas, annoyed at the insult these words implied.

"I was fond of that woman. She was ill, but she belonged to me; I could have had my fill of her for days, weeks, months. I was selling things so that I could buy nice mutton chops, eggs, beer, and suchlike. I really spoiled her!"

"Dammit all, what's that got to do with me?"

"You could help me, Loas. What I want to know is whether it's true you know charms to bind a woman close. . . ."

"But you don't believe in that sort of thing!" Loas broke in, getting even by keeping the wretched man on tenterhooks.

"Sometimes a chap doesn't know what to believe."

By that, Loas knew his friend was really down in the mouth. "Yes, I know some charms. And I can do other things, too," he answered more sympathetically.

"That's what I've heard tell. Now, be frank with me, my friend; that's all I ask. Is it true that you've had speech with the devil? In fact, did he get you the money for the donkey?"

"I can't explain everything, Vieirinha. There are things that I mustn't talk about."

"And that donkey's such a fine animal! That was a bargain, if you like. Whether it was the devil in person, or someone on his behalf, who gave you good advice is neither here nor there. What does matter is that it was a fine bargain."

"Do you think so?" Loas persisted, now really walking on air.

"Yes. I knew that donkey."

"People talked a lot about it, didn't they?"

"Yes, but they've stopped gossiping about it now, of course. People get tired of talking about the same thing. Envy wears itself out, too. Just like women, my friend. They've got no staying power, and so . . ."

"So there was talk about the donkey. . . . Wouldn't you like a nice slice of ham? . . . No? . . . Well, it's only now that I'm beginning to realize how work was held up for lack of a donkey. Just take a look at this crop, Vieirinha! So they spoke well of the animal, did they?"

"Nobody's got anything against the animal. You've got a fine bargain. A mild-tempered beast, Loas. Soft as wax. I often saw it when it was carrying its mistress to the doctor at Arraiolos. She had leprosy and could hardly see, but the donkey always took her there all right."

God in heaven! What abrupt change did Vieirinha see in his friend's eyes? Why was the silence that fell between the two men so big with size, surprise, and tension? Loas stood there, his face rigid with shock; then he had to lean against his friend as though his legs were giving way under the burden of the news.

"Did you say 'leprosy'?" he asked faintly.

"Yes, didn't you know? The doctor at Arraiolos gave her injections for months on end; then the family took her to a leper hospital. I've never seen her since. It's an ugly disease. I saw a lot of it in the Amazon."

Loas was still pale and dazed. He felt something like a whirlpool round him, carrying him giddily along, threatening to submerge him.

"You saw the donkey with the leper? Are you sure you're not mistaken?"

Whatever was the matter with old Loas? Rather puzzled, Vieirinha confirmed what he had already said: "Yes, it was this donkey, my friend. In these parts, there aren't two as sweet-tempered as yours. Don't you believe me? Isn't it true you went to the farmstead at Malhadas to buy it?"

Loas, his eyes bloodshot, nodded an affirmative. He had moved over to the cork tree, and was now leaning against the trunk for support. Surrender and weariness had come over him to sap his strength. His lips were so dry that he couldn't seem to open them. With an effort he forced them apart, and with an effort forced out the words:

"Did you ever see the leper?"

"I passed her sometimes on the road to Arraiolos, with her face covered. Nobody ever saw her at the farm; the family kept her shut away in a room." Quite at sea, and suspecting that something terrible had happened beyond his comprehension, Vieirinha tried to turn his friend's thoughts away from it. "I never thought you'd be buying a donkey so soon, friend Loas. What I wanted was for me to give you a donkey, that I swear. But how can a man twist this devil of a life to his own purpose? And these bitches of women, too!"

With one gesture Loas cut short Vieirinha's chatter. Suddenly he raised his head, his eyes burning.

"Clear out, Vieirinha! Be off with you!" he shouted. "Take yourself off, you monster!"

Retreating in amazement, Vieirinha stumbled over a stone, and nearly lost his balance. This swift change of mood was extraordinary. His poor friend must have gone stark mad all of a sudden.

"And don't let me catch you on this holding again! I'm going to close it up on all sides. I'm going to enclose it with thick hedges of bramble so that no thief can come here again, stealing my peace of mind!"

Vieirinha hadn't the strength to protest. He looked at the sweat bursting out of Loas's crazy forehead; he looked at his demented gestures and, like a dog that has been driven off, began to walk slowly away without turning round.

177

14

So the donkey had belonged to a leper. The tarnished hands and clothes of the sick woman had been in contact with the animal's flesh, had contaminated it with their own persistent, treacherous taint. The family had shut the leper up in a hospital, and, so that nothing of her unclean presence should be left behind, had sold the animal to the first simpleton who fell into the trap. The poison, pustules, pollution of that cankered body had kept close company with the animal, and were now incubating in the bosom of his own family. Incubating in grisly silence.

The donkey had passed on the noxious germ to people, to the earth, to the newborn wheat, to Alice's frail body, Barbaças' dark hands, to the very air they all breathed. A loathsome germ without form or smell—but now he, Loas, knew of its existence; he could feel it everywhere. In his troubled imagination the torpid, repulsive presence took on foul shapes. It was an insignificant seed that grew bigger each morning, expanding as mushrooms swell up in dank places, and would burst out one day in sores riddled with pus. Leprosy was in each one of them, viscous, lurking, sapping their vitals. Who would be the first victim? Would it be Barbaças who handled the donkey's feed and ran to gather up the dung that came from its viscera? Or would it be Loas himself, who had driven it at the plow, repaired the saddle on which the leper's buttocks had rested. No, it wouldn't be Barbaças; he was as thick-skinned and impervious as any crustacean, a wild thing so resistant to disease that he'd withstood even tetanus. But what about Alice? She had led the donkey back from that contaminated farmstead. She had carressed it with hands and lips, lost no opportunity of riding on its back. Alice, with her sweet, fragile body, unable to withstand such a malignant disease. Alice! Alice! Why hadn't his anxious thought settled straight on her, without beating about the bush? Alice, my poor little girl! shouted all Loas's tormented nerves. He felt as though he'd like to batter his brains and flesh against stones, trees, stars, against that thing not yet identified, in which the cause of the catastrophe had found cover.

Loas half closed his eyes at the creeping, insidious thought. His whole being gathered itself together, coat abristle, like an animal awaiting another beast's attack. What was going on in his mind? Dream, insight madness—tragedy only? There was somewhere in him an obscure, evasive zone that he was in the last resort afraid to probe, an inaccessible inferno from which lava flowed, fleeting shafts of light that suddenly illuminated his thought, then as suddenly left it dark. What had been the origin of the catastrophe? There lay the secret enlightenment —better, perhaps, left obscure—that he half glimpsed in flashes. All he was waiting for was that instant when he would catch the revelation in all its clarity and horror. For him, the donkey had been the materialization of a long-cherished dream. But the dream had borne canker at its core, had been pregnant with evil. And the donkey had passed the malediction on to others. Ah, Vieirinha, damn your eyes!

Loas moved about the holding like one crazed, the monstrous secret suffocating him; and no one, seeing his condition, ventured to ask what was the matter. The family gathered in front of the house, drawn together in the same amazement, anxiously waiting, silently watching the master of the house as he strode to and fro, nobody daring to ask the reason for his haggard unrest. Loas didn't come home to sleep that night, and all the others sat up till dawn, waiting for him in vain.

The next day they felt worn out.

"Mam, what's the matter with Dad?" Alice asked. "Why is he angry with us all?" Joana lay the girl's head on her breast and rocked her till she fell asleep.

Loas had wandered off, tramping for miles in search of the weariness that would dull his agitated nerves. My God, he was thinking, what was going to happen to them all? As head of the tribe and sole possessor of the secret, what course ought he to take? Sometimes he imagined that when he got back to the holding he'd find the family standing there, all of them disfigured with pustules, waiting in a row, stark stiff, as though for execution. He could see them in front of him, larger than life, angry, hideous as only his frantic mind could paint them. The donkey had belonged to a leper. It had perfidiously spread infection over the holding. Carried on the wind, the infection would travel farther afield, insatiable, rushing like wildfire over the heathland. He could feel it on the march in the formless obscurity of the night, without body yet obscene, reaching out toward a reddening sky. No! It couldn't be true! Why had Vieirinha come and told him about it? Accursed bird of ill omen, blast him! No! It couldn't be! He, Loas, wouldn't let it happen! Rather than see the heathland plague-ridden, he'd bury the donkey in such a deep hole that even the roots of trees couldn't reach down to absorb its poison. But would he have the heart to do that? Didn't the donkey stand for crops, shrubs, the untiring fertility of the land? Didn't it stand for plowing clear furrows through the fallow, cradle for seeds, fertilizers, and his own belief in earth's yield? The land lived and breathed through the lungs of creatures who threw in their lot with its destiny. To kill its possibilities would be to mutilate himself, bury his dream in that same deep hole beyond the reach of searching roots. . . . No, he'd never have the heart to do it. Why had that damned Vieirinha come with one of those truths blacker than lies?

Suddenly, a doubt cut like a flash through Loas's nightmare. Perhaps Alice hadn't been contaminated yet. Recently, both Alice and Barbaças had put on weight; and the rosy-cheeked girl seemed to shoot up from day to day. The joy of having a donkey on the holding appeared to have made her more robust. So, could it be possible? Yes, maybe there was still time to avoid calamity. If he told the girl to keep right away from the donkey, and if the rest of them were properly careful, that might do the trick. The leper woman's family had lived side by side with the disease, yet they looked as healthy as anybody else. Damn it all, could that be a way out?

Loas felt a rush of relief that wiped the black misgivings

from his mind. He'd get back to the holding as quickly as he could. And if it should become necessary for someone to keep watch with him, he'd tell his wife what had happened. For anything concerning Alice, Joana was a she-wolf. He could rely on her vigilant, unobtrusive cooperation.

15

During the night they burned the old saddle and harness. Loas picked them up with a pitchfork, sick at the thought of how many times he'd clutched them closely to him. Joana lighted a bonfire at the far end of the holding, while her husband dug a big hole, because neither of them had the least intention of throwing the ashes into the manure sump. After that, it'd be necessary to persuade Barbaças to go and have a good bathe in the stream, and leave the dirty old clothes he'd been wearing for years behind him. Joana went to town to sell all the products that were saleable, and with the money she bought a suit and shirts for the youth.

Loas in the meantime had been thinking up a good tale to convince Barbaças to take himself off and get rid of his filthy rags. He'd tell him that one of these days the family would have to go to market to choose half a dozen ewes, so that they could have wool and fresh cheese on the holding. He'd tell him he was a good lad, who'd given up loafing about the town in order to lend a helping hand to a friend with no thought of profit for himself—he'd even generously refused the offer of a legacy guaranteed before the notary. Now, when they went to market, the family must look decent, clean, and respectable. "Fresh cheese, Barbaças," he'd say. "And a nice new shirt, to show them we aren't idle have-nothings!"

But it was no good. He wouldn't say that, or anything like it. He no longer had the heart for such tales. The muscles of his face seemed to have lost the habit of smiling and forming empty words. He was a different man. So he just told Barbaças plainly that he'd go with him to the stream, and give him some clean clothes to put on after his bathe. And that's what he did. He wanted to be quite sure that after Barbaças had scrubbed himself in the water, he wouldn't touch the tainted clothes again. He watched him from the willow trees on the bank, and only when the youth threw off the last piece of clothing (so greasy that it lay floating for some time before it was drawn into the foaming dam race) did he feel one anxiety the less. When he threw the new clothing to Barbaças, at the same time taking a good look at his dark skin, it was as though the family had got rid of the last scab of poison.

Now it was necessary to look after the girl, with unwavering vigilance keep her from any contact with the donkey. Isolate the pestilence in such a way that it would wither like a neglected flower. Then, perhaps, the sun and wind of blazing days on the heathland would burn the disease from the animal's thick skin. But from now on, they would use the donkey for indispensable tasks only. To plow the earth. For the rest of the time they'd leave it by itself in the high-lying distant part of the holding, in a place open to the winds.

But he knew it wouldn't be easy to convince Alice. She was used to climbing the garden wall and jumping from it onto the donkey's patient back for endless rides, till they both rolled over in the threshed straw, the whole day spent in skips and capers. Then, at night, when Barbaças was careful to go and fasten the stable door, she was the last person to say good night to the donkey. Sometimes, her eyes already heavy with sleep, she'd ask him if he hadn't forgotten to leave the bucket full of water, and the manger well filled with maize feed. And almost always his short replies didn't satisfy her, and she'd go to find out herself. Nevertheless, at all costs, and whether she liked it or not, they'd have to curb the girl's passion for the donkey.

Joana began by telling her daughter she was growing into a little woman, and from that time she'd got to help in the house. She didn't think much of girls, Joana said, who spent their days in baby play or, like gypsies, riding on animals that ought to be at work. Alice wept as children do weep when you try to make them understand that certain things, which seem innocent enough to them, are really very wrong. The next few days, with a naïve seriousness in look and gesture, she tried to imitate her mother as she went about her work. Now and again she'd quickly glance in the direction of the donkey, as though it had led her astray to commit dark misdeeds. But she couldn't keep this superior attitude up for long, and so, giving her parents the slip, she ended by searching the donkey out on the other side of the hill in the out-of-the-way place where they had hidden it.

A gentle grief shone in the animal's moist eyes, a look of appeal veiled in resignation. The girl took hold of the tether in her left hand, and with the other offered it a handful of grass. The donkey crunched it slowly, casting a melancholy glance all round. It looked at the green mantle of the hillside, at the trees, at the wisps of cloud—as though afraid of finding hostility or censure in the girl's face. When it bent its head the next time toward Alice's hands, it opened its sensitive nostrils and whinnied gently.

"What's the matter, my pet?"

And the girl nuzzled her cheek against the donkey's nose.

"What's the matter? You can smell the grass; that's what it is, isn't it?" Alice thought it must be feeling sad. There was pasture on all sides, on hillocks and fallows; even the sandy slope was covered with broom. What the donkey wanted was freedom and affection, such as it had before. Poor pet! She was so sorry, she must give it a hug.

But she didn't always get the chance for these stolen meetings. Loas would shut it up for days on end, until at last Alice had to go and consult Barbaças.

"Did you know little girls shouldn't play with donkeys?" she asked.

"Don't be silly! All little girls play with donkeys," he answered.

"But Mam says they don't."

"Well, they're just having us on, and I'm getting sick of it. Your dad wants me to scrub my hands every time I've had anything to do with the donkey. He's got a bee in his bonnet about cleanliness now. I've just about had enough of it. But one of these fine days, just to show him, I'm going to sleep with the donkey."

"When will you do it, Barbaças?"

"What do you want to know for?"

"So that I can keep out of their way and go with you."

"That's just crazy. You're all crazy. That's what folk say in town." Alice looked down, hurt. She didn't like Barbaças to talk about her parents in that way. She jumped up with tears in her eyes, and ran and hid in the house so that she could have a good cry.

Startled, Barbaças watched her run away. Whatever was the matter with the girl? Somehow, she seemed more grown up in her ways now. And ever since that day when Vieirinha called, people on the holding had looked and talked differently. A strange unease, a feeling of storm ready to break, was growing up round them, isolating them day by day.

Meals took place in silence. Sometimes Loas stared fixedly at Barbaças' hands, hands that had just finished tending the donkey. He saw them swollen, monstrous, purulent. Pus running from hairs and nails into the broth, passing with it onto all their plates. His stomach heaved with sickness, and he had to rush from the table, livid as a corpse. Then he would wander over the holding, feeling the burning, tumid earth pulsing beneath his feet, something of base sensuality in its vigor. The earth was a lewd, turgid womb whence flowed streams of lust, and their poison turned into the sap that fed the roots of growing things. All the holding, everything germinating from it, was befouled. No amount of lye would cleanse it. People, land, trees, would have to wait, condemned, while the pestilence slowly devoured them.

Now that his eyes were opened, Loas noticed many things that hadn't troubled him before. Barbaças' filthy manners, for instance. He had to admit it now; Barbaças had always been filthy. When he ate, food dropped from his cracked lips; he dipped his fingers in the soup, picked the meat out with the eager greed of an animal. To eat with him was real self-denial. How could Loas protect a pig like that from the menace of the disease? But even if Barbaças had been a clean sort of chap, hadn't he, Loas, thrown him as a sacrifice to devouring leprosy? Yes, it was all true. But who else was there except Barbaças? Joana, Alice, Loas himself? Joana was his wife, Alice's mother.

Alice was the flesh of his flesh. How could he sacrifice them? But he himself it was who'd been all in a fret till they'd got an animal on the holding, and so was responsible for the whole thing. Could he be so cowardly as to sacrifice somebody else in his place? Where was the solution? It was enough to send you crazy! Ah, Vieirinha, damn your eyes, why the devil did you come with news like that?

It was during the night that Loas racked his brains desperately in a nightmare of mental conflict. At daybreak, the pure light of morning cleared the landscape of its terrors, specters, and nausea—people and things came forth unsullied. Sometimes he would pull up a blade of corn and crush the root between his fingers, looking for signs of disease. But there was nothing abnormal. So powerful and wise was the earth that, in its womb, death was transformed into life. It was he, Loas, who was losing all sense of proportion. For months the donkey's body had been baked in the sun, cleansed of foul germs, and in the new saddle and harness there were no crannies where disease could lurk. Thus, the whole trouble was over and done with. The only thing now was to look after the girl. That was all.

So, having reached peace in his own mind, Loas, in great good humor, called Barbaças, and they set to work with a will.

But one afternoon, Joana caught Alice asleep beside the donkey. She didn't tell her husband. She took the girl aside where she could punish her without witnesses.

"Why don't you sell the donkey?" she asked later, during a sleepless night.

"It's wanted for the work. I couldn't get on without it."

"You could buy another."

There you are! Why hadn't he thought of this simple solution? It was really amazing that Joana should have such a good idea and find words for it. That woman had always been extraordinary. Now he came to think of it, lately she'd been taking a more active part in life on the holding, bit by bit making her presence felt. How was it he hadn't noticed the change before?

Loas got up from his straw mattress and opened the window to let the relief he felt at Joana's suggestion spread over the holding and through the night. Sell the donkey—send the leprosy carrier away. Sell the donkey—exchange it for a sound, healthy animal that wouldn't be a threat to anybody's happiness. Sell the donkey ... but the more he considered the idea and turned it over, the more his fancy ran riot. By all means sell the donkey. Why not do the business through a gypsy? He might even manage to exchange it for a jackass or, later, with the money from the harvest, for a pair of mules. Then once again he'd drive along the roads with a fine pair of bays, with bells on their collars. (Hadn't he promised Barbaças that he'd get a saddle with bells on it for the donkey? And what had he done about it?) Later, with the passage of time, he'd end up by freeing the holding from mortgage and getting a really reliable motor for the water machine. Joana should have her vines, and a more extensive, more luxuriant garden in which beans and turnips'd shoot up overnight.

The dream went on increasing and multiplying till the room wouldn't hold it. Barefooted, and with his shirt open, he went out into the cottage garden and breathed in the fragrance of the earth. The smell of the corn, green though it still was, penetrated everything to the core. From hour to hour, he could feel the turbulent growth of the corn crop. The silence of the plain was only a mask. Beneath it, grain was swelling slowly, tirelessly. This slow, sure growth was reflected in people's eyes, in their concentrated, expectant looks, in the grandiose serenity of the southerner. They knew that however slow earth's gestation might be, it would never forsake them.

The holding was no longer the waste land it had been the year before. Barbaças had been a wonderful helper! How he had changed! Had the spell of the earth caught him, too? And since they'd had the donkey to break the sterile crust, bringing the sap hidden in the depths up to the surface of the holding, seeds germinated in a very different way, as though in a hurry to grow and be gathered. The donkey was an intimate part of all this revival. If another one came ... Would it be quite the same thing if they had another? But Loas shied away from these questions. He wanted to skirt round them, too fainthearted to face them squarely and come to a decision. He needed Joana, Vieirinha, anybody, to point a direction. But which direction, blast it?

Not noticing where he was going, he found himself near the stable. He opened the door quietly, like a thief, or like someone trying to take an enemy by surprise. And there, waiting for him, he saw the liquid, contented eyes of the donkey, serene as the night outside. Those eyes seemed to have guessed what was passing in Loas's mind, and accepted it with deep humility. Those eyes were resigned, human.

Loas stood leaning against the doorpost. No, that wasn't a donkey you could exchange for another one. On the holding, people and beasts were too closely associated in the epic task for them to be coldly replaced or hired. Had he ever accepted a hired man on the holding? What was a hired man? Somebody who didn't and couldn't share in the land to which he hired out his strength. Earth didn't need only hands; it demanded the whole heart. He had induced Barbaças to leave his loafing ways so that he could give himself up to the holding, and end by feeling that it belonged to him, too. He, Barbaças, and the donkey made up one indivisible whole. The animal had come to fill in the spaces of his dream that had been only agitation and anxiety up to that time. To send the donkey away was to destroy the foundation of the dream. And so, Vieirinha, how came he to do it?

Pale-faced, breathing hard, sweat beading on his forehead, Loas twisted his finger joints. In the dusk of the night, the donkey's eyes looked enormous, as if about to burst into tears. The look seemed to fill space and Loas's very soul, flare through his conscience. He must reassure them, dominate them with a curse or a caress. He must do something: drub the donkey pitilessly, then throw himself at its feet and weep together over the fatality that united and divided them. Or else, get away again. Suddenly, he banged the door behind him, hurried along the paths through the corn, and spent the rest of the night far from the house, up at the top of the holding, anxiously waiting for daybreak.

16

Barbaças was beginning to think that the behavior of Loas and his wife was very strange. Loas wandered about moping, without a word to say for himself. He didn't talk; he kept himself to himself, and didn't go in for any flights of fancy. Both he and Joana, Barbaças thought, were trying to push him out of the family circle. They were always giving him some kind of work that would keep him out of the way; and at night, if he came to sit on the stone seat as he used to do before, near Loas or Alice, some pretext was always found to make him shift. He was no longer free to go on poaching expeditions with Alice, or to ask her to go with him when he gave the donkey its feed.

"Where are you off to, my girl? Your place is at home."

His suspicions already aroused, and each day bringing some new surprise, Barbaças also finished by noticing that, at table, he always had the same plate and that Loas insisted on serving him each time he stretched his arm toward the soup pan. Also, as though by chance, his seat at table always seemed to get farther and farther away from the seats of the other people in the house. They were all close together at one end, as though huddling away from some danger. And sometimes Barbaças caught Loas watching the movements of his spoon with a look of disgust. What the devil was happening on the holding?

They were strict with Alice, too. They wouldn't let her go into the stable, or go with the donkey when it was taken out to plow. The girl looked wan and dispirited. Could there be something the matter with him? Was there something about him that put people off? Barbaças went and examined himself carefully in a glass. Had they caught sight of some sign of disease? He'd always heard tell that people were afraid of contact with consumptives because consumption was a fatal, very catching disease. But consumptives cough, spit blood, are pale and thin. Whereas he felt stronger and sturdier day by day. Was it because they were just stupid? No, they were folk who had dealings with the devil, that was more like it! There'd been something strange about the holding lately, an atmosphere of witchcraft, plotting, whispering in corners that was really sickening. Oh, no, this didn't suit him at all! Loas had better be a bit more civil, or he'd soon show them he hadn't forgotten the road to town.

The town? When he called those former days to mind, his thoughts became gloomier. The town had forgotten him. The last time he'd been there he'd been treated like a stranger. But even if this weren't the case, would he really and truly be capable of leaving the holding? No part of it belonged to him, yet the bonds linking him to all that took place on it were stronger than deeds drawn up by a notary. He'd got clear of Loas's silly talk only to find himself caught in a bigger spell. As though he were the stem of some plant that took root, grew, branched out, a stem springing from a seed that had lain withered and sterile till then, waiting to be fertilized. Why get into a fume at the odd behavior of the people round him? The master of the house was full of whims and crotchets. Well, his crotchets would pass. And although Joana, in her unobtrusive way, was at present crabby and looked at him askance, it was only the reflection of the hole-and-corner mystification that lay dismal over the holding.

One afternoon Joana had to go to town for the week's supplies. When she got back, she couldn't find Alice either in the house or anywhere near it. Loas and Barbaças had been out in the garden all the time, fixing the canes to support the climbing beans, and neither of them could say where the girl had hidden herself. Loas answered grumpily, annoyed at having his work interrupted, pleasant work for hands that took pride in their skill. Then, as if the implication had just struck him, he suddenly straightened his lank torso and stood there preoccupied. His wife, he could see, had gone back to have a look through the stable door; then he watched her disappear after a time on the other side of the rise. He knew what that meant. Lately a bond of understanding had arisen between them that the previous years of habit had been unable to produce. It had been created by their anxiety, by one secret shared, rather than by affection.

Joana found Alice careering along the road. Alice and the donkey emerged in a cloud of dust; and the more quickly the donkey ran at the girl's excited shouts, the more she urged it on. When Alice saw her mother, she went very red and slowly slipped down from the donkey's back. She'd got used to the feeling of guilt now associated with being with the donkey; it had become a secret desire for a forbidden pleasure; and so she ran away from her mother's scolding, making toward the house. Joana picked up the halter and led the animal back to the holding by the least conspicuous path. Events had got the better of her capacity for resistance or resignation.

That night, when Alice was asleep, Joana drew back the covering from her body and examined it closely for any sign of disease. Till then, she'd been afraid to face such an examination, but now she felt hard-pressed and desperate enough to put aside her fears. On Alice's abdomen she found a little water blister with a ring of red round it, and although she'd foreseen that sooner or later she might find something revealing the latent presence of the disease, she felt staggered and crushed. She went and shook her husband, who was sleeping coiled up like a worm.

"Sell the donkey!" she said to him.

Loas rubbed his startled eyes.

"What's the matter? What is it? Has somebody stolen the donkey?" he stammered, his face full of dazed anxiety.

"We've got to sell it."

"What's that?" he asked again, still heavy with sleep.

"I've just found a blister on the girl's body. She still goes on playing with the donkey."

Loas scratched his scalp savagely. His bare feet came out of the bed; his head drooped over his skinny ribs.

"Blast it, Joana!" he exclaimed, then went on in a plaintive, timid voice, "Do you think the blister means anything?"

He would have liked to ask other questions, too, but he was afraid of the answers.

"I don't know, but we've got to settle it once and for all."

"Yes, that's right. We've got to settle it. Blast me, we've really got to settle it once and for all. We'll take the girl to the healer tomorrow. And you, tie that damned donkey up safe somewhere."

"Sell it."

Loas took a deep breath.

"Sell it! Sell it!" he retorted with a violence that seemed to throw the blame for everything onto Joana. "And what then? Don't you know we need the donkey?"

He buttoned his shirt, stuffed it into his trousers, and went out to pace restlessly through another night.

17

That matter of seeing the healer was really a man's job, but Loas was unable to stop Joana from going with her daughter. With both of them away, Barbaças would remain in charge of the holding.

"Listen, Barbaças. Alice has got a blister on her belly. We're going to take her to the healer. You look after the donkey and . . . the holding."

"All right."

A good thing the lad didn't trouble to ask a lot of awkward questions. From the holding to the healer's cottage was quite some distance. Barbaças couldn't understand why they should get rattled over a little blister, and, what's more, not use the donkey to carry the girl. But that was their affair. Loas could break his back carrying her, if he liked.

The healer's cottage lay over toward Spain, on the outskirts of a dust-baked, remote village. First a few good miles of scarlet oak and olive plantations, then bare dusty plateaus not far from a river the dry tortured landscape would never lead you to expect.

Joana, Loas, and the girl first caught sight of the village in the midday heat. They had left behind the regions of good deep earth crossed at times by woods that reminded Joana of the kind of countryside she had known in her girlhood. Each time they came to these woods, she would breathe in the light pine-scented air, holding her breath to keep it with her as long as possible. The ruins of a castle marked the village, with a cluster of white houses round them, so white they seemed to have come fresh from the brush, standing haughtily by the asphalt road, which, seen from a distance, seemed to simmer in a dazzling dust. Still farther on, almost abruptly, the burnt land lost all vegetation, and merged far away into the blue lower slopes of the frontier mountain ranges.

Loas felt numb and heavy about the legs. This long while he'd been carrying the girl pickaback on his shoulders, and fatigue made him want to find fault with something.

"Don't you think it's time we had something to eat?"

Joana stopped and opened the packet of food. Loas smelled the bread and bacon, and lost interest.

"What I need is something to drink."

Alice quickly held out her hands for something to eat, afraid her father's remark would put the meal off till later.

Loas watched the pleasure with which she bit into the bacon. There was certainly nothing wrong with her appetite, and good appetite meant good health. That was what he conveyed in the almost cheerful glance he exchanged with his wife. Now that they were near the healer's cottage, he felt he'd like to turn back. He was afraid to have their fears confirmed. Would the man know anything about such diseases? No, that wasn't what he wanted to know. He couldn't even believe the girl was ill. No, she wasn't ill. Then would the man be able to tell whether she'd caught any infection? But infection meant illness. And with the girl's appetite like that, dammit all, it wasn't possible!

Loas couldn't take his eyes off the child's movements, the speed with which she got through her lunch. Feeling his eyes on her seemed to make her eat more and more quickly, and this in turn helped to allay her parents' fears. Good appetite meant good health. Could Barbaças possibly be ill, always nibbling at anything he could lay hands on, picking on the sly any fruit he found ripening on a tree? Could anybody laughing, eating, and leaping about like Alice be afflicted with such a disease? Laughing? No, she didn't laugh these days. She seemed out of spirits. She ate well; she had a good appetite; but she wasn't as lively as she used to be. Maybe it was sickness that damped her spirits. No, she wasn't ill. And that damned donkey had already got through all the fodder they'd laid by in the autumn! Animals must have wonderful resistance against disease. And what if animals aren't liable to catch leprosy? . . .

194

Dammit all, was that likely? If so, the donkey had come to the holding as sound as any other. And so Alice . . .

"Alice has finished. Let's move on."

Joana abruptly put a stop to this ray of hope. The healer would tell them. Healers are born under a sign, and what they say is sure. Now he was eager again to get to the healer's cottage. And so he set off once more with no thought for his weary muscles.

"Listen, Joana. I want to ask the man a question. Don't forget to remind me."

"What man?"

"The healer."

Some tomfool idea of his. And Joana stepped briskly ahead. At the first cottage they came to, Loas asked where the healer's house was.

"At the bottom of that fallow. Quite near. You can follow the cart track."

The cart track. Everybody knew that. People came from all over the province, and from still farther afield. Farmers, knowledgeable men, people from all over the place. He must be a man who knew a thing or two. What would he have to say about the girl?

Joana was now crossing a patch of stubble left from green barley crop. Farther on, vegetable furrows, waiting for winter. Then, suddenly, in front of them, a tiled roof and arrogant bright yellow walls, trying to look different from the usual low-built white cottages.

They had to wait a few minutes, Loas holding the girl tight as though shielding her from some threat; then a man came down the slope at a leisurely pace and opened the door. He was young and rather chubby, waistcoat negligently un-buttoned, and not at all surprised at the visit.

"What do you want?" he asked carelessly.

"I've brought my daughter," Loas explained, stuttering over the words.

"Come in here." Not an invitation, an order. Loas went and stood closer to his wife, both of them humble and abashed.

The healer offered them two chairs, and they sat down as

stiff as ramrods (Dammit all, why was it a man couldn't feel at ease there?), while he drew up a canvas chair and lounged lazily in it. Loas, out of politeness, had removed his hat, but the healer, as though conceding a favor, invited him to put in on again.

Loas looked at Joana, Joana looked at Alice, and Alice, feeling scared, took refuge at her father's knees. Which of them would be bold enough to begin?

"Who sent you here?"

"Nobody."

The man scratched his ears with a pencil, swinging his legs carelessly. He seemed bored.

"Where do you come from?"

Loas turned to his wife again, and she answered briefly: "Not far away."

"I don't know you. Isn't there anyone you can go to in your own district?"

Shy but fascinated, Alice looked at her father.

"There's a little man who sells a few herbs," Loas answered deprecatingly, "but he doesn't know much. You're the man people talk about everywhere."

The healer smiled his agreement. When he smiled, you could see that one of his canines had grown over the next tooth. Alice couldn't keep her eyes off it; the unknown man reminded her of an angry cat.

"Good. Now tell me which of you is ill."

Again Loas looked at his wife for support, and, as she lowered her eyes, the healer took advantage of the pause to cut in again himself.

"I can tell you that," he said, passing his hands over the dust that had gathered on the small table laden with medicine bottles. When he noticed Loas's astonishment, he spoke directly to him: "What doctors have you been to?"

"Me?" asked Loas.

"Yes, you. Sometimes you pass very bad nights, don't you?" Loas scratched the back of his neck, unable to find a suitable reply. "And there are days you don't feel as fit as others. Sometimes you feel a heaviness over the eyes. And there are times when you get angry over nothing at all."

Suddenly, Loas looked straight at Joana. The devil take the woman! So she'd gone behind his back. He felt he'd fallen into a wretched trap.

"Damn it all!" he barked out at last in a voice that had thrown off all polite reserve.

"Now, now," said the man without any change of expression. "Your nerves are out of order. You suffer from nervous irritative neurasthenia. Have you taken any tonics?"

His plump face and sanguine look challenged Loas's meager, puzzled glance, and settled on the farmer's hands fidgeting restlessly on his knees. Loas was on the point of putting them out of sight when the healer caught them.

"Let me have a look at your hands.... You know, sometimes the illness you've got is so bad that it even weakens the parts."

Joana got up, determined to put an end to the misunderstanding, when the healer stopped her by pointing his finger at her face.

"And you're the one who's got to look after him. If you hadn't brought him to me, it was more than certain that the parts would've weakened altogether. Some people even get 'pileptic St. Vitus's dance, which leads to 'pilepticism."

Loas put his hands to his parts. A cold sweat broke out on his forehead. Dumbfounded, he didn't know what to say or think. The man had guessed everything! Yes, all those things he'd mentioned had troubled him for quite some time: bad nights, sudden rages, heaviness over the eyes—and as for the parts, of course, during the last few years ... Devil take her, Joana had laid the trap for him! But he saw now it was a good thing she had. Otherwise, he'd never've believed there was anything the matter with him. And if he'd done nothing about feeling queer, he would've ended up with 'pilepticism!

This time he looked at his wife with humble gratitude, and just at that moment she swiftly picked up Alice's frock before the girl could make any difficulty about it, and said sharply:

"You're mistaken, sir. It's the girl who's ill. She's got this blister on her belly."

For a moment the healer lost face. His nostrils quivered, and a glint of cruelty showed in his look.

"I was aware of that," he said. "There's quite a bit of it about. But her father's illness had to come first."

"Is the blister serious?"

The healer showed his gums in a mirthless smile, revealing the overlapping tooth. With glittering eyes and dilated nostrils, as though seized with lust to give pain, he answered with grim severity:

"Yes. Very serious."

18

     Loas felt that this talk with the healer needed reflection. And it wasn't with stiff tired legs and the child riding on his shoulders that a man could straighten out his ideas. This half-hour past he'd been on the point of telling Joana that he was going to sit down by the roadside to rest a bit, and she could go on in front with the girl in her arms if she'd a mind. And so the moment came when he passed his hand over his forehead in a weary gesture, gave the signal to halt, as if wondering what to do next, and set Alice down on the ground.

     "You go on, Joana. You go on. I've got a pain in my guts." Maybe he had got a pain in his guts, and elsewhere, too. Without further delay he'd got to think the matter out there and then, in the quiet of that solitary place, turn everything over the healer had said. The devil take it, strange dark words he'd spoken. Could it be true that he'd got nervous irritative neurasthenia? Yes. He'd got it, all right. The man had picked on his brusque changes of mood, his feeling queer, his bad nights. So the rest must be true, too. And that tale of weakness in the parts . . . Dammit all, the man'd hit the mark there! He'd have to be careful. He was ill, very close to that 'pilepticism the healer had talked about, and he'd never suspected anything like that. . . . And what about Alice? How could he forget her health was more important than everything else? Well, the healer had begun by telling them there was an epidemic of these blisters, no doubt so as not to worry them with the true nature of the disease, till, he, Loas, had taken him into a corner, out of Alice's earshot, and told him about the donkey, about its coming from a leper, that it'd been running about all over their holding, and they couldn't keep Alice away from it.

"Morphew, did you say?" the man had shouted, darting a grim look at Joana. (What had the healer got against Joana?) *"Morphew?* Then it's hopeless!" He'd said that the donkey must be fumigated immediately, and the girl, too, with branches of furze in quantity roughly equivalent to Alice's weight. They would have to make a bonfire with the furze and hold the girl and the donkey over the flames till it had all burnt down to ashes. And after the treatment, the girl must be prevented from going near the donkey ever again.

"Won't the fire burn her belly?"

"That may be," the healer had opined, "but it'll burn the morphew too."

"And . . . and . . . who's strong enough to hold the donkey with its belly singeing?"

"Well, the owner. That's you, isn't it? And aren't you the girl's father?"

Yes, the man was right. But what if the donkey took it into its head to kick out, and gave him a kick in the parts?

"But . . . does it have to be the girl's father?"

"Well, no, it doesn't have to be."

That's what he wanted to hear. . . . And so now, with the wide silence of the heath all round him, he'd got to think up some way of carrying out the treatment without risk to his own vulnerable body. A kick in the parts would be the last straw. Would Barbaças be willing to undertake the job? Earlier on, he might have. But lately, he'd been given to looking down his nose when told to do anything. Pigheaded, he was, suspicious. It was quite plain he was beginning to boggle at things. He'd want to know the reason for the fumigations, and would immediately jump to the conclusion it was some way of having dealings with the devil. No, he wouldn't be able to count on Barbaças. If only the healer hadn't mentioned that question of the parts. . . . (A sharp fellow, that! He'd seized at once on that most secret thing!) Otherwise, of course, he wouldn't have wanted anybody else to take his place in the treatment his daughter needed; but as things were, it was clear he'd have to be careful. . . . What about Vieirinha? Bless me, Vieirinha was the chap! You'd only have to tell him that these performances with donkeys and furze were charms to win women's good graces. . . . A good thing Vieirinha was that way inclined! Before going back to the holding, he'd take a turn by Vieirinha's hut. The chap was still strong enough to hang on to the donkey's sides and keep it in place over the fire. They'd begin the fumigation treatment that very night.

Having solved his difficulties, Loas got up much lighter than when he'd sat down, and set off again almost cheerful.

Joana and Alice were now about an hour's walk ahead. Alice had to run to keep up with her mother, and she'd pull at her skirts now and again, trying to make her slow down or come out of her silence. Joana was walking along in such a hurry, she looked as if she wanted to put the biggest distance as quickly as possible between herself and the healer, or between herself and the sun-baked heath they had to cross before reaching the pinewood. She was racing along. Trying to get away from the healer's sickening verdict? *Morphew, leprosy!* Running away from the flat heath, from anxiety, from Loas's simpleminded, vacillating speculations? Where was Joana running to, with no thought for the girl's weary legs?

Their bare feet kicked up the dust on the road. The dust rose up, settled on their faces, on their clothes, and kept pace with them till they reached the broom-covered ground. Two weeks of clear sky were enough to bring the dust clouds back over the plain and the roads. Dust, dryness, solitude. On all sides the warm odor of wheat, sensuous and still, mingling with the smell from stretches where stubble lay moldering till the plow would bury it again under the soil, when sowing time came round. Men's thoughts, too, lay stagnant in the low land where there were no storms, rain, mountains, trees, or winds to churn them up and clarify them. Running away from the plain, from the wheat, Joana was running away from her own brooding thoughts.

Each year, as soon as the weather dried up, foretelling the torpid months when earth and sky were embers in a fire, Joana became restless and even more taciturn than usual. With a keenness the passage of time never dulled, the longing for her own part of the country woke up in her. The swarthy monotony of the plain, always the same year after year, like prison for life, could never appeal to her; however long she lived there, and however often she saw the same landscape, the persistent sameness only made her long more and more for the varied harmony of her childhood's home, where the days, the colors and odors of the earth, never stagnated to sediment. There, colors followed each other nimbly in fugitive richness, passing like fleeting butterflies, with light pure mountain breezes blowing them from north to south, mingling them, forever renewing them, so that they never outstayed their welcome and the senses never tired. The sky was never still, but gave color, now with light, now with shade, to an exuberant world in which people, shaped by the ever-changing landscape, were brisk and sociable.

The curse that had fallen on the holding added its weight to the heavy brooding of the plain; both together formed a muddy something that clogged the air. Like the plain, Joana's lungs were clogged, too. Mud, nothing but mud. As though plain and plague together had swollen up like a dough with yeast fermenting in it. Joana breathed deeply in a desperate effort to throw off the oppression. Her whole body longed for the rugged strength of mountains, virile winds that quicken the senses, trees that purify the air one breathes.

Each year, when the smooth sky curved gently over the earth in its few months' sleep, Joana was stirred into a feeling of rebellion against the plain. She would leave the holding, make her way over estates and fallow lands, and take refuge for a few hours in the woods. And when she got there, it always came over her that her domestic problems were in some way bound up with the plain. This wandering away had begun to be something of a mystic pilgrimage. She had forgotten almost all the prayers she knew in her girlhood, but it sometimes came about that she held strange talk with saints when she took refuge in this green oasis of majestic trees. Lost amid the mysterious rustling of the woods, she would call upon some saint by name, as though calling upon someone in her own family. From this flesh-and-blood appeal, the saint would better understand her longing to return to the north country. But as she became more and more immersed in her surroundings, the gods in some way became one with the trees and leaves, and even with the murmur of the wind. And finally she made her supplications without distinction, or simultaneously, to the woods and to the gods.

Alice noticed that they were getting farther away from the road to the holding, that the woods were rising up and drawing closer to them. Like her father, she looked upon the top of the hill, where the trees reached up to the sky, as a forbidden place. Joana had to take the girl by the arm and drag her along so as not to leave her standing behind. The child had been born on the plain, a shoot of its turbid languor. And Joana dragged her along with more and more determination.

"I'm tired, Mam."

"We'll soon sit down for a rest."

They sat down in a clearing among the eucalyptus trees and pines. The dry ground was carpeted with violet-colored flowers. Joana greedily breathed in the scent of grass and leaves —but even here the rich soft odor of the plain gradually penetrated. Rising from the depths of the purple savannah, feeling its way along the last light before dusk fell, the musk of the plain reached even here. Joana got up again, and taking Alice by the hand, went even farther into the heart of the wood. Here the trunks rose so close together that there was no gap revealing the plain. Alice looked round with more fright than curiosity. Where did her mother want to take her?

"Do you like it, Alice?" Her mother's voice was soft, eager, remote.

"Like what, Mam?"

Like what! The child was a real sprig of the plain, she'd never understand.

Years earlier, before Alice was born, Joana had brought her husband here. She'd hoped that, caught by the magic of the woods, he'd make up his mind to change his way of life and move far away from the plain. But Loas, looking at the solemn lush-green trees, had felt challenged by a secret, mysterious world—and had taken himself off before she could find courage to ask again. Neither Loas nor his daughter would ever understand. Nor their daughter—flesh of her flesh, with the quick blood of the north country folk running in her veins! How deeply she had wanted her child to respond to the deep call of the past! Perhaps if Alice had been in the habit of coming here, the still air of the pines would have freed her from the torpor of the plain and the taint of disease! But what was the use of wishing? The child had the torpor of the plain in her blood. Joana was alone in her passion for the woods. She knew it was so. And, swallowing hard to keep back her tears, she began to think about her own part of the country as though she had nothing else left on earth. As if her own part of the country were nothing but color, leaves, trees. As if her longing for the past were only a yearning for a color, a yearning for a wood.

19

"But why is it necessary to bring the donkey and the girl into it?" Vieirinha asked again.

Loas had found Vieirinha inside his hut, lying on a mat with apples and melons spread round him so odorous that the man himself smelled like garden fruit. Fat as he was, and in such surroundings, he looked like some pagan god. Loas lifted one of the melons to his nose, to hide the fact that it was hard to find an answer.

"It's a secret," he said at last. "It's no use trying to guess. When I set about reading St. Cipriano's book, or during certain talks with the devil, I do nothing but obey. And that's all. I'm scared stiff of asking questions."

An indulgent smile flickered over Vieirinha's lips.

"But, my friend, a man has to ask questions. A man can't allow anybody, human or demon, to shut his mouth for him."

"But these aren't men, Vieirinha. What'd I gain by asking questions?"

Vieirinha put one fist on the mat and heaved himself up.

"Well, it would be like putting the questions to yourself, and that's already something."

Just one of Vieirinha's funny ideas. But the talk reminded Loas that he hadn't managed to get the explanation he wanted from the healer. Was leprosy catching? The devil, wasn't it the same as if he'd asked the question? The man had said he must fumigate the girl and the donkey, and then keep them absolutely apart. That, of course, made it quite plain. He'd seen the look the healer had darted at Joana—like accusing her because she hadn't kept the girl in the house, and hating her for such negligence. And he was quite right. Joana was dense.

But now everything was going to change. He could swear

to that. After seeing the healer, he felt that peace had come back to him. And to the holding, too. Now there was a definite enemy to fight, he wouldn't be just flailing his arms about blindly. The stubborn optimism of his nature surged up inside him again in waves of incorrigible well-being. The accursed disease was at last going to meet an adversary who would prove to be one too many for it. He felt vigorous, cheerful, eager for the battle that would be a new epic in his life. Dammit all, was it really possible to reach the point of feeling pleased because something terrible, something devastating had befallen the holding?

He'd been asking himself too many questions about the whole thing. And here was friend Vieirinha prodding him on to more questions! He felt so full of a number of contradictory feelings that it was on the tip of his tongue to blurt out proudly to his companion, "We've got leprosy on the holding!" Then, when he saw him knocked all of a heap, he'd add: "But we're not the sort of folk to sit and twiddle our thumbs. We'll fight it tooth and claw." And Vieirinha would go spouting all over the town that those people on the holding were as brave as lions.

But that wasn't the point. What he had to do now was put the trick over on Vieirinha, persuade him to take charge of the donkey during the fumigation. If the chap could just sniff the possibility of making a few conquests, he'd do his damndest before he'd let the donkey out of his grasp. The healer hadn't specified how many treatments were necessary— but Loas was convinced that if Alice's blister were dried up, the whole disease would be wiped out. And thenceforward Alice could be quite sure she'd never be allowed any further contact with the donkey.

"Well, then, Vieirinha, can I count on you?"

"I'm almost ashamed to admit it, my friend, but I feel ready for anything. Only, it does seem idiotic to bring the donkey and the girl into it. Are you sure you've got it right?"

"I've been wondering, too, why the girl and the donkey come into it. Of course, they're both females. But, listen, I've

206

got it now: The girl stands for innocence, and the donkey for the beast. It's so that the furze smoke'll drive both from your path. Otherwise, it wouldn't be proper."

"That's a good idea you've got there, my friend. There're no flies on you."

"I can count on you, then?"

Vieirinha footed away the melons that cluttered the exit to the fodder plot, and, with Loas following after, went outside to look at the motionless, stormy sky.

"You're a real friend, Loas. I hadn't realized what a good friend you were. You came to offer me a service. And then you ask whether you can count on me!"

"All right, Vieirinha, I—"

"And you're ready to bring the girl and the donkey into it, too, just so that I can spend a few happy hours with some strumpet or other."

"Well, not quite that. I—"

"But you've already forgotten that it was old Vieirinha who squandered the money you gave to Barbaças for a donkey; that it was old Vieirinha who got the lad put in prison. . . . Such a low-down trick, Loas! No, I don't want you to go to all this trouble for me. I'm not worth it."

"But you want a woman, don't you? Damn it all, Vieirinha, it was all arranged! You're not going to back out now. . . ."

"Yes, I'm going to back out. I'm not worth all that trouble, just to get some bitch or other."

"But I've got all the words for the spells ready."

Vieirinha shook his head with grand determination. And Loas, seeing it, realized it wouldn't be easy to make him swerve from his orgy of repentance. He coughed discreetly, waiting for his friend to notice, when he came to pause, that nobody was contradicting him. Oh, no, he wasn't going to let Vieirinha, with his belated twinges of conscience, bring his plans to nothing. Let him talk himself out. And so Loas, to pass the time and curb his impatience, began to think of other things. The vegetables that Vieirinha had planted round the hut had

come on well, and a heady scent lay sweetish in the air. Flies
and bees came down from the sky, unable to resist the warm
perfume of fecundity. They came down with a dry humming
sound and, when they got near the two men, formed into a
ring and flew round them in ever-narrowing circles. Loas
waited for one of the flies to settle on his companion's head,
then cautiously stretched out his hand, at the same time signing
to Vierinha to stand still so as not to disturb his prey. Vieirinha, annoyed that Loas was not paying more attention to him,
broke off in the middle of his discourse to watch. And when
at last he could go on, he discovered to his disgust that he'd
forgotten what he was going to say. He was about to give vent
to a few home truths—but Loas was already after a second fly.
With one hand he held Vieirinha's elbow, the other hand
raised to make his catch. His movements were silent and supple
as a lad's and it was a real treat to see him.

"Don't move, Vieirinha; then I can get this one, too."
It was so catching that Vieirinha was soon engaged in the
summer sport.

"If flies were only birds, my friend, what a dainty dish
they'd make!"

Loas smiled complacently. Now he was sure it'd be safe
to come to the point.

"We could get going with that plan tonight, Vieirinha.
There'll be moonlight."

"Eh, what's that?"

"Doesn't it appeal to you?"

"But I'll be putting you to the deuce of a lot of trouble
just for me. I'm quite sure I don't deserve it."

Loas patiently wagged his head; he was quite aware of
everything his friend wanted to say, and understood his
scruples. But with a magnanimous gesture he waved them all
aside.

"It's no trouble at all, my friend. In fact, there's nothing
I like better than working some well-prepared spells."

Now they were off to the holding to collect the child and

the donkey, but Vieirinha still had a thing or two to get off his chest. Far behind them, the straw-thatched hut under the dark, viscous sky had an orange glitter about it, the glitter of corn. Vieirinha turned round time after time to give an appreciative look at the place, his hermit's refuge at certain seasons.

"What do you think of it, my friend? Don't you like my melon patch?" But that wasn't what he wanted to say. "Look here, Loas, when you drove me away from the holding that time"—Loas looked a bit put out—"you were angry with me. You hadn't forgotten all that to-do about the donkey. I know I deserved it all, my friend. Or was there some other reason, perhaps?"

Loas measured the danger. If he gave Vieirinha a further pretext for a new orgy of self-accusation, his plan would be jeopardized once more. He cast round desperately for an excuse.

"We all have our off days, Vieirinha."

"Yes, days when we pick on our friends' mistakes . . ."

"It wasn't that at all, blast it! It was something quite different. Can you guess what it was? Do you want to know?" But not lighting on any quickly thought-up reason, he fell back on his Sibylline manner. "It was something I'm not going to tell you."

"But I'm not blaming you. You were entirely in the right. I'm a wretch, nothing but a filthy pig."

"It had nothing whatever to do with that, dammit! It'd better tell you what it was. I'd got a pain in my parts."

Loas put his hands to his trousers, and by a strange coincidence, at the same moment, he felt a sharp pain shoot through him as though his parts had shrunk to a frail string crushed between pincers. He felt that was the end. Had the healer deceived him? Was his disease the dreaded morphew?

"Do you suffer from it now?"

"A bit. Sometimes. Yes, I've got a pain now. And when it's like that, I say things I don't mean. I'm sorry, Vieirinha." Loas's face looked as drawn and pale as wax.

"And on top of it all you say you're sorry! Sit down for

a spell and rest. . . . I never thought of anything like that, my friend. That's bad, that's bad," said Vieirinha, sympathizing with him and helping him to sit down.

"You know a lot of things," Loas began in a formal tone, "so tell me how people catch diseases."

"They catch them from germs in the air. The germs get into our mouths, noses, and ears. And we give them out again. They're carried through the air, and other people breathe them in."

Loas sat unraveling the meaning of these words, and, not to disturb him, Vieirinha remained silent.

"So it's no use killing anybody who's ill," he decided at last.

"Kill!" exclaimed Vieirinha, staring at his companion with dismay. "Of course not. But who kills sick people?"

"It isn't only people who fall ill. Animals get sores that are catching. Don't some people kill mangy dogs?"

"I don't see what you're getting at," Vieirinha answered, half in disgust, half in pity.

"And those germs you talk about, do they infect the earth, trees, and wheat, too?"

"You're asking the devil of a lot of questions!"

"But you said just now we ought to ask about everything."

"I didn't mean foolish questions."

"Let me go on asking questions, just for today," Loas begged with a glassy stare, his hands still clenched in his trousers pockets, "even though I know that questions do sometimes get us more mixed up than before. Why do I want a holding and mules and machines? If I kept on asking myself why, shouldn't I finish by losing the desire for them?"

Vieirinha's head was swimming. Deep down, his friend's talk quite frightened him. He ought never to have come.

"No, no, my friend. You'd find a stronger reason for fighting for what you want. You'd fight to more effect. There's something you want. There's something I want. There's something we all want, and we go after it blindly. We all feel the need of something. A need," he said again, in a feverish voice.

210

"You say 'fight,' Vieirinha. Fight who?"

"With yourself. You've got to begin by struggling with yourself."

"With myself?"

But Vieirinha wasn't listening anymore. He'd shut himself up in his own sad thoughts. His face looked old. He was as drained and withdrawn as an old man. His words, however, were still echoing in Loas's ears, and drew him into a bottomless well of speculations. Struggle with yourself. Vieirinha's words swelled and filled out and began to glow in his mind. However obscure the words, he took them for a revelation.

"Tell me some more, Vieira."

"I don't know much, friend Loas. What else do you want to know?"

"How should I know? Just tell me anything that comes into your head."

"About the jungle?"

"The jungle? No. Tell me about things that are true."

"So you think I've been telling lies, do you?"

Loas looked at him wearily and explained what he meant in a small, gentle voice.

"That isn't what I mean, Vieirinha. I mean you should talk to me about things I can understand, things that help me. . . ."

"About women?"

"Now, Vieirinha, I've got a pain in my parts, so I don't want to hear about women. I'm ill, and I don't know whether I ought to think about women."

"Well, then, why shouldn't we fumigate your parts, too? Do you think you can live without women? Surely, that isn't possible?"

And Vieirinha clutched his friend feverishly by the arm. Loas saw a look of crazy, insatiable desire on his face that made little furrows on his ruddy cheeks, gave a moist look to his eyes, and made his nostrils quiver. Loas was deeply touched. How could he have thought of playing on his friend's weakness, taking advantage of his tragedy to use him as a tool because

211

he, Loas, was a coward? No, he wasn't acting right in this, because Vieirinha's desire was not mere sensuality. It was something deep, something terribly dramatic.

"Damn it all, Vieirinha, I'm nothing but a monster! Don't look at me like that! I've just been fooling you all along the line. The fumigations aren't meant for you."

"But didn't you want me to hold the donkey firm?"

"Yes, that's right. I wanted you to hold the donkey that came from the leper woman."

And having got it out, Loas looked defiantly at his friend, saying nothing further, but his look full of meaning as he gave time for the whole significance of the dreadful hint to sink in. Throughout these last months Vieirinha had seemed to attach no importance to the fact that the donkey had been in close contact with a leper, but now Loas wanted to make the whole drama clear to him, and confess the low trick he had meant to play.

"Do you understand now, Vieirinha?"

"Yes, I think so, my friend."

"And can you see why I've been so fed up with everything?"

"Yes, I can understand that, my friend. But I think you've let it get on your nerves. You're not old enough yet for that to happen to you. Try with some other woman! Sometimes a man gets stale. . . ."

"With some other woman?"

"Only once, of course. Your Joana would have to agree it was just a health measure."

"But what are you talking about, Vieirinha? Why do you think I came to you when I talked about holding the donkey for me? Don't you really see the point yet?"

"Yes, I see the point, as I've already said. You've got a pain in your parts, and the devil or somebody else advised you to fumigate your body. And you need a friend to hang on to the donkey's tail. You needn't have beaten about the bush. But what beats me"—here Vieirinha put his finger to his lips in sudden perplexity—"what I still can't fathom is what the donkey and the girl have got to do with it."

After this remark, Loas was just as puzzled as Vieirinha. It was astounding that Vieirinha should go on being stupidly unaware of the terrible threat of leprosy. You could talk to him about lepers, put the facts under his very nose—and not a quiver or thought of horror showed on his oily face. Vieirinha could listen to talk about the donkey and the leper who had owned it with much more composure than when you talked to him about strumpets. How was it that people could at one and the same time be both shrewd and stupid? It was useless to go on giving hints, and Loas couldn't get up enough courage to tell him bluntly what it was all about.

"Yes, that's what I can't understand," Vieirinha repeated, rather vexed at his friend's continued silence.

Loas narrowed his eyes as though the bright reflected light of sunset troubled him. A snipe settled on the stump of a young ilex tree and kept a wary eye on the two men coming along the road. Loas frightened it off with a stone.

"In fact, I don't understand it at all," Vieirinha said again.

"You don't want to understand! You don't want to understand anything. Be off with you!" Loas burst out, stamping with his boots, like a horse pawing the ground.

"You're always sending me off now, and I'd like to know why. But I'm not going. And I'm not going to ask any questions, either. All I require to know is that you need me to hold the donkey."

Loas shrugged his shoulders. Well, so long as Vieirinha, even though not understanding, insisted on being friendly, he'd carry out the healer's advice to the very end. Let Vieirinha go on thinking the fumigations were necessary because of the pain in his parts. He didn't care. But this feeling of indifference wasn't peace, only abdication. He'd lost all confidence, enthusiasm, and peace. This talk with Vieirinha had only opened up new vistas of doubt and perplexity—but for the present he only felt tired. He'd let himself go with the current. He'd carry on with the fumigations.

20

They had spent the late evening cutting the furze and securing the donkey over the bonfire. And the climax of it all was an infernal din, when Alice, fastened to the animal's crupper, realized that her father and his friend had not found the proper way of keeping the creature pegged to the sacrifice. Shouting at each other, and licked by the flames, they all looked like demons running about in hell.

When it was all over, Vieirinha felt deaf from the noise, and his eyes smarted from the smoke. The donkey, with its legs astraddle, looked as if it were in rut. . . . They had come away worn out, looking silly, annoyed with each other, perhaps ashamed at having played their part in something wrong.

Making their way back over the heath, their shadows were etched on the road by sharp moonlight, and looked like the furtive shapes of evildoers.

The silence of his two companions got on Loas's nerves.

"Shut that girl up in her room night and day," he said to Joana. "We've got to burn the disease out. There's a faith inside me that tells me we've got to sweat it out completely, till people in our house can open their mouths and breathe freely again."

Loas spoke vehemently through his teeth, yet at the same time anxious for approval. Vieirinha in the rear—limping along from a kick the donkey had given him when a shower of sparks from the furze had scattered on its belly—heard the words quite clearly, but they didn't seem to mean anything at all. In fact, friend Loas had never had his wits quite in the right place. And the best thing he, Vieirinha, could do then, hungry as he was and with a pain in his buttock, was to make off for his hut without further fuss, and not wait for a meal or expect some rational explanation for the strange behavior of these folk.

Loas saw him moving away, but made no attempt to stop him. Later, he wouldn't let Barbaças put the donkey in the stable, but tied it up himself in a makeshift pen right in front of the stone bench where everybody knew he would keep an eye on it.

The moonlight washed over the treetops, and the plain lay motionless in a silver lake. The silence of the night, the trees, the crops, all seemed caught up in a trance. The palpable presence of the plain was as if concentrated in a tumid odor bursting from the pores of the stillness. Loas breathed it in with an almost lascivious pleasure. It's an unpleasant smell, he thought. Why does the earth smell so bad? But he breathed it in with sensual satisfaction.

There stood the donkey in front of them; and Barbaças and Joana were so still and silent they looked like specters in the moonlight. The silence was oppressive. He'd better say something.

"Listen, Barbaças. I never asked you what you thought of those people at Malhadas. . . . "

"The folk who owned the donkey?"

"Yes," Loas replied, rather embarrassed.

"The man was half crazy. He kept stuffing me with oranges."

"That's what I thought, too. But they looked healthy enough, don't you think?"

Barbaças grunted an affirmative, but next moment, feeling nettled because he could see no sense in the talk, he added, "But I can't really remember, now."

Loas's nostrils were still quivering. The earth, or the moonlight, still gave off that smell. Was it the stench of a huge corpse rotting somewhere? The smell of bodies after copulation?

"The earth's tainted with disease, Barbaças."

"What do you mean, Master?"

Thoughts of the hard-baked earth of the summer months, withered grass, dust, rankled in Joana's memory. Her own mind

215

was like a dusty road. Had her husband understood at last that the plain was devouring them in its dry cracks and fissures?

The night breeze whispered over the holding, carrying wafts of smell. Was it the smell of burnt flesh? Loas got up and moved away behind the water machine, as though to make water. But he walked stealthily on, as if afraid of waking the earth up. He wanted to lean down over the ground and make sure, catch in his own nostrils whether the odor came from the grass, the leaves, the sated plain.

"Aren't you coming to bed?" Joana called.

Loas came back to the family group, but a feeling of restless excitement was beginning to rise in him. The donkey, still tethered, was stretching its neck toward the bucket of water that Barbaças, half afraid, and watching for his master's reaction, had brought and placed near it. After dipping its nose in the water, it swung its head from side to side, as though it too could scent the obscure odor that was troubling its owner's nostrils.

Loas got up again and went to the animal to stroke its crupper. The donkey lifted its head toward its master, and Loas saw something like the glitter of tears in its mild, troubled eyes, the moan of a wounded beast, or someone in lonely, desperate death agony. Maybe it had a presentment of the disease that was sapping its vitals. And it was then that Loas put a name to the smell that lay over the holding, filling his nostrils. The smell came from the donkey. It was the smell of leprosy. Again panic came over him.

"Have you put the girl to bed?" he asked Joana, just to say something to take his mind off the obsession.

His wife nervously pushed back her hair, black soft hair that as a girl she had oiled with olive oil to make it look glossier.

"Do you mean have I *locked* her in?" she asked. "Have I got to lock her up for the rest of her life?"

"Let me alone!" he shouted at her.

Joana went inside, followed by Barbaças.

The breeze was still rustling through the moonlight—light tremor of long cilia of wheat, grass, hay, and the restlessness of animals; but the whole thrill of it now turbid with the pollution of the contaminated plain.

Loas covered his head and nose with his hands, as if by so doing he could protect his brain and senses from the surrounding pestilence. He took a few steps over the holding, and, finding himself in front of the water machine—another ghost petrified in the moonlight—he fell to kicking at the mass of metal rusted by the presence of time. Then he laughed softly to himself. The machine was the symbol of all his failures, but he was still there, unchanged, ready to begin again right away. But where did he go wrong? Vieirinha had given him vague glimpses of an explanation. He'd got to free himself from the dross mixed in his own flesh. And the donkey, that poor dream come to nothing, was it just more dross to be got rid of? *Sell it!* But if he did sell it, wouldn't the ashes still be with him? Damn it all, perhaps the dross was all inside himself. *Fight with yourself! You've got to begin by fighting with yourself!* Wasn't the episode of the disease one of those many dark gulfs into which his irresolution plunged him, and which alternated with those other cyclic waves of rootless, aimless hope?

Loas looked round for support, and found only the shadow of his trouble. He tried to reconstruct in his mind all the events that had happened during the last weeks. Lifting his head so that the freshness of the night would clear his brain, he tried to remember what the holding and its inhabitants had been like before. How far away it all seemed! Suddenly he felt an irresistible need for action. He darted about the garden, the kitchen, the stable, and for lack of anything else to put his hands to, began pushing thistles into the rabbit hutches. But that wasn't enough to work off his restlessness. The night seemed to be expanding and contracting in a panting pulsation that was becoming unbearable. The night was like a huge lung that was being forcibly deflated, while waves of moonlight beat down on the straining creases of suffocation. Impossible to breathe in this place.

Loas had to go out for some fresh air. He took the donkey into the stable and saw it look in vain for green stuff in the manger. Barbaças kept the feed on a high shelf where the donkey couldn't reach it, and Loas stretched up and got it a measure of barley. Somebody else would have to take Alice's place for these tasks.

The donkey began to munch the grain, but without enthusiasm. Oh, so it's growing dainty. But the grass is getting dry and yellow. If it doesn't rain during the waning moon ... Loas was thinking. He'd better look up what the almanac said for the week. Now, with a good water machine, the holding would always be green. Perhaps Vieirinha could give him the name of some city chap well up in machinery who was neither a tippler nor a humbug.

He caught sight of a length of rusty wire near the donkey's hooves and, lingering on inside the stable, as though unwilling to go outside, tied it slowly to the bars of the manger. Then he got another measure of barley from the shelf, and at last went out, casting a stealthy glance at the donkey's belly. Another time they'd have to be more careful with the fumigation, and see that the flames didn't reach the flesh. But it's for its own good, he said, half aloud in excuse, as if there were someone there to hear it.

Now he'd go and shut himself in his room.

Stretched on his bed with his eyes closed, he couldn't sleep, though he was dead tired. Insomnia pulsed in his forehead like a thick hard vein. Anxiety had taken hold of him once more. Loas knew he'd find real peace only when a ray of light made everything quite plain. *Fight with yourself.* That's all right, Vieirinha, but what do you have to do to drive off ugly phantoms? Sell the donkey? Lock the girl up all her life as though in a prison? The devil, Barbaças was forgetting to put the feed in the manger. ... But if the healer was going to cure the disease in a few days' time, was it worth all this questioning and anxiety? What part did the disease play in the whole crop of problems that he could as yet only vaguely glimpse? And why did that smell lie over the land?

Suddenly the smell was in the house, too. The smell of the animal, of the holding, of disease. Loas thought of it creeping like a snake over sand, and he could hear the rustle of the earth yielding and shrinking in fear as it advanced. Holding

218

his breath, he listened to its approach.

He wanted to sit up straight to face the disease when it got to his bed, but his muscles were paralyzed. His arms and legs had turned into heavy lumps of flesh that were nothing but a burden, and he lay there till the smell moistened his skin like warm, viscous dew. He was bathed in sweat. And suddenly he fell asleep.

When he opened his eyes again, it was early morning, though the light creeping over the windowsill and peeping into the room was still moonlight. Behind it, however, a mild light could be sensed that would soon be dawn. Loas still felt drained, but he also felt refreshed. And although he tried not to think of his nightmare thoughts, when they did slip into his mind, he was relieved to feel they no longer harassed him. He was free of them. And, once the scarecrows of indecision were vanquished, he felt vigorous and incredibly clearheaded. With a few more fumigations, the girl would be cured and the disease would be expelled from the donkey's body. All the rest of it, leprosy, foul smells, had only been born of his fear lest disease should come and destroy the resurrection of the holding. In a few days, they could start all over again. That's what the healer had said, and healers were men born under a sign who were never mistaken. And that pain in his parts was of no consequence at all. If the worst came to the worst and it began to trouble him again, he'd follow Vieirinha's advice. That wretch of a Vieirinha! There was a real friend for you, and knowledgeable. He'd hung on to the donkey's tail; he'd almost hung on by his teeth just to make it stand still over the fire, though he knew quite well he wasn't making the effort in his own interest. Maybe Vieirinha was the sort who could settle down on a holding if you found him a wife for his bed. He'd have to think it over. True, Barbaças had a better pair of arms, but he'd never be the company that an intelligent man like Vieirinha was, who could keep you interested for two winters running just with tales about the jungle. Vieirinha knew a mort of things; perhaps he could even contrive to get the machine going.

"I'll get Vieirinha to come over today," Loas promised himself. He'd make him an honest, generous proposal, and give him an interest in the holding, seeing that Barbaças, like the blockhead he was, had let slip the opportunity for an agreement before the notary.

Sitting on his bed, waiting for daybreak, Loas felt that he wanted to get into immediate action. Work and sing away as he hadn't done this long while, because he could at last see clear through his problems. Very soon he would gather the family together in the garden, and tell them of his plan to call Vieirinha onto the holding. Of course, Barbaças, touchy and jealous as he was, would make a long face about it. He'd already been surprised because they hadn't taken him along with them to the healer's, and he'd certainly be even more surprised if he knew Vieirinha had taken a hand in the fumigation. (Hadn't that donkey given Vieirinha a good kick in the belly? Was it the belly or the hip? Anyway, it had been a merry night, after all!) But even if Barbaças did resent it, he wouldn't go through with the bluster of going back to town. He'd swallow his dissatisfaction because now, most of all, he'd feel the fear of a dog that doesn't want to be kicked out. How people on the holding had changed!

Yes, all this had got to be decided early. But how slow the morning was in coming! How long time was when there was nobody with a nimble tongue to make it pass quickly! Somebody like Vieirinha. Joana was asleep, Barbaças was asleep, and Alice, tired out with yesterday's jaunt, would certainly not wake up till the sun was high over the house. He mustn't forget to have a look at that blister, first thing, when she woke up. However, there they were, all asleep. How could people sleep so soundly, when the earth all around was quick with life and activity?

The long wait began to get on his nerves. He went to the window to see what time it was, and saw that the leaves were dripping with dew and that mist still hung in the branches of trees, waiting for the wind to disperse it. With this mist, perhaps the pasturage would last longer. The donkey was a devil for greenstuff.

At that moment, Loas heard the stealthy movement of steps under the window. Had Barbaças got up? No, that wasn't the sound of anybody belonging to the house. Whoever was down there didn't want to be heard. Damn it all, what if some thief were hanging round the house or perhaps round the stable? Of course, somebody was getting ready to steal the donkey. Loas fastened his pants up in a hurry and, on tiptoe to take the robber by surprise, went to the kitchen to get his shotgun from the peg. Whoever it was, he'd lay him out with two bursts of shot. Who the devil could it be? Somebody who knew his way about the outhouses, for sure. What if it were Vieirinha? Wasn't he the only one who knew where the donkey was kept? Well, well, he'd always had a suspicion that Vieirinha was not altogether to be trusted. If he'd been so keen to lend a hand, it must have been because he'd had his eye on the animal for some time. In that case it'd be Vieirinha who'd lie stretched on the ground. He'd make an example of him for all those thieves and loose livers from town!

When Loas got outside, with his gun at the ready, he clearly heard the creaking of the stable door. Oh, so the thief wanted to be peppered inside the trap? Perhaps he'd get what he wanted! Ho, there, Vieirinha, you just come out of there! Out of there, you filthy swine! . . . Holding his breath, Loas crept behind the young holm oak, finger on the trigger, waiting any moment for that scarecrow of a Vieirinha to come out leading the donkey by the halter. . . . But the minutes went by, and the stable door remained closed. Strange that the rogue should take so long to fix the halter. Had he scented the danger? Loas decided to lie in the grass, hiding his gun level with the ground. Sooner or later the fellow would have to come out, even if it meant waiting there the whole day. He'd much rather sight at him from a distance like this than get in a huddle with him in the small stable. Come out of there, you mad dog! No, better not shout. But what a relief to bawl insults at him in his own mind.

The door creaked again. The barrel of the gun emerged above the blades of grass, taking aim at the intruder, just as Alice, listening to make sure that all was silent round the house, stepped out of the door. Alice! Loas's finger lay frozen against the hollow of the trigger, and a sob came from his throat.

Alice made her way carefully by the garden wall and the house wall, moving like a transparent shadow, and finally disappeared through the cottage door. But her shadow image seemed to remain behind, fluttering like cold wings in the half-light that lay over the holding.

Loas didn't know what oaths to let fly, with his lips and in his heart. Alice, he was now sure of it, during all this time, had been getting up from her pallet each night to come and sleep near the donkey till dawn. The breath of their bodies, their sweat, had mingled in contamination. Leprosy had been in the flesh and blood of the girl this long while, and forever. To the end of time leprosy would be part of Loas's dreams, part of the soil, part of the grain. He wouldn't sell the donkey, as Joana had advised him. Wherever they took it, the animal would carry the devouring plague into the sap of the plain. Streams of impurity to find their way back to the holding. To sell it was no solution. He'd kill it. Loas heard the donkey pawing the ground in the stable, as if it had guessed what its master meant to do.

And then red sunrise flushed over everything, setting the mist aflame. To avoid thought, Loas stood looking at the sky for some minutes. Dawn had taken the gray curtain by surprise, rending it impatiently apart. It seemed to Loas that from one moment to the next, everything would go up in flame under the furious sun. Kill it. The sky, too, had come to share in the massacre. But it wasn't merely the massacre of the donkey. He himself, the holding, his dreams, his aspirations— all would be involved in the ruthless death pang.

"Joana!" he shouted, to spur on the anger inside him, an anger that he must keep flaring. "Joana! Joana!"

Two sheep dogs, slow and suspicious, got up from the dusty road that skirted the cottage and, roused by Loas's shouts, looked round for the head of the flock.

"Joana! Blast it! Joana!"

His wife, hair disheveled like a witch's, appeared at the

222

window. Seeing her husband with his gun in his hand, she ran out to him. He clutched her by the arm, and with an anxious affection that was not his usual habit, led her to the stable door.

"Bring the donkey out. I'm not selling it."

Joana sensed his tense desperation, and her heart contracted inside her. Tight-lipped, she heard him, without comment.

"Did you know the girl spends the nights side by side with that accursed donkey?" he went on.

Without answering, Joana opened the stable door, gripped the animal by its coat, and pushed it outside.

"Here it is. Kill it, Loas."

The animal blinked in the morning light, then went forward slowly and quietly, like a dromedary, toward its master. Loas held up his hand to stop it. Like this—no. He couldn't kill it now; he would kill it, but he didn't want it to collaborate in its own death. Earlier, with the barrel of his gun hidden in the grass, watching for Vieirinha to come out, that was different. But not like this. He'd got ready to settle Vieirinha's hash without his suspecting anything, and he wanted to destroy the donkey and the plague in the same way. Damn it all! He'd rather it'd been Vieirinha on the prowl. Now there was no question of thieves. There was just Vieirinha, who'd never been anything but an honest chap all the time, and the donkey, and the girl. No, it wasn't Vieirinha. Vieirinha had no part in this.

Loas was moving back all the time, as if setting the butt of his gun more firmly against his shoulder, while Joana, stiff and bleak, stood awaiting the shot; but he went on asking himself why Vieirinha's name kept turning up in his thoughts. And a sudden flash illumination shot across his mind: Vieirinha had never shown any distaste for the donkey, though he'd known the truth right from the beginning. Hadn't he been the one who'd told him in the first place it'd belonged to a leper woman? Yet he'd never shown any distaste for the donkey. Why? Dammit, Vieirinha knew all the time that animals didn't catch the disease! Though friend Vieirinha was pernickety, he'd never shown any disgust, because he knew the disease had been left behind at Malhadas.

"Joana! Joana! It isn't necessary to kill the donkey!" Joana was so amazed that her breath stuck in her throat. Her man was just the same as ever: weak and infirm of purpose. For the rest of their lives they'd be stuck in the muck of the plain, of the disease, of his irresolution.

"Don't put a face on like that! I tell you, it isn't necessary. Vieirinha knows that donkeys don't catch the morphew, though I've only just tumbled to it. Alice can play with the donkey as much as she likes!"

The gun in his hands fell slack, the barrel pointing into the grass. Still rigid, Joana moved toward her husband, while he now fell back, scared of her crazed, stony look.

"It isn't necessary, Joana. You'll see the fine place we'll make of this holding. Now's the time to think of your vines and the pine trees and everything you want."

She caught the word "pine trees," and, like a sleepwalker, turned round toward the hillside. Even from this distance, she could feel the spines of the trees combing the wind. Loas saw what she was looking at, knew what she was thinking.

"If the wheat should catch fire one day, and if the cottage caught fire, too, we could run and shelter there, Joana. But that won't happen. There'll be so much water from the water machine that the holding will be a real green garden."

But with a sudden lunge she pulled the gun from his hands. Before he realized what was happening, a red-hot crack of sound echoed through the quiet morning. The donkey swayed over the dewy ground. It made one last effort to lift its hind legs, then fell groaning on its knees. One of its eyes was shattered, and from it ran a slow, thick trickle of blood that soon collected in a warm blotch on the ground. The blotch spread and trickled off in veins over the black earth. Not only the donkey's blood: the very holding was groaning in a sweat of blood, a sweat of death agony. There was a sharp wind, too, a vagrant wind that blew from the mountains of the north country, and rippled the viscous coagulation.

224